A Prejudiced Resentment

American Cultures in Recovery

A NOVEL

Bob EagleClaw Parkins, Ph.D.

© Copyright 2004 Bob EagleClaw Parkins. All rights reserved.

No part of this publication may be reproduced, stored in a retrieval system, or transmitted, in any form or by any means, electronic, mechanical, photocopying, recording, or otherwise, without the written prior permission of the author.
Printed in Victoria, BC, Canada

Note for Librarians: a cataloguing record for this book that includes Dewey Decimal Classification and US Library of Congress numbers is available from the National Library of Canada. The complete cataloguing record can be obtained from the National Library's online database at: www.nlc-bnc.ca/amicus/index-e.html
ISBN 1-41203316-0

TRAFFORD

Offices in Canada, USA, Ireland, UK and Spain
This book was published on-demand in cooperation with Trafford Publishing. On-demand publishing is a unique process and service of making a book available for retail sale to the public taking advantage of on-demand manufacturing and Internet marketing. On-demand publishing includes promotions, retail sales, manufacturing, order fulfilment, accounting and collecting royalties on behalf of the author.

Book sales in Europe:
Trafford Publishing (UK) Ltd., Enterprise House, Wistaston Road Business Centre, Wistaston Road, Crewe, Cheshire CW2 7RP UNITED KINGDOM
phone 01270 251 396 (local rate 0845 230 9601)
facsimile 01270 254 983; orders.uk@trafford.com

Book sales for North America and International:
Trafford Publishing, 6E–2333 Government St., Victoria, BC V8T 4P4 CANADA
phone 250 383 6864 (toll-free 1 888 232 4444)
fax 250 383 6804; email to orders@trafford.com

www.trafford.com/robots/04-1143.html

10 9 8 7 6 5 4 3 2

Prologue

THREE CIRCLES OF Appalachian cultures and history; a spiritually-based recovery; and, a modern-day political theme combine to complete for the reader a circle of human experience in this truly historical novel.

For the first time, Appalachian Indian history, and the resulting clash with Western European culture, are elucidated. This region of mountains running the entire north-south length of the United States served for over 100 years as a cultural and historical fortress called the American eastern frontier. That history is written not by facts-and-dates by the traditional European style, but instead in the Native American style of cycles and circles called trends of history and cultures.

A memoir-inspired political theme in today's world reveals that history in Appalachee – the Native name meaning "unending mountains" – repeats itself. The cultural clashes of 200 years ago through today finds the people in a spiritually-based culture of recovery – both from their own history and from themselves.

The three epics of history, politics and spiritual – not religious – recovery, combine to complete a triangle and circle of information for the reader.

History and spirituality are not often good bedfellows, but they are both good experiences in this wholistic and integrated novel, perhaps because they represent a whole person's life. Based on the life of EagleClaw, the Native name of Dr. Bob EagleClaw Parks, born in a coal camp in West Virginia and destined to always "land on his feet" in life, this main character's life story carries the epic now being compared to a North American sequel to Victor Hugo's *Les Miserables*. And once again out of the hills of Appalachia comes a real life experience of recovery superseding even the known theme of *A Beautiful Mind*.

It has been said that this country was not founded on the Ten Commandments. It was founded on killing and taking land from Indians. And that extreme denial, it is amazing. And "it" is amazing – the factual truth that continues in that land called Appalachia into now.

Those three circles of information come together in this autobiographical production labelled *A Prejudiced Resentment* and subtitled *American Cultures in Recovery*.

Any real or imaginary relationship in the novel to historical characters is just that – a characterization. The author reveals through these characterizations the spiritual axiom that Creator's Will, or Providence, occurs with or without those characters of our uniquely Appalachian American history. Thus, for the reader, a cultural and historical feast may be experienced in that circular process described in Native American culture as "...absolutely everything that goes around, comes around."

–the author

Chapter One

The Downbeat

"It can be amazing what can happen when a man develops a resentment and then acts on it, especially when he is in position with the government over contracts," his friend Yianni said to him. "We have seen that so many times in the government contracting arena. It is astounding what the results can be, especially when two bureaucrats combine their thoughts over another individual, right or wrong, and then act on their unidentified emotions and insecurities, which can range from salary comparisons to either real or imaginary shortcomings in physiological areas, if you catch my drift," Yianni said and smiled.

"You know what I mean by that, I'm sure," Yianni said and smiled again.

"Yes," Dr. Parks, a Ph.D. kind of doctor, adjunct college professor and small business owner in the government contract arena of business nodded his head, "and several women and some men I have known in my time understand your comments in ways most men never can," he added.

The two men, Yianni, a lawyer employed at a four-person small firm in downtown, part Portuguese and part Italian; and Dr. Parks, part Cherokee and Shawnee Indian and part Scots/Irish blood mixes, had come to admire each other in a friendly way that could only be described as spiritually based – two men secure in their physical appearances who had discussions outside business matters that "just happened" – that neither was religiously based in life, but that both were spiritually-based, secure men. They seemed to have known each other in another time, another place.

What the two were discussing was the illegal interruption of a major contract of Dr. Parks' firm in January as the direct result of a resentment of one bureaucrat, a long-term acquaintance, and the prejudices and resentments of another bureaucrat, one state, one federal, who had combined their discussions and efforts with each other then acted on their misguided emotions.

Although the two bureaucrats were from very different levels of government, the synergistic effect that had occurred as the result of their prejudging known contract actions had resulted in their ending the contract and filing federal criminal charges of fraud.

They then sent their employees looking for hoped-for errors and omissions in the consulting work performed under contract and tasking orders in order to justify and rationalize their own unspoken resentments against Dr. Parks and his small minority-owned business. "It's not paranoia if it's real," he had been advised by those who knew.

The two bureaucrats on meeting had agreed to have their other bureaucrats bring a legal action against Dr. Parks and his business partner, whom both bureaucrats suspected of being a "partner" in a larger sense; Dr. Park's two younger children; and, of course, the corporation – an extreme action for anybody in government and one that could only be described as vindictive.

The federal bureaucrat, working in the environmental enforcement arena, said he knew a little-used law called the False Claims Act which could wreak havoc on any small business, but was a civil matter. The state bureaucrat said he wanted a charge which was criminal and could "make that crazy Indian worry about being put into a jail cell." Both expressions had been repeated to Dr. Parks by staff members in private conversations after he quietly asked friends what the uproar suddenly was about after seven years' satisfactory work on the state contract.

Dr. Parks had been told by friends in both camps that "you just have something about you that the guy has never seemed to like, for some reason."

"Mr. Yianni, if you will draft the case for my damages and provide a copy on a disk for my review, I will pay the requested retainer and sign a contract for one-third contingency fees to your firm."

"Let me know," he added, "and I will make comments and you folks can take the case from there," Dr. Parks said in leaving to return to his office.

For the past seven years he had operated a successful start-up venture in the northern part of the state and had obtained clients including Dupont, US-EPA, the Department of Energy and about 180 other contracts for both private industry and government work. The seven years before that time he had been an employee of a federal contract firm and had learned the business of federal and state contracting.

He often described the two learning experiences as two "seven year cycles of spiritual growth and decline and rebirth."

At two years in business, he had won the state asbestos building inspection contract, one that paid less than federal contracting but one that provided the same billable hours wages for employees. The administrative-multiplier was capped at 1.6 at the state level and was substantially less than the federal work for the company. But for a start-up firm it helped pay the rent and kept folks paid on payday.

But his real goal for the initially successful US-Small Business Administration start-up firm was government contracting at the federal level.

After becoming known by personnel at state agencies, he was contacted and requested based on his technical and business skills to bid the state contract. The bureaucrats needed to meet federal quotas, or at least to give the appearance, of locating and sharing 25% of a federal allocation to a minority-owned small business. The contract was to be a minority business set-aside, he was told, to meet those federal guidelines. At the federal level, he and his business had achieved US-SBA Section 8a status as an Appalachian Indian-owned firm which showed his competence at the federal contract level. The printed state asbestos building inspection bid confirmed the minority setaside provisions.

He had complied with all the necessary paperwork and rules and was approved as one of three businesses which could be called for work. Contract specifications were for up to one-half million dollars of work per year for inspecting buildings to be demolished for new highways for potential asbestos-containing material. They were 'words on a page'.

Contracts in government can be very different from contracts in business, he would learn. Entrenched bureaucrats who either have or form opinions on nearly everyone they come into contact with, by the time they reach administrative levels, may sway huge amounts of dollars of work up, down, across or out. And when their prejudices and personal resentments get fired up, and they act on those mental conditions and emotions, both many good and many bad things can happen – usually to the ox pulling the load – the contractor, or in his case, the consultant – and said ox was about to get gored. And like the real definition of the word suggestion, he mused, much of the culture still hadn't learned that two professions contract government work.

Contractors are those who perform levels of physical skill based on knowledge. Consultants are those who hold technical skills and produce a product for the contractors to use. The word consultant had been ill-defined in the culture his entire lifetime, usually jokingly. But most categories deserved respect, such as engineers and environmental testing scientists. These professional services categories, based on educational attainment, are called consultants. Most deserve respect as skilled businessmen.

Dr. Parks had earned that respect. But respect is put aside when ego-driven non-professional bureaucrats labelled enforcement officers need to make themselves look important and can always use the universal excuse, 'I was just doing my job,' he would learn.

But the self-willed, offending bureaucrat is protected, strangely enough, by the 11th Amendment to the US Constitution, we are told, or at least until one goes through a pre-loaded and usually unfair administrative review process conducted, alas, by other bureaucrats.

But fortunately, in plying the law in the United States, we also are told by lawyers, "For every wrong committed there is a righting action."

"We shall see, shan't we" Dr. Parks said to himself, reverting to his 12-step recovery program thinking begun and continued the past 17 years and today as a reply to unanswered questions. It was a regularly used expression by his sponsor Ed H and it worked for him, too.

Dr. Parks had learned after closing his first SBA-guaranteed loan to the bank – not to the business – that politicians can be bought, or at least donated to, but that bureaucrats with a personal prejudice and/or resentment are protected in most cases by that 11th Amendment to the US Constitution, as well as the administrative review process for complaints of misfeasance or malfeasance. And, that usually the small business will be out of business long before justice is served by that administrative review process set up to punish the bad actor bureaucrat.

He had not only learned that sad fact already, but he also had recompense that the proverbial ox can be gored, yes, but that sometimes, in his experience, the bad actor bureaucrat can be *"hoisted to his own petard"* in the words of Shakespeare out of the Middle French logging industry, by other politicians, euphemistically called elected officials, especially when the complaints become repeated. And when the complaints begin to allege taking unnecessary state trips for pleasure and accepting bribes while hiding behind a 12-step program, something will happen, such as hoisting up and out, often euphemistically called retirement.

And because he too had worked 17 years in government prior to contracting himself out to a private firm in the federal contract market, he had leaned some other principles

– not necessarily of the moralistic kind, but those of the practicing variety – that, like computer science, it only takes a 00 personality combining energy with a 01 personality to result in a parity check.

Two bureaucrats from two separate power bases, acting together, will result in a synergistic impact on the receiver. Thus, the very definition of the French term *resentire* – to re-think, to re-feel, to re-send messages–in a word, resentment, when acted upon, can often have astounding effects, and especially for bureaucracies seeking something new to talk about each day instead of performing work.

"We aren't workers even though we're engineers by training," he had once heard a contract manager say. "We provide oversight to the contract and we expect someone else to provide oversight for the actual work. We are not workers in that sense," the contract manager had once explained to him.

"You consultants do the work and we judge your actions," he had it explained. He had found most people who work in government admire both consultants and workers but are afraid to become one of them due to the perception of lack of job security, even though the pay in private industry is better. "Better safe than sorry – or successful," he had once heard.

Thus, his 17 years working in government had provided several lessons learned about upper echelon government employees – one of which was they work to provide oversight for contractors who do the work of government.

"We offer opinions and act not on our prejudices but on contract language. The human factor is eliminated in that manner," he had been told in a required contracts management course conducted by, of course, a government contract manager who had never worked outside government. He had never signed the front of a paycheck, just the back.

For fun in his mind, Dr. Parks ran the numerology in a comical application that had come from both his European culture as an American and his Native American culture and spirituality – 17 years as a government employee, year of the Locust, time for a rebirthing; 7 years as a federal contractor large business employee; and 7 years a small business owner; and, now two years having to defend himself in court – and simultaneously bringing counter charges for the huge amount of dollars lost by his business as the direct result of a prejudiced resentment of two bureaucrats – both personal acquaintances both before and during the contract period.

"What a mess," his lawyer had said before excitedly taking his case and seeing a payday, he hoped, for 33 percent of up to $5,000,000. "It's an uphill battle, but there is still a document in existence and on display in the Smithsonian Institution called the US Constitution and with what has arbitrarily been done to you and your firm, we will bring them to justice, that illusive term even for us in the legal field," the plier of the law had promised, offering the contract.

Chapter Two

EagleClaw

BORN IN A COAL camp in West Virginia of English and American Indian bloodlines and cultures, he had learned early in life that people are full of secrets they keep much of the time, his wonderful Christian Indian grandparents included.

Even though the grandmother was half Cherokee and half Irish, she called herself Irish from her social training from the last century, that if "white" is on your birth certificate, we don't talk about a racial mix from the past. Likewise, his grandfather, called Indian George in the coal camp, claimed also to be Irish, based on his last name Wright. All the land where their families had lived was ceded to a man named Wright, so Indians there took his last name. He was their new chief, so to speak. It was one of the ways Indians had taken their European names.

In the family Bible were all the pictures of visibly Indians with European names, a common occurrence throughout Appalachia – that land the Indians called Appalachee – unending mountains.

When George Washington surveyed the Kanawha and Ohio River valleys as a government contractor to King George III of England, he had Latinized the spelling on his maps from the Indian word Appalachee to Appalachia. The *ia* represented 'land of' and the common double ee in Indian language for proper nouns was largely eliminated.

Likewise, on the new maps drawn by the new surveyors the original Canoy, again dropping the double ee spelling and pronunciation, the rivers, Great and Little, became

Kanawha, and later three more different spellings of the same word were to be found on maps drawn by English and later American government contractors. And the French used a fourth, Canaugua, the Indian town located adjacent to Gallopolis, the first town the Gauls surveyed in the Ohio Valley. The French wanted to locate their first new town where Canaugua was located because of the view of the confluence of the Great Kanawha and Ohio Rivers, an awesome sight for miles, but the Shawnee said we don't think so. So the French moved two miles downstream.

It has been said in several ways that our history books are written by the victors. That fact certainly applies to Appalachian Indian history. The place names are there but the history books aren't.

The people, an estimated 300,000 West Virginians alone not counting the additional 12 states or parts recognized as Appalachia, often are mixed-blood Indian descendants who often don't know their history because it has not been written yet save some roadside historical markers around the states, mostly of "bloody" Indian battles lost, of course, they say, by the Indians.

And the history of the state's many Indian chiefs, Pocatalico, Logan, Cornstalk, Red Jacket, Blue Jacket, and even Tecumseh, born near Clarksburg, has not been written even to this day. A key indicator of a culture's history is who the cultural heroes are. But if the cultural heroes are left out of the history books, then the cultural genocide of Native Americans which occurred about a hundred and twenty five years ago in West Virginia and the United States is nearly complete.

And that's what happened when West Virginia, a bastard child of the Civil War, became a state, by both default and by geographical isolation and because the federal government needed its mineral resources and its one east-west railroad, the C&O, which ran from Parkersburg on the Ohio River to Chesapeake near Washington.

People apparently didn't count for much in the economically depressed but mineral-rich state, except as they became necessary to mine coal or cut timber or work in the steel mills or chemical manufacturing plants of the past in the state.

Both of Dr. Parks' parents had grown up living mostly on beans and potatoes and had washed their clothes in the creek. They dug coal and worked willingly and tried to get ahead by working hard. They were a product of their cultures, one thrust upon them by European landlords who saw them as expendable commodities, but their own history, culture and mores of a Native American culture was largely denied to them.

That European culture was fear based, starting with its religion, but the Native culture had been spiritually based and allowed that man has a spirit which none but Creator may rule over. The cultures represented a clash of the wills of men and would require over 100 years to restore after its destruction. But it would be reinvented in a wholistic and integrated manner and would represent an improved new American culture someday.

Wholistic and integrated were terms Dr. Parks had developed as original thinking, he believed, while writing his Ph.D. dissertation, then applying the philosophy to practical application for small business principles. The whole, which he always insisted on spelling with the w, not the higher-flying h, represented the whole thing of anything, and the 25-cent term integrated represented its very definition of respect for all the parts. Thus, life itself is wholistic and integrated, or at least should be lived that way, he believed.

He taught hazardous materials handling and health and safety classes for large chemical giants and for students at the Jesuit University using the philosophy. It worked.

And it worked in business or on any life problem – so long as the other players played by the rules. They didn't always do that, though, people in all cultures have learned. And so that's why we have always had codified regulations and laws, because some government players not only don't follow their own rules, let alone practice their own culture's ethics when exercising those rules, Dr. Parks would learn.

Thus, Dr. Parks' physical cultural backdrop was one he had worked to leave behind. But he took his ethics with him.

At 17 years old, in 1959, he left his grandfather's log house without indoor plumbing to work his way through college. He welcomed change. He left home to change and to achieve the American and Appalachian cultural dream – to "make something of himself," in that America he knew existed because he could see it since 1954 on television. Change came rapidly in the 1960's.

The coal camp where he was born in his grandmother's bed, Plymouth, had been developed by an English corporation for mining coal. Workers were hired, one step higher than whored, from the local population of mixed Indian and European integration that had occurred since the days of his great-grandparents. Indians had been digging coal out of the sides of the beautiful mountains and burning it there for thousands of years.

The maternal great-grandfather had come over from Ireland during the potato famine to seek his fortune hunting and trapping furs and seeking a remaining Indian woman left behind after the Indian males had fought to the death, died from the European diseases, or followed Tecumseh to Chillicothe or Canada to fight with the British about 1812.

The Native women were left behind with the children in their chink log houses just like the one he grew up in, made from the natural resources of the land of logs with clay soil and small rocks between the logs and cemented outside for permanency.

The same foods found growing when the Europeans came were still being grown by him as a child in his own garden – tomatoes, potatoes, green beans, corn, squashes, and pumpkins – all the "good" food we Americans eat today from our American Indian heritage in this country.

That heritage, nearly lost on the dominant Western European culture in America, had been both continued and reborn in his and his family's relearning and regaining some of the culture. But much more of the spirituality had been regained in the past several years that he had operated his own "American Dream" of operating his own small business. His three children were now past college and a couple through medical schools, with some of dad's inspiration and some more financial assistance.

He had earlier founded and helped develop a resurgence of Appalachian Indian history and culture by assisting the growth of a new Indian tribe, this one inter-tribal and state recognized, Appalachian American Indians of West Virginia. They were on the World Wide Web as AAIWV, but not to be confused with the Japanese .com saying "this is not a tribe at all," and membership had grown to 7,000 mostly mixed-blood Indians with 74 kinds of Native America linages on file. They now called themselves Ani, Cherokee for "the people" and an acronym for Applachian Nation of Indians. They knew who they were but had their heritage denied by laws on the books since the state was formed – a state that denied the very existence of Indian blood, culture, and history in the state, let alone the spirituality that the European religionist culture could never quite comprehend.

"Those savages believe in spirits, including one in the human body," he had been admonished while a child. But he could never at any level of honesty, especially self-honesty, the most important, find acceptance for the denial of the Native American spirituality when the dominant culture preached of the Trinity and its thee components, God the Father, God the Son, and God the Holy Spirit, and they are all one.

Instead of a God is Love definition in that mountain religion, the preachers taught God is going to return someday and set the world on fire. People received souls at death and they remained in the grave until judgement day, then rose up and the good ones were saved and the rest burned in a hell forever. Native culture practiced smudging four days after death to send the spirit on to Creator to be cleansed by him. The smudging, a prayer process, was carried out just in case the soul was confused or didn't want to leave this plane to go back where it belonged, to its Creator. No concept of burning in a hell forever existed.

"There is no dichotomy – they are both right, there is only one race – the human race, not four of them as Darwin taught based on racial characteristics – and each has a spirit which has a direct correlation to Great Spirit, or God, or Jehovah, or whatever name from whatever culture we choose – and that is spirituality, he had learned.

Once he knew that, he then also knew his greater purpose in life was not one of government contracting, but instead one of seeking spiritual growth. And in his line of work as a small business operator for the past seven years he had been provided the freedom to gain that spiritual growth. His life ledger was balanced in the correct direction, he knew. He could even define the balanced ledger in a greater cultural term – living in God's Will.

Thus, drawing on his Native spirituality, spiritual growth opportunities provided by a 12-step program, and continued seeking, life had allowed him to face many obstacles that others would view during the present crisis as failure, or at best fearlessly but not without painstaking by its true definition.

But that was not his thinking even in the face of others doing the wrong thing to him and his small business, even in a state where small business is touted as big business – and very American, and other dichotomies and paradoxes in that uniquely American culture.

Denial, both of history, and by governments and its bureaucrats, is a thread that runs truly through the entire culture from its history to its contract doctrines, he had learned. That culture seeks to blame the victim when something goes wrong, as has been said.

But could he change that? Yes, in some very small way,

he hoped, but was that his obligation? Again, yes in some way, he had learned and accepted. It was a part of practicing the spiritual principle of acceptance. And in a larger way, he recognized that was his purpose now in whatever form it was to be presented to him by his own Higher Power of his own choosing and definition.

The problem was, he wasn't sure of the costs, but he was sure of the rewards, so the ledger would ultimately balance, even if the scales of justice did not. At least that was how it seemed in the early stages of his being victimized by a prejudiced resentment of the two powerful bureaucrats. But as his sponsor had always said, "We shall see, shan't we?"

The very coal camp land where he was born had been surveyed by George Washington while Indians still lived there. The Natives, his ancestors, were given smiles, liquor and European diseases in return for their friendly helpfulness and allowing the survey "parties" to simply bury lead plates as mapped evidence – plates usually dug up and never found again in most cases. He now owned one from his parents land that was once owned by George Washington in the Kanawha Valley near Poca. They were said to be recorded as "talking leaves," and would have a later cultural and devastating public health effect on entire populations of Shawnee and Cherokee people living in towns there at the time. The public health effect, was not one of the lead, but the European diseases which killed an estimated 70 per cent of the local population after the surveyors came through the valley.

Thus, a new history was to be visited upon his ancestors and thus their descendants as the direct result of the European diseases spread by the government contract workers for King George and by the future "father of our country" George Washington. To this day around this land formerly and unfortunately not-chosen name of the new state, Vandalia, one sees signs proclaiming "George Washington slept here."

Some things never change, and that is true of our first

president through the last the governor of West Virginia. They, as have many other men, had trouble keeping their flys closed. George had a girlfriend called Winona, a common Indian female name, on Wheeling Island – the daughter of Chief Cornplanter of the Seneca. Those people had been hired out, by Webster's broader definition, by the British to establish Seneca towns for British protection down the Ohio Valley for protection against the "ferocious" Shawnee. It is called a buffer zone. This one was between the men of two European superpowers of the time, the Brits and the French. Local folks were but pawns used in their goal-setting. Both ultimately failed miserably, but the real losers were their local pawns, the Native Americans. But many survived through integration and are still here in the form they are in today. DNA doesn't really change, it just adapts and blends and then resurges with the human race.

Thus, the pro-British Natives established towns from Pittsburgh to Wheeling Island then down the Ohio River Valley and into Raven's Woods in then western Virginia, English land.

George and crew then surveyed. He was a 19-year-old British government contractor. They surveyed from Wheeling, an Indian name meaning land of the white skull, as best the first white invaders could surmise. Washington's Woods began in Wheeling and ran south, again into Virginia, Augusta County, Ravenswood, then along the Ohio River west to Kentuckee, land of the Cherokee, and later up the Kanawha Valley to lay claim to the best land, a rich valley populated by Indian towns. After the survey parties came through historians later wrote that "not that many" Indians were left after 50 years. The European diseases took care of that cultural and political problem. And would one after that experience seek association with death? Not likely, of course.

In between, on the Ohio side of the river, French-claimed land, the Shawnee met their brothers the Seneca from "the Five Civilized Nations" up north in peace-not-war and laughed together, Shawnee oral traditions tell us. They all had plenty of Creator's Turtle Island, they agreed. The buffer zone was acceptable to the Shawnee who had witnessed too many deaths already to the European diseases and the ravages of alcoholism and other "White Man's Diseases."

Near Ravenswood, George left a bastard son the Indians called, of course, George Washington. Until about 17, he was a tall, lanky Indian with light skin and high cheekbones and forehead. He was later murdered by John Wetzel, an Indian Fighter who had moved to the Wheeling area and was allegedly trapping for furs near Ravenswood. The state later honored Wetzel by naming a county after him. Wetzel and his partner had doubled back at night after a day trade visit and committed the murder.

What an embarrassment, Wetzel must have thought, an Indian George Washington bastard son, as he and a partner plied their trades as Indian Traders for King George III, who paid $25 per Indian scalp sent to London, a hefty sum in pounds back then.

Some of those scalps were discovered several years back by the British Museum. Curators were horrified.

It was a lucrative sideline while they were in disguise as fur traders. But their primary trade was as King George III government contractors delivering fear to the Native population for claiming and protecting English land from those who owned it for thousands of years – about 13,000 years, carbon date testing now verifies.

As the direct result of the fear-based cultural traditions of the English scalping, the French and Indians, the Shawnee, would later move mostly to the other side of the Ohio River, where the Brits in America wanted to keep them, at least for a time. And America would later name a little understood war after them, the French and Indian War. It's always been a misnomer, but the better to bury that side of our uniquely American history.

Dr. Parks recalled that in his own cultural history that George the younger could have authored a now historical song called "Nineteen and I like it." He remembered being 19 himself – not just being 19 and liking it, but having spent the summer in rural areas of West Africa with a cultural exchange program called Operation Crossroads Africa.

He later learned the organization was funded not just by individuals and civic groups and his college but also by the CIA to promote western cultural ideas. Some things never change.

What a price in Washington's day for instilling fear into local populations west and east of the Ohio river and even nearer the English Customs House in Wheeling. Crossing the Ohio at Wheeling meant going into another country – at least until the French and Indian long war ended after the American Revolution. Put the Indians in the enemy camp for PR purposes, the English had decided, and George was their primary contractor both for surveying and for later leading the Colonial troops to Pittsburgh, where he failed miserably in battle.

Later, George Washington continued his government contracting to King George III for more survey work in the Kanawha Valley, and thousands more Indians died at Buffalo and other towns in Appalachee of the European diseases after his survey parties traveled through Indian towns there.

Local records later revealed that Washington's provisions while surveying the Kanawha Valley included barrels of biscuits, barrels of survey instruments, and barrels of rum. Thus, the survey parties traveling through early West Virginia were just that.

Later, history reports the first white man in the Kanawha Valley, before George came, was Gabriel Arthur, who left lots of Native American kinfolk with his last name who today still revere him at family reunions there. Life is change, Dr. Parks had learned, but history repeats itself in cycles and circles and absolutely everything that goes around comes around, his Native culture and spirituality had taught him. Many Arthurs were now his cousins there. And they knew they were Indians and Europeans called Americans.

George's family was later assigned 10,000 acres at West Virginia's Lost Colony on the Ohio River between Ravenswood and Pt. Pleasant, near the end of the Kanawha Valley. Some Europeans from Virginia were moved there to plant orchards and build a mansion, but those folks later disappeared and contact with them was lost during the American Revolution. They no doubt integrated with local Indians in the Ohio Valley during the Revolutionary War, and as the Indians more and more moved to the western side of the river for safety, not a lot of Indians remained in western Virginia but moved to Shawnee territory in Ohio.

But many later escaped back across that magnetic river and into the woods with relatives when the sad Trail of Tears came blowing through their lives later in history. Their descendants today are called West Virginians all over the state.

Today, only the historical roadside marker remains along US Rt. 35 south of Pt. Pleasant and west of Ravens Woods for that lost colony. But the people are still there, people like Dr. Parks' family and thousands of other West Virginians who know who they are with pictures in the family Bibles, O-Negative blood, coal black eyes and hair in some instances, but not others, and very knowing of exactly who they are as a people. Many now carry Indian roll cards of the state-recognized intertribal tribe of Indians from whence they came – Appalachian Indians by blood, genetics and spirit.

Thus, with rationalization and justification ever present in the human mind until truth is forced upon them, usually in recovery from themselves, this land was supposedly just used by those Native Americans for hunting and fishing and burying their dead. And those Indians went back to wherever they came from, but losing a zillion arrowheads and leaving thousands of burial mounds along the way. And a bluejay is red. Historians for the state actually wrote that 50 years ago in state school textbooks.

That is what Appalachian Indians today call "the big lie"

in their known history. And that's actually what Appalachian Indians were taught in school as they were growing up, and the state archeologists verified the "fact" because they were supposed to, one supposes. Indian "camps" is the common expression that otherwise professional archeologists in the state used until recent years. Indian camps to coal camps is thus the state's longer history for 200 years. Its prehistory, often largely destroyed, though, is a known 13,000 years of the misnomer, Indian history.

Yet the people were taught to never tell they had Indian blood by their Indian grandmothers who had been taught "it was a racial thing," and "they will hold it against you," – a common story throughout the state today.

But here's the rest of the story, and it's one of how many of us "breeds" were born here, Dr. Parks could tell his children.

Your great-grandmother, whose tin-type picture photo copy we have, lived on the family homestead in the Ohio Valley near the end of Teays Valley, that ancient river path. But as if enough travesty had not occurred in the family, the Trail of Tears was developed by that dark US President Andrew Jackson, in the early 1800's before we were a state.

Jackson's very life was once saved by a Creek Indian in a battle as a younger man, but Jackson's military and its government contractors drew maps throughout the country, not just in North Carolina, for the Trail of Tears, to solve 'the Indian problem' in the United States once he became president.

But In western Virginia and the Ohio Valley, much integration had already occurred and blood is thicker than water.

"Your great-grandmother Indian, and this has not been that long ago – just three generations back – my mother knew her – lived in the chink log house homestead still standing today, just like the one I grew up in," he had told his children. He had shared that culture, history and spirituality with them, not in a proselytising way, just sharing, and his three adult children were now in good places in life in part, he believed, because or it.

"During the Trail of Tears Gen. Winfield Scott wrote a letter that's still in the Smithsonian archives, stating that the rough land in western Virginia is "so poor no white man would want it anyway...so we are not attempting to remove any but a few Indian males there." Your grandmother's Indian husband of the time was one of those captured and driven on the Trail of Tears. They were Shawnee, who fought back. So the survivors then called themselves Cherokee in order to survive.

"Your great-grandmother, who was pregnant, was allowed to stay at home with the promise she would come along later, which she never did, of course.

"A few years later, after the land was safe for Europeans to come into the area for hunting, trapping, and, of course, stealing a continent one state at a time, your Irish grandfather, escaping the Irish potato famine, came into the area.

"He later married your great-grandmother and that is how all of us got here. We are Scots-Irish and Cherokee and Shawnee Indians in the form we are in today."

So if one wonders what ever happened to the Indians in West Virginia, and many folks have after reading the historical markers throughout the state, beyond death to the European diseases or killed in the "bloody Indian battles," the answer is we are still here in the form we are in today.

Manifest Destiny has been superseded by God's Will, it seems.

"Baby, we're back," Dr. Parks reminisced to himself.

---------- Chapter Three ----------

Recovery – In A Spiritually-Based Culture

IN THE BLOOD-LINE and cultural restoration he and his family had helped initiate, spiritually-based names had become a part of the restoration. His name EagleClaw was arrived at after a spiritual seeking process well known in Native culture. And just as his Christian cultural name is a real name, his Native name EagleClaw – not to be quoted like a nickname – is well recognized in many communities. Both his names, Christian and Native, are both real and surreal.

In English culture one is usually given three names, then called something else. Charles Robert Parks is called "Bob." But in Native culture, spelled in European grammar, his name became EagleClaw, with all the spiritually-based significance and realization of cultural legality inherent within his *wasicu* birth certificate.

Indians never believed one needed to be certified as being born. After all, they were here. And after that, only licensures, laws and ethics were important, such as his drivers license, his tribal card, and his professional licensures, which were abundant. And all were important. It's just a higher level of the spiritual principle of acceptance, he allowed.

His great-grandmother's tin-type picture shows her with starched high English collar, copper skin color, feathered earrings and a carved wooden Indian bead necklace that was held safely in his grandmother's top chest of drawer when he was a child living there, along with her buffalo horn comb, which he now owned. Indian history was never to be spoken in the grandparent's house, the grandfather had pronounced, but his grandmother always told him who he was in private, that he had Indian blood but to never tell anyone because they would hold it against him, whatever "it" might be. "It" was prejudice of the racial and cultural and religious variety, he presumed.

And as he went to grade school there were many Indian appearing children in his classes–all with European names, of course, and all with "white" checked on their birth certificates.

When West Virginia was set up as a state, the law said that you were only either "white" or "colored." It remained that way until a state constitutional amendment required by the federal Civil Rights Act of 1964 mandated that such "archaic" language was to be removed from the state constitution.

Thus, if one were part Indian and part white, or just Indian, he or she was white. But if one had any percentage, a drop of blood by a US Supreme Court decision, of African American blood, one was simply "colored." None of those old Virginia "mulatto" confusing races of people here in the mountains. You were either one of us, and most chose to be, or you were one of "them."

Two races, not the human race, then, became the mountain standard. And even though an estimated 100,000 full-blood Indians still lived in the new state at the time of statehood, Indian was not a birth choice. And don't even think Native American. We are all Americans now, we were taught at Thanksgiving. Thus, that Indian holiday of gratitude to Creator became an American holiday, which it truly is. The Indians knew who was coming to dinner at Thanksgiving so they wouldn't starve to death."...and there's only a few of them – what could a few newcomers possibly hurt in this vast land Creator has given all of us," they humorously asked themselves. But we all have to live and learn, Eagle-Claw's mother Rosalie always said to him and his siblings.

She too always participated in tribal affairs at powwows and gatherings with her children. She too knew her grandmother but only at a distance. Her grandmother was the one who later moved off the homestead to the backwater area near Red House, but was shunned in no uncertain terms as a short, dark-skinned woman whom their own "Irish" Christian mother had been advised to keep clear of out of fear that was unspoken. They were allowed to only go to the old Indian woman's door to visit, but not go inside. She later died alone. She always told folks exactly who they were and that keeping secrets was not ungodly but unhealthy. Some truths keep being told.

Shawnee women like his mother Rosalie were easily physiologically identifiable at powwows in Appalachee because they nearly all have flat butts, he had once said to his mom. She knew, she said. She knew. Cherokee women were often taller and their personalities were usually more vibrant and they insisted on remaining that way. They were the ones who told next-to off-color jokes and could get away with comments to men and no real man would challenge them for fear of intimidation possibilities, and respect. The Cherokee as a culture require respect for women as the nourishers, protectors, and in fact, providers of life.

History books record the Cherokee women poignantly asking Christian missionary men here why they were here away from their women. Are things too short for your women there, they would chide. Cher is a Cherokee woman.

Shawnee women were more caretakers while Cherokee women didn't always presume the missionary's position as necessarily correct for them. Both commanded equal decision-making authority in their positions in the tribe on all important matters, whether making love or war. If a divorce came, the man found his hunting and fishing belongings outside the door upon returning home. Women, next to Creator, owned all property and decided where the family would live. The community, or the village, raised the children. Women raised the gardens and the men hunted and fished. Yet European men thought they could improve on that culture, it has been said with a smile.

But these recognized subcultural differences, and many others, EagleClaw would catch himself saying in later life, collectively was "just a cultural thang" with the Appalachian mountain nasal accent reminiscent of The Beverly Hillbillies syntax variety of the English language thrust upon his ancestors, who were survivors.

Thus, a whole culture, along with two whole languages, Shawnee and Cherokee, a culture of love and music and spirituality, cultures based on one word, respect, had been driven from the land of his birth not so long ago in America's sadder and more shameful side of its history. But the people and the artifacts remained. Thus, truth remained.

And history was being re-recorded, and the two languages, all but lost, were now back in writing and being learned by disparate tribal groups. The Shawnee language had gotten down to one old woman on the reservation in Oklahoma who still knew it all, and a successful effort was now underway to re-record that knowledge. It was nearly lost art. But the Cherokee language had been salvaged last century by a written syllabary of George Sequoyah Gist. It is now available on disk.

So much for the "Indian Problem" in the new state in the late 1800's. So long as one claimed to be Cherokee and Christian and wore two safety pins crossed in the form of the Cross, one might be relatively safe. However, in the new state, only 100 years old a few years ago – two 50-year generations – an Indian could not own land or "congregate" on a public street else be legally shot by the county sheriff, as some were in Bluefield, else be 'shipped' to Oklahoma, as happened as late as 1950 in Wheeling.

Pockets of starving Indians around the state in communities identified by Gov. MacCorkle were offered the first state assistance as Indians in the 1930's, with his verbal pronouncements that they were to be hired to help build roads to be kept from starving, and, thus, in the process, were given legal notification of existence – albeit inadvertently. Affirmative Action was not in the language yet.

While still the State of Virginia, prior to 1863, several reservations existed around the state for leftover Indian populations who had not yet become acculturated and who suffered from diseases ranging from tuberculosis to diphtheria to alcoholism and were better "out of sight, out of mind" to the civil Virginians.

But to the new West Virginians, the Virginia reservations, such as thousands of acres of level land at Institute in the Kanawha Valley, the Shawnee Reservation, and other tribal properties, were very economically inviting. They were now new state properties.

And besides, they had to do something to contain the newly-freed African-American population in the new state after the Civil War. So such land as that in "the Colored Institute," now owned largely by the county and the state and called Shawnee Park, went to black populations, but colored Indians were welcome. Most of that land is today occupied by a land-grant well respected educational institution, West Virginia State College, recently renamed West Virginia State University. The balance of the former reservation is owned today by Kanawha County and is used as a golf course. One Indian burial mound is left standing there where dozens formerly existed, leveled for industry, a fair grounds and the county poor farm for left over adults and orphan children last century.

In other locations around the new state, such as at Delbarton, the 10,000-acre Birch Cherokee reservation, alas, after a fire at the county courthouse required reconstruction of all property deeds, the local coal company was 10,000 acres larger.

And along Elk Tiskewah River, two reservations at Indian Creek and at Pinch from "Pinched Gut," the Indian historical name given by the hungry Indians who lived there to describe their physiological condition during the Great Depression, local politicians simply purchased the land at tax sales, then sold it to other individuals who developed subdivisions and small farms. Today, the Indian burial mounds remain at locations including at the Pinch Reunion Grounds, and are revered by local residents, many of whom know their heritage and why they have coal black hair and olive skin and O-type blood, a medical "indicator" of having Native American bloodlines.

Thus, the state's real history was one of "taking" by perception for the public good. Public was usually ill-defined in the new state except as it related to history defined by its original two-syllabic root derivation of the term. And since Indians no longer existed, how could they own land? That law, too, was passed by the state Legislature, and included any man white or otherwise who married an Indian woman. The law and many other ethnicity anomalies were not removed from the state Code until 1967 and quickly forgotten. But the new federal Civil Rights Act required sharing the wealth with the same categories eliminated 100 years ago in this and many states. No problem. Those folks no longer exist in the new state born of the Civil War. They're all white or colored, according to our laws this year.

And thus, Dr. Parks the government contractor, a leftover Indian and European in the same body–a cognitive anomaly–was to be eliminated by prejudiced resentment, the two white cultural products of European descent with insecure emotions about their insufficient physiological anatomies, would decide. They now knew who EagleClaw was as an American male. It had all been declared in truth called a federally-designated USSBA Section 8-a owned company.

EagleClaw had been told his body language spoke a book on security, friendliness, education and his more than sufficient manhood. After all, you have heard those rumors about Indian males, and in many cases, he found, they were true, others not so true. But they are true in all ethnicities, and untrue in some and then there are the myth-breakers in all ethnicities, he had found. It's all on the individual, whomever that individual may be, and whatever "it" may be.

But he knew he had his and that was all he needed to know. He had observed that both bureaucrats seem unreasonably uncomfortable in his presence, and overly formal in most occasions where simple, friendly communication was all that was required. He had something about him the two were just uncomfortable about, he observed but did not comment on. He just didn't consider it a problem – at the time.

Others, however, and he suspected the two bureaucrats in question, were prime examples of jealousy and various forms of envy–especially one bureaucrat crime investigator named Pearbottom. He appeared to believe he had gotten cheated genetically, he believed, and blamed others silently in whatever manner available to him for his shortcomings.

But others' shortcomings were not his responsibility, he had learned well. He just didn't consider such matters as his responsibility. His responsibility was to meet contract conditions.

But just what was that "R-word," responsibility, he had often wondered. And in his legal and contract affairs, he had none unmet that either he or his business partner could identify because both he and his partner, in discussions, knew they had done nothing wrong. So why worry about the strange line of questioning which had come his way while meeting with the state client personnel last month as to why recent work assignments had declined on the state asbestos building inspection contract.

He had once read out of his European cultural tradition that a man named William George Jordan, from *"The Majesty of Calmness,"* had said that the only responsibility that a man can't evade in his life is the one that he thinks of least.

Jordan had said that his personal influence, when he is on dress parade, when he is posing to impress those around him, is woefully small. But his unconscious influence, that silent, subtle radiation of his personality, the effect of his words and acts, the trifles he never considers, is tremendous.

"Every moment of life he is changing, to a degree, the life of the whole world. Every man has an atmosphere which is affecting every other man. So silent and unconsciously is this influence working that many forget that it exists," he had said.

Jordan added that "Into the hands of every individual is given a marvelous power for good or evil – the silent, unconscious, unseen influence of his life," he called it.

"This is simply the constant radiation of what a man really is, not pretends to be. Every man, by his mere living, is radiating sympathy, or sorrow, or morbidness, or cynicism, or happiness, or hope, or any of a hundred other qualities."

Jordan, of course, had it right, but didn't finish the job. Fear, that four-letter f-word, should top the list of the human negative emotions, either generating it or absorbing it, he had learned as EagleClaw. It tops the list of the 12 off-the-beam emotions, he had been taught by at least two of his spiritual sources, both by his Native spiritual teachings and by his 12-step recovery-from-self spiritual teachings.

But Jordan also had said that life is a state of constant radiation and absorption: to exist is to radiate; to exist is to be the recipient of radiations.

So in essence, he had it right again, he just didn't get it all, Dr. Parks surmised. But he knew he hadn't yet gotten it all spiritually, either, so why should he expect others to have "it" all in one package – whatever package containing "whatever," that one-word prayer he had learned to utter to Creator.

Heady stuff, EagleClaw thought, and not incomparable to his own Native American spirituality teachings, now available in books and on-line from the same publishing house that provides most 12-step recovery literature to Americans. That fact was a sign and symbol that the whole culture was changing for the good one person at a time and one day at a time, he thought to himself. Life is good, he knew, so long as all life called the medicine wheel in his Native culture – medicine meaning spiritual medicine – is kept in balance.

Through proper thinking, which leads to proper action, and by helping others, the basis of his serenity, he had achieved in part a wonderful result, a growing spiritual awareness. And by continued seeking, and by his actions, he would continue both that cultural and spiritual growth process, not just for today, but for his life. It's called recovery. It was one of only a few spiritual axioms he could identify in his life. He called it all a spiritual principle.

What another circular pattern, he thought. It was the government contractors, George Washington and Winfield Scott and their ilk, who had done in his ancestors and an entire culture and spirituality that was now returning and being practiced around the state through powwows, school education programs, archeological exhibits, law enforcement to the felony level for disturbing Indian grave sites, thank Creator, and a legally recognized state tribe of Appalachian Indians. And although only a few of many tribal ancestries were anywhere near full-bloods, it in fact didn't really matter.

They were still here in the form they are in today. And anyway, it's all about Spirit, he knew.

Yet, here he was – a government contractor, with minority designation based on 'proof,' yet being prosecuted, he suspected, but didn't know how to prove, because he had Indian blood.

And that federally recognized 'proof' was based on his being a card-carrying Indian, not one but two blood lines, and 'two-spirited." And again like the powerful impact of the computer numbers 00 and 01 and the synergistic result requiring a parity check, his impact on others was often more than met the eye, he was sure, just like William George Jordan had said. It's enough to make a European-cultured bureaucrat nervous, he thought.

Indians are the only minority Americans who have to "prove" to the government who they are. Ask any African-American. Can we trust that government? Ask any Indian.

But the process is one of self-certification, since Indians didn't, and by law couldn't, keep written records of who they were. Thanks to more than due diligence in the past by the American Civil Liberties Union, the Supreme Court case law now regulates the entire matter and is available in books and is practiced well throughout the country. And acceptance is the key, it has been said.

EagleClaw had recognized that it was only after he had declared his "Indianess" that he had suffered any noticeable prejudice at all. But maybe there was more. Perhaps there was perceived sexual bias by insecure males. After all, those blue eyes, genetically predominant in Native Americans after just one blood mix via the recessive genes; a blue-eyed Indian with a black mustache. But John Wayne's Indians never had any facial hair at all. Therefore, he must not be telling the truth. And he is a healthy racquetball player with a good genetic build and bigger than normal cheekbones – makes a European boy nervous, doesn't it? So there's got to be some catch, the two bureaucrats could surmise.

It is not a matter of jealousy – that most awful of human emotions – with the bureaucrats – or was it? He didn't know.

Envy was another possible emotion for them, he thought, especially for that which some males do or do not possess. But what he knew for sure was that a Federal Investigation was now underway he had been advised by a subpoena with a purpose of bringing federal criminal fraud charges against him and his corporation, as best he could surmise. It's not paranoia if it's real, he repeated to himself.

It was time to discuss such matters with his lawyer, who guessed the enforcers thought something like "So, obviously, he isn't sampling our asbestos right and he's making money off the government in the process, and that's called fraud. Perhaps if we ask enough questions, we'll get something on him..." as EagleClaw's criminal defense lawyer Ben Wanton had suggested to him, based on language in a complaint and later in subpoenas.

"After all," Barrister Wanton had said, "that's human nature. If one asks enough of the most doubting questions, humans begin to wonder what someone really has done wrong. Even if they can't prove that you composited samples of asbestos composited building material and suggest you sent more to the lab than necessary to make some more money, maybe they can find something else to nail their prejudiced resentment to. Maybe you didn't pay your taxes or something. Maybe you are overcharging on your government audits. Maybe they can find something. And they do, after all, need the billable hours to bill to. And the economy is really down here for other environmental firms and there's not much else to justify their budget allocation for the upcoming year," Wanton had said to Dr. Parks. "And they can always say they're just doing their jobs."

"Since there isn't much going on economically, we don't see as many real environmental violations as we used to see since they're mostly today laid off from work," he had added.

"And besides," his lawyer had told Dr. Parks, "the new Bob Byrd Federal Courthouse here has four, mind you, full federal court staffs where they used to have only one – four judges with four staffs with four investigators and four courtrooms that have to get used for something, else their Congressional re-allocation can't be justified. So they have to find something to keep themselves busy. And the EPA staff – we never even had one in the past here until the new large federal courthouse was built, so they have to do something, even if it is wrong."

"And two minds saying one thing on separate unrelated occasions can have a synergistic effect when the two come together with a prejudiced resentment lurking," he added.

"But truth, regardless, always surfaces."

But the bureaucrats thought just a little differently, Dr.

Parks had been told later by a friend in their office.

"But until then, let's let our vivid imaginations continue our work against Dr. Parks. Bet he'll never testify in court against us again," Ben Wanton half-joked, referring to the government-protected bureaucrats and referring to the primary fact that Dr. Parks had served as an asbestos expert witness for a client but in opposition in a court case of the same EPA bureaucrat in federal district court in Wheeling the past year.

"That's something you should remember to think about in this Federal Investigation," Ben Wanton had said to Dr. Parks in ending their first discussion of the potential federal criminal charges of compositing asbestos samples and submitting false documents in order to get paid.

Chapter Four

In the Small World of Government Contracting

"Mr. Parks, we are here to interview you in your office and that is the purpose of our unannounced visit. You may either be interviewed or we will take you downtown and arrest you for mail fraud on federal criminal charges. Which would you prefer?" the local EPA enforcement officer asked of Dr. Parks while flashing a gold Federal badge.

He and a second individual had banged on Dr. Parks' office door adjacent to his home demanding he identify himself verbally three times while holding his inside suit pocket forward for no apparent reason. They appeared visibly nervous at their duties.

They insisted on the use of the word Mr., carefully avoiding the Dr. word. No big deal, Dr. Parks thought, usually reserving the term for his college classroom instruction. He actually preferred and was more honored to be called EagleClaw but normally just introduced himself in most circles as Bob.

"May I have one of your business cards?" Dr. Parks asked of the two.

"We'll get to that after you agree to be interviewed or be arrested and taken downtown to the federal courtroom," Nicholas Pearbottom said, adding "we have more important business to conduct with you at the direction of my boss in Wheeling."

Dr. Parks said he didn't seem to have much choice and asked if this related to the alleged federal investigation of his firm's five year contract with the state of West Virginia for inspecting buildings for new highway construction for suspect asbestos-containing materials.

Pearbottom said it was related but admonished "you should not make such presumptions." Parks said he had not suspected that the Wheeling EPA linkage for enforcement would so overtly erupt, since his asbestos environmental consulting work was regulated by OSHA – not EPA.

"We are enforcement for the environment," Pearbottom said, "…and we question your methods of sampling and believe you composited asbestos material and then sent them all mixed up as samples to a lab to make more money. You can either be charged with that or we will charge you with mail fraud for sending them to a laboratory across state lines and wire fraud for receiving the faxed analytical reports."

"Is that a presumptive indictment of guilt before the talk about sampling methodologies occurs, or just a stinging indictment?" Dr. Parks asked.

"We are here to ask the questions and I will write the report as a technical document and let others decide on it's content," Pearbottom answered.

"Mr. Pearbottom, are you technically trained in asbestos so that if I give general answers to questions that may require technical explanations, such as Transmission Electron Microscopy, will you automatically understand, or will I need to back up with more keep-it-simple explanations as I do to jurors when I am an expert witness in a courtroom?" Dr. Parks asked.

"I know enough to ask the right questions and formulate answers," Pearbottom replied. "I have your reports for $13,000 worth of work on West Virginia Highways Commission contracts, and we see glaring errors which the state technicians say you have made a lot of money on and that is considered fraud under federal law."

Dr. Parks could see that the case of a stinging indictment was already lined up and said he would answer any questions asked. He wondered if he should call a lawyer, but decided that honesty and his "God's Will" attitude would result in the truth being arrived at, and continued the discussion by asking what the questions were.

"Well, first," Pearbottom replied, "we believe you mixed up samples and sent, say, 25 samples from the Logan job from house plaster to a lab, thus enriching yourself unjustly and making more money on samples."

Dr. Parks repeated Pearbottom's words verbatim back to him, recognizing a bluff was occurring since no more than seven samples of any suspect asbestos-containing material is ever sent to a lab for any size building for a like-appearing material sampled, such as wall plaster, even for, say a 30-story building.

"You have the lab results and that plaster was required by its square footage figures to have five samples sent to the lab," Dr. Parks said. "So why are you suggesting that 25 were sent?"

"I've already spoken with my boss in Wheeling and he said you sent 25 samples in after you composited the material to quickly get off the job and make more money and that is federal fraud to the EPA," Pearbottom replied.

"I have a question," Dr. Parks said,"...is this interview being taped in order to help you write your memo to your boss in Wheeling?"

"Look, Parks, if you think this is a frame-up of some kind, we can go downtown and you can give your answers to the federal judge. I have already spoken with his Justice Department lawyer and she knows you by your articles in *the Valley Gazette* about the Indian stuff with your nickname "Eagle claw," which he added to the official record, along with the misspelling, and quoting it, as a nickname, "... and all about you, and Judge Goodrich thinks you may be some kind of freak. We already know you don't have a Ph.D. except for a piece of paper from some country in Africa and we at EPA have already been embarrassed enough in West Virginia in the court systems about college degrees and we plan to use this case to correct, shall we say, some of our own press and history," Pearbottom said.

"Aren't you a former deputy sheriff from Boone County, Pearbottom" Dr. Parks asked.

"No, no, you must have me confused – not Boone County. There's another guy with a similar name who was a past president of the West Virginia Deputy Sheriff's Association and he was from one of those coal mining counties and you must have me confused with him," Pearbottom replied.

Dr. Parks said maybe so, but a friend of his, a lawyer and prosecutor in Boone County, had referenced Pearbottom's questionable environmental enforcement in the county as a deputy sheriff who had little or no environmental training but nevertheless held opinions and acted on them as a deputized employee in a federally funded retraining employment program, who had allegedly collected bribes from local coal officials to be quieted, but then had used the alleged environmental experience to be hired by the US-EPA to perform background investigation work for criminal enforcement, Pearbottom's present job.

"That's preposterous," Pearbottom replied, "and we need to move on with my questions and have explanations to your highways work. We have films of your work and two technicians with state government at both Health, where you used to work, and at the Division of Environmental Development, who have already agreed to testify against you. They know you from the past and they don't care for you. They say you used being Indian and having a Ph.D. as a consultant to cover up your activities for making money and that you aren't any more qualified than them to be doing this work. They both say they are astounded that one large job by your small business makes more money than their state salaries for a year. And just because they don't have college degrees they are laughed at for having to do asbestos enforcement work with no support from the rest of the state government, so I am going to help them in this case – both my boss and me – so let's get on with the interview."

"I have about seven questions to ask you and then we will let you know about our report after we give it to Judge Goodrich and the Justice Department," Pearbottom continued.

"Who is your boss, Mr. Pearbottom" Dr. Parks asked.

"Marvin S. Reicht" he replied.

Dr. Parks smiled, then paused and replied, "Oh, yes, I know him well. We used to work together at EPA in Wheeling, me as a hazardous materials scientist and technical consultant and him as a criminal enforcement officer. Is he still concentrating on asbestos potential violations or is he looking into the real issues for protecting public health and the environment rather than pesticides and other hazardous material which have had improper disposal in old buildings in Wheeling?" Dr. Parks asked.

"I don't understand hazardous materials and don't have any training in that line of work so I don't talk about that much with Mr. Reicht" Pearbottom said.

"I just wondered what the more serious implications were presently," Dr. Parks said, lowering his tone. "We used to disagree regularly on the seriousness of pesticides such as DDT in soil where new housing developments were being built with children playing in the dirt in backyards in Wheeling and why EPA worried more about a barn being torn down with potential asbestos roof shingles than DDT where children are playing."

Pearbottom, straightening his solid black suit coat at the right inside pocket, shuffled in the swivel chair that, like he and his fellow traveler, had been occupied immediately by them in Dr. Parks' three-desk small office. Pearbottom's guest from the federal highways administration, who had flown into town just for the interview, had sat uninvited at Dr. Parks' desk chair. Dr. Parks sat at the technician's desk, and Pearbottom occupied Thom Botts' chair and desk.

Dr. Parks and his business partner had moved into that property after he had down-sized his business contract bidding purposefully after moving from Wheeling to Charleston.

That move, three years back, was for the purpose of getting mostly out of the environmental consulting business except as an expert witness in the state and federal court systems and instead to ply his substantial technical expertise in a state government position where he had worked for 17 years in his earlier environmental career and where he needed to complete his state retirement plan.

His technical expertise had become substantial after helping EPA clean up over 300 Superfund sites throughout the eastern United States and abroad.

He had worked as an EPA contract employee during seven large profit years for the federal contractor in the Superfund Program, then had completed a Ph. D. degree.

He resigned close to contract renewal time, then started his own small business consulting practice in Wheeling, only to learn that the "big dogs" at the federal contract level eat "small dogs" for breakfast when they aren't needed to meet small business federal contract conditions, nay, goals – which they seldom are in reality, he had learned by the school of hard knocks. But the US-SBA wants one to think so.

"So how long have you and your corporation performed this type of work?" Pearbottom continued. Dr. Parks replied about 27 years as an individual, and for the past 14 years as a government contractor, either at the federal contract employee level or for his own corporation.

"Well, then you must have made lots of money. I see your three children all have college degrees and a couple medical school degrees. Did you do that with asbestos government money?" Pearbottom asked.

"The answer is yes, they have those degrees – but what does that have to do with this asbestos criminal investigation interview?" Dr. Parks asked.

"Well," Pearbottom said, "We believe – well, that's just not important here for now. We will let you know our decision or the US Justice Department will be in touch with you with a subpoena soon – for both you, your corporation, your children and your business partner. By the way, this Mr. Thom Botts, your partner, where can I reach him? Doesn't he work for the state now?" Pearbottom asked, rising from his chair. "If you give me his number I will call him in advance and ask him these same questions, since he worked for that same money from us and the state as you did."

Dr. Parks wrote a note with the telephone number and handed it to Pearbotton.

"We will be in touch through the court system with you. You'll be hearing from us," Pearbottom replied after the note was handed to him, saying he would let himself out.

Dr. Parks pulled a numbered job file from the earlier asbestos expert witness job the year before in Wheeling. He had served a lawyer for his client as an asbestos expert witness in the case in Federal District Court. EPA had lost the case and the newspaper article was attached to the front of the file cover. The charge was amazingly similar, criminally charging a businessman there with asbestos violations and trying to send him to prison. History often repeats itself in both cultures and individual circumstances when resentful men don't meet their personal goals and get their feelings hurt, he surmised.

Testing for point-counting for definitively locating the asbestos material, according to EPA-Wheeling's experts shipped into town from out of state, had not been performed by them. And thus the criminal case against a local businessman there was lost, even though the businessman's corporation agreed to pay a small, undisclosed fine to ease the embarrassment for the government, his lawyer said, but also probably to avoid the costs of a threatened civil trial. That "double jeopardy" had somehow become legal, regardless of what the U.S. Constitution states, ever since the OJ trial obsession on television. It was now law by case law and the Constitution was overruled by case law in the country today. Everyone knew that because they saw it on tv. But Dr. Parks' case was not an OJ case at all.

Dr. Parks had testified as the expert witness for the defense that the point-counting procedure for asbestos is federal law, yet EPA had not followed its own rules in the court case. He simply went to the federal courtroom and spoke truth, not opinion, by Webster's, not legalese, definition.

EPA officials never admitted they acted vindictively and were actually after a local asbestos removal contractor who had been hired by the businessman being charged. They were just sending a message via the press, they believed, Dr. Parks' lawyer-client had advised him. There's more than one way to re-send messages, he had replied. "Whatever happened to plain old on-site inspections, like other state and federal agencies do?" his attorney asked.

"These federal criminal investigators don't look for facts," he answered. "They mentally invent their own suspicions then recall them as accusations of fact."

That trial was covered thoroughly by the local press because the local businessman was well known and the message was resent again and again via the aid of local EPA staff press releases to newspaper reporters, even though several were present in the courtroom.

Pearbottom's boss Marvin Reicht's resentment at losing that and several earlier law cases was well known to local lawyers in the small city.

Reicht's office is known as the Wheeling Field Office of US-EPA Region III, Criminal Enforcement Section. He is a field guy, said to be wanting to move up in the ranks and he's not supposed to lose his first few court cases, EPA contract officials had said to Dr. Parks in earlier years when he worked for them and had their confidentiality as a contract employee.

On a Friday evening about three weeks later, Pearbottom again knocked, not at the office door he knew, but instead at the residence front door, with subpoenas for Dr. Parks, his two younger children, business partner Thom Botts, and, of course, the corporation.

The list would later be expanded for presumptive intimidation purposes to include several professional staff associates, including the archeologist, the chemist and the industrial engineer. They had performed environmental technical work on field projects, but not on asbestos projects under current surveillance.

"Hey, Pearbottom, you missed my mom, my grandmother, and my sponsor," Dr. Parks wanted to say, but held his tongue.

"Criminal charges – interesting, Pearbottom, when the False Claims Act only provides for civil penalties. What are the criminal charges?" Dr. Parks asked.

"Oh, as a reminder and just for sure we threw in the federal NESHAPS law for mixing up the samples and it provides for either civil or criminal charges, Mr. Parks. But I don't have to answer your questions, I'll just hand you the papers this time. Besides, it is not me this time it is the state that wants you in federal court. I'm just doing my job serving the subpoenas to you."

Dr. Parks' suspicion from his Sixth Sense was that Pearbottom was simply lying to him.

"You don't even have to sign them." Pearbottom replied, thrusting the papers between the storm door and the residential front door.

Next day Dr. Parks went to see his lawyer Ben Wanton again.

"And how about the Congressional intent of the False Claims Act – isn't there supposed to be a Whistleblower purpose for that federal law?" he asked. "Someone called a Relator?"

"Is there someone in, say, Philadelphia, maybe a Charlie Kay, or maybe a Mike Springer, or a Rudy Shoup, who has filed a complaint to get a third of the Whistleblower award provided for in this *qui tam* law they are using, instead of maybe the state asbestos law, which I drafted and shepherded through the state Legislature about 17 years ago before the folks at EPA even regulated asbestos except in schools, and to announce over and over that it was a killer mineral?" he asked the lawyer, whom he had developed a closer relationship with over the past couple months. He left the meeting with the lawyer with more questions than answers.

Pearbottom had chosen to deliver the subpoenas himself. The federal assistant prosecutor could have had a deputy sheriff or a civilian hired for such purposes under most conditions serve the subpoenas which were not required to be signed by the recipient. Pearbottom had said he was on overtime and still had his paperwork to do back at the office and promptly left.

He remembered seeing Pearbottom once briefly but distinctly in the past in the Wheeling area, at an adult book store at Dallas Pike, on a Friday or Saturday evening but in a world-away environment from this day. His stomach turned. It was not a pleasant memory. He never forgot a face, although he didn't know at the time he would see that face again. It had not been seeing his face that caused his stomach to turn over from the unpleasant memory. After leaving he never went there again.

Dr. Parks had been carrying three empty laundry baskets from the basement to bedroom closets when he answered the front doorbell of his residence. It was after work hours. He eventually put the baskets on the floor, extended a hand to collect the subpoenas, nodded, and again looked Pearbottom in the face in an attempt to make eye contact. It didn't happen. And it was just as well, he thought.

A quick review of the paperwork had revealed the suspected: people in either the company or the family charged, including company associates; all the family except the daughter in Alaska, listed and charged with the same paragraph – creating false documents for billing the government and charged by the United States with creating false documents and fraudulently billing for that service – knowingly, of course.

If one weren't in a program of honesty, the intimidation might have worked. Courage is not the absence of fear. Dr.

Parks left for a planned meeting at 5:30 pm and entered a couple minutes late and as it happened, sat beside one of his lawyers. Dr. Parks passed in discussion, demurely and with a slight smile, holding the subpoena envelopes in his hand, not on purpose so much as hoping to catch a quick moment for further review.

Dr. Parks would later end another session with the lawyer Ben Wanton by telling him about the manner in which Pearbottom had left his home that day after again personally delivering papers to Dr. Parks. Pearbottom had lowered his head on exiting, presumably to avoid eye contact with him.

Dr. Parks' conversation, including smiling demurely and lowering his entire head and shoulders in order to look up slightly into Pearbottom's face, had made the criminal investigator nervous, he commented. "No doubt," his lawyer said.

The next day Dr. Parks was scheduled for an appointment with Harry Breeze, Esq., whom he had asked to come in on the case for his filing a $5 million damages suit against the state, as well as filing a bad faith claim against his professional liability insurance firm, which had denied responsibility for providing legal services, a common story in the state presently.

Breeze announced he would be filing the bad faith claim later that week. But surprisingly he said he had learned that someone at the state was now suggesting to the Justice Department that Dr. Parks had accepted a bribe from the asbestos removal contractor. It was their last ditch attempt at rationalization and justification of false legal charges against him and his small business, Harry suggested.

"Some things never change," Harry said as Dr. Parks left.

Chapter Five

A Prejudiced Resentment

WHEELING, W.VA.: *The Times-Record* and the *Wheeling Intelligencer* reported today the loss of a criminal prosecution case brought by local US-EPA Enforcement Officer Marvin Reicht. The criminal charges were leveled against a local businessman who owns several local businesses and local buildings.

Reicht, known locally as a pistol-wearing, badge-flashing officer, was moved here from the Philadelphia Office of EPA to bring asbestos cases where enforcement was complained to be lax by a senior citizen employment informant often described as "on a tirade" in his asbestos technician job.

Reicht and others reported being highly embarrassed at the loss in the case. Dr. Bob EagleClaw Parks, an Expert Witness in the case for the defense, testified Wednesday in Northern District Court here that EPA officials simply had not performed their own required testing for "point-counting" of the suspect asbestos material, according to Court records. Thus the case was lost by EPA, even though the businessman's corporation agreed to pay a small, undisclosed fine to ease the embarrassment for the government.

EPA officials admitted in cross-examination that they were actually after a local asbestos removal contractor who had been hired by the businessman, according to court records from last year. EPA's Reicht admitted in an interview that he had been unable to convict him in earlier trials.

That press release was copied from the web site and attached to the file Dr. Parks had kept when moving offices as a part of his growing expert witness for asbestos suits around the state.

Most of the small business's work in the past two years

had come from working not so much for lawyer clients, but from engineering-related work activities. The firm was categorized by federal and state Standard Industrial Classification Codes for state and federal tax purposes as SIC Code 8744-Architectural and Engineering-Related corporation, not unlike other federal contractors in the engineering-related disciplines.

He had worked seven years earlier for a similar firm, and the codes had been assigned for bidding purposes on federal contract and subcontract categories published in the Federal Register.

Substantial work for the firm also had come from one client who at times required commercial property environmental site assessments, or Phase I's, as they are known in the industry, in Texas, Florida and other states having a viable economy. He regularly flew out to that "rest of the country" where somehow environmental law is respected due to potential liability for property purchasers, unlike here in the mountains, as a local bank loan officer had once said to him.

In the Mountain State, the Division of Environmental Development is staffed by industry-friendly political appointees, in power only a short time, and who do not expect to stay there very long except to build a career for the chemical or coal industry in the state in the future for themselves.

In a state where Coal is King and wild women are tamed by putting a governor on them, environmental law is more philosophy, more newspaper headlines, than reality, and enforcement is best completed through press releases by government bureaucrats wanting to promote themselves through a Peter Principle to better positions elsewhere.

One might have to work in a coal camp awhile, but one doesn't have to stay there. And while there, if you're a governor into taming a wild woman who happens to be a state employee, don't forget, please, to at least properly file those 500 e-mails in the family computer which go through the same server as the one in the state office–unless, of course, your hands are full and one has only one free hand for the keyboard. Men of all cultures understand that, as do women.

That thought occurred in Dr. Parks' mind after the national news disclosed that fact during his own Federal Investigation about the state's Governor Wisecoff.

"The philosophy of making money here goes something like, now I will prosecute over here with a small business firm unable to defend itself while you guys who make the donations make $20,000,000 over there in that coal county by mountaintop removal while the environmental legislation is reviewed by the court systems. Thus, we can't have enforcement until new case law is written. And that may be awhile in our experience – say, a generation or two," his lawyer had volunteered to Dr. Parks in discussion in his office. His best thinking got him here, he said, and that was part of the reasoning for the prosecution, he surmised. Facts didn't always make him feel any better, he replied.

"Meanwhile, with a court case or two, the local press will write the word environmental every day over and over and at least the voting public will think something is being done to control environmental conditions. Besides, God meant for these mountains to be leveled or He wouldn't have placed them here and allowed the Pittsburgh corporations to have bought the coal rights years ago," the lawyer added with a smirk.

"But meanwhile, we speak of law enforcement in the third person, and look for that small business to prosecute and make some headlines, the philosophy goes. That's where your problem comes in." he concluded. Somehow truth had been spoken to his own law case, Dr. Parks surmised. But it didn't make him feel a lot better. It was just entertaining awhile.

EPA-Wheeling's field office is located in the Methodist Building in downtown. That church group's founders Charles and brother John Wesley came to Appalachia to save souls of savage Indians two generations back. Roads, chapels and edifices are named after them around the state. When Dr. Parks was a child attending the local Methodist Church, the revered Methodist Hymnal even included two or three songs sub-labelled Indian songs. But those were revised in the 1950's when a new song book, blue not maroon, was purchased in volume after a fund raiser labelled a Pie Social raised the necessary funds.

The church Boy Scout Troop donated $20 of its $23.44 treasury to the cause. The old hymnals were shipped to Africa after the Methodist Youth Fellowship raised money for shipping costs. It was a good religious thing to be doing, they were told – more important religiously than, say rollerskating, or camping out with the troop leader.

Young Parks later at 19 years old had helped build two classrooms at an English Methodist School for Boys in Sierra Leone with the Operation Crossroads Africa cultural exchange program. The English headmaster there was later murdered by local Temne tribesmen for alleged child sexual abuse. After his wife returned to Birmingham, England, the school site became a Sierra Leone Civil War battleground site, American newspapers reported. The location and fate of the Methodist hymnals from West Virginia is unknown.

Methodism as a religion in the state has been prominent since the time of the Wesley Brothers, when Indians and coal miners needed their souls saved. And some, including the Wheeling Methodist Church, later learned the financial art of investment in buildings in order to have money to pay its preachers when its small churches went out of style in Appalachia in the 1950's with the coming of television and with the mass exodus of people needing work.

Thus, the office building with a church sanctuary on the third floor serves several purposes for the church group today, including rental space to US-EPA and others, including Dr. Parks' environmental consulting practice.

Government agencies such as US-EPA and state environmental and health agencies rent space in the comfortable and not-for-profit structure. And so also did Dr. Parks' firm as an environmental firm. And so it happened that Dr. Parks' office became located 20 feet across the lobby from EPA-Wheeling's Criminal Enforcement Officer Marvin S. Reicht.

Dr. Parks' office there had simple four inch letters with the firm's name, while the substantial Superfund tax dollars paid for Mr. Reicht's office entrance. It was camera-ready, and secret codes for locks were located behind bullet-proof glass installed after Reicht's arrival there from Philadelphia.

At times, the two discussed and disagreed on environmental sites for enforcement in the area. Dr. Parks' firm performed environmental hazardous materials site assessments, and found at times astounding amounts of buried hazardous wastes from the past, often in concrete vaults, and his work often ended when he told the truth, via written technical reports, of his findings.

No property purchases are suggested when hazardous wastes are found, after all. No firm wants to purchase a Superfund site and no lending institution wants to finance one with its or FDIC-sourced dollars. The L word in CERCLA, or Superfund, Liability, is too prominent, too great, and too financially painful. Respecting client confidentiality, Dr. Parks wondered how often in the future he would be subpoenaed without pay and have to tell the truth in court. Not to worry, though. It hasn't happened yet, he remembered.

"Not much," he had been advised by his long-term local legal counselor when he asked about his CERCLA, RCRA or Superfund responsibility to report threats to public health and the environment. As an attorney, he also worked by contract for the city, as did his two lawyer sons there.

"We have money for development, but not for environmental cleanup, especially when there isn't a Responsible Party with deep pockets," he was advised. And after all, he had already learned from Wheeling city officials that federal environmental law doesn't apply there, anyway. Dr. Parks had maintained a field office in the Methodist Building for one year after moving his office to Charleston. He returned at first to work there one day per week and to finish out a few remaining contracts to the former office. In a chance conversation which occurred while they were outside to smoke, Dr. Parks was advised by a friend of the following conversation: "But we need press attention to go after the asbestos cases," Reicht had instructed Pearbottom shortly after being hired. The real Superfund pot of dollars is going to be spent in current years in the Republican states, not West Virginia. The Justice Department wants 4,000 cases of asbestos press releases throughout the country now and next year.

"And I have a lead for you...and I want you to be very thorough and assess every single action for criminal and civil and personal and everything else against that environmental freak that moved last year from Wheeling to Charleston. He's a small business operator and does a state contract for inspecting buildings for asbestos for the state road commission. I want you to be proactive in enforcement since that is what your paycheck is all about, but I also want you to use the state government people, especially the asbestos technicians, to build a case. I want you to destroy this Tonto because he caused me to lose my major asbestos case here last year. Do an interview and charge him, his children, his company and any employee you can with compositing asbestos samples, first so we can be in on the act as feds with fraud under a little known *qui tam* act. I'll explain that later. I'll be down to Charleston next week to meet with you and then you can come here for a staff meeting Friday evening for the details. Meanwhile, I want you to get to know a Joe Dunn at the state highway office, who is the contract manager. I have already talked with him and the DED asbestos technician to stop any permits for any of his work. We want him dead in his tracks and we have already arranged to watch him do a couple contracted jobs in Logan and Huntington. By the way, the highways people who grade his work like him, I am told, so we'll have to involve someone else there to get the goods on him. There are a couple guys in the Technical Section at Highways who just love free drinks and I'll give you their names and numbers.

"This Joe Dunn at Highways also said he has some doubts about the so-called Dr. Parks after figuring out who he and his partner are from 17 years earlier. He said he has tried not to assign him much work but had to send some since Parks' firm is the designated minority firm for the contract, so there are some problems, but there are now three other firms doing the asbestos work and Parks is the fourth firm, but he is supposed to be the asbestos minority set-aside business.

"We want to watch him like an eagle on these two jobs and film what we can, then we'll ask that his work be resurveyed after he turns it in. Joe Dunn says he won't be paid for it though and we think he may be hurting for funds anyway so this should finish him off financially and then we'll see him in court with the Justice Department, which doesn't have much to do there anyway. I have already met with their people here in Wheeling and we are going to nail this bastard. Bet he'll never be a witness against us in court again. My friends in Philly, who he used to work for, and caused them to lose a major contract they say, want him out of the picture, too. Springer and Shoup both have a resentment against him for leaving at contract time. They needed his resume to help win the new contract to include the Wheeling office and he shouldn't have left them when he did so that they could continue to make good money here."

"My buddy there Mike Springer and his buddy Rudy Shoup who he used to work for say he has friends left at EPA, so don't leak any information to them or the state agency. I'll be talking with their deputy secretary Bill Adamson at DED there after we begin the Federal Investigation to see if they can come in on the set-up process to help us. We send them a lot of money every year. And I already have a poor bastard at the DED who is on an ego trip, if we can keep him sober, who'll help us and he'll involve the guy over at Health, who still has a resentment against Parks because he used to be his boss, then was trained by them and EPA and left two years later to make a bunch of money for himself and his own company. He started his own firm to make a bunch more off EPA. Then he won a $2.4 million dollar subcontract with our Superfund contractor and my buddies there, but they wouldn't send him any work, then he sued and settled for God knows what. My buddy Mike Springer calls every day from Philly to see how we're going to get him."

The entire conversation had been repeated to Dr. Parks by a friend around the corner from the outside smoking area several days after the conversation occurred.

"Dottie Kay Spott," Dr. Parks said to her, "Who told you all this, not that I don't believe you at all. I might have suspected that kind of imaginary conversation had taken place, but I never suspected someone like an old friend like you would actually tell me that kind of truth," Dr. Parks said to his trusted friend.

"Rudy told me that himself in a fit of confidence and liquid lubrication the last time he was over and we went out after you know what and he had too much to drink, as he does regularly anymore, it appears," Dottie replied.

Dr. Parks knew "what" and remembered the two had been more than friends while Rudy Shoup was his "big boss" at Western Environmental & Engineering. Dottie was married and stayed in the marriage for the children's sake. Her husband was a fellow with severe back injuries and more than sufficient painkiller medications to subdue all nerve endings. Dr. Parks was sympathetic and considered the confidential information in a non-judgmental light. Sex was no longer an issue in their marriage, she had said often.

The next month Dottie had driven to Charleston to bring her daughter to a high school competition twirling event in the state, and had asked to use the guest quarters at Dr. Parks' home. The two renewed an old friendship, and the information today was deemed to be confidential – but the dichotomy of information that is truth and the disparity of Dr. Parks' pain and losses – emotionally and financially – were separate issues in his mind. Creator and time and truth would hold the answers, he had decided at the time, and time was on his side – and maybe a couple friends like Dottie.

Shortly after Dr. Parks had received a standard-appearing tasking assignment for the Logan and Huntington jobs, the work was performed efficiently, referenced expenses in all category were pre-approved by standard rates and contract and federal and state regulatory standards had been met as in a hundred other tasking assignments for state and federal contracting.

The work was performed and turned in to the Division of Highways Consultant Services Section. Standard CPA-audited admin-multiplier rates were used and the hours and travel and analytical expenses were the most competitive available. He often wondered if he was charging enough after hearing of dollar amounts available by computer utilized by his competitor Pittsburgh firm, which had to drive or fly people in from Pittsburgh offices at expenses hugely higher than his capital city location.

And as is standard for most small business owners, a drawdown for expenses on plastic was completed for the work performed, and a check from the state was expected about 30 days later as they had done for the past five years. But when no check arrived, Dr. Parks called the accounting section, and was told they had not even received approved invoices there. They were held up in Joe Dunn's office, he was advised.

He then called the folks who had become professional acquaintances over the past five years of working for them at the Consultant Services Section. He was told there were some problems with the government regulators not wanting to issue a permit for his work and that he should call Joe Dunn. "He holds the key," he had been told.

"We'll get you a written report in 30 days," Dunn told Dr. Parks. Two months later no report was forthcoming.

"We want you to meet with us and our lawyer," Dr. Parks said to Dunn. They met, Dunn became the classical bureaucrat and wrote a letter report saying what they had discussed with seven points of discussion in his office being reiterated in a memo. Dunn said nothing about discussions with EPA bureaucrats, only that the state DED would not issue a permit on Dr. Parks' company's work – lying by not telling the whole truth.

"Our work does not require a permit," Dr. Parks reiterated. Dunn was silent on the comment. A letter to the Governor's office was sent, it was then sent over to Highways, where Dunn later drafted for another person's signature the standard reply that the work was being re-surveyed and a report would follow but that no payment could be made and that possibly the entire rules for asbestos sampling would have to be rewritten by the highways Technical Section, since they could not understand the perceived "discrepancies."

A field visit had resulted in more questions than answers to their inexperienced technicians, Dunn had commented, since they didn't understand asbestos or how to follow an inspection.

"Now I don't know anything about asbestos," Dunn said to Dr. Parks, "but it is my opinion that I should be able to follow an inspection." Dr. Parks said many state employees newly working in the asbestos technician field had told him that they 'didn't know their asbestos from a hole in the ground' but that they had an opinion."

He added that even inexperienced state employees have a right to their opinions, of course, but that the rules are available in writing and not a lot more should matter when those expansive rules have been followed for a generation now. "The reports require trained, certified personnel and are not necessarily written in a manner a layman would understand just by picking them up," Dr. Parks replied.

Dunn said nothing at any time about his conversations with the EPA-Wheeling bureaucrats, only that the DED state bureaucrats would not issue a permit based on Parks' work.

"Again, none is required, never has been, that's for the demolition contractor, which we don't do, as you well know. We are technical consultants and tell the removal contractor what is there, within reason under a magnitude of state and federal rules, which we follow to a tee, rules I helped write," Dr. Parks said.

Dunn replied he took the word of the regulators, since they decide if a project moves or not, and that is serious business to him, for moving millions of construction dollars from the Governor's office by the next state election.

Dunn, Dr. Parks had observed over the 17 years he had known him in circles outside government contracting and the last five in government contract circles, had made himself very important by appearing solemn when wanting to give the impression of seriousness and in fact solemnity.

Dunn came from that extended northern European culture as a guy who had after years battling drunkenness, divorce and degradation, developed solemnity as a character trait in order to keep his highways engineering job. He was serious and one didn't even have to ask.

That cultural and personal characteristic had baffled Dr. Parks as a kind of clear dishonesty, anathema to his Native culture of spiritually-based honesty as a manner of being happy, healthy and free in all his affairs.

In his European Culture 301 class in college he had studied the European culture as best as one could relate to it, and had submitted a study report on a guy Molly Ivins later in life had written about once in a column from Ft. Worth while he was there performing an environmental site assessment of a commercial property.

Dr. Parks remembered Joe Dunn at the time, then wondered the next year during a lead presentation how God was forcing such honesty through a man who played an astute bureaucrat role through several political administrations where dishonesty is openly required of state road administrators in the state.

Dunn had the kind of Teutonic mind, and physiological appearance and personality, that didn't allow for the difference between being solemn and being serious. "There is a kind of Teutonic mind which you find not just in Germany and Switzerland, but also in America," Molly Ivins had copied in a writing of John Cheese, a British actor.

"...that Teutonic mind believes you have to be solemn if you are being serious. But in fact solemnity is, I think, in many ways the enemy of the kind of process of learning that comes from being open, because solemnity is allied with pompousness."

Through scores of years of continuing adult education, Dr. Parks had come to identify and admire those in powerful roles who possess what he termed a scientific mind. But he distrusted inherently those in powerful places with Teutonic minds, usually accompanied, he had learned, by some innate lack of native intelligence but with a strong self-will to succeed in their professions, or at least in the role they had been assigned as bureaucrats.

Joe Dunn had a Teutonic mind, he observed. Many rooms are filled with sick bastards, he had experienced in years of spiritual growth, but it is those who profess solemnity next to spirituality who are often the sickest, in his experience.

In his first year in recovery, Dr. Parks' sponsor had instilled the following thought as step one of recovery: "Always remember and never forget: there are sick people both in these room and outside these rooms. In fact, we are all sick to a degree, or we wouldn't be here in recovery. People are going to do what people are going to do. And you may quote me on that. That's been my experience and will probably be yours."

When Pearbottom had acted on the bureaucrats' spate of

self-will, nothing was discussed about the other "two's" in the "on-going" Federal Investigation. Now, two years later, the "two's" and their synergisms became more readily apparent when the list of witnesses against Dr. Parks' company was sent out after the secret criminal investigation proceedings.

Dr. Parks and his business partner, Thom Botts; Dr. Parks' two children, neither of whom participated in the work, but was good for intimidation; two state DED and Health red-faced, white shirted, and gray-suited older men labeled asbestos technicians; two EPA enforcement officers passing out press releases and quoting questionable education backgrounds; two former federal contract employees, Springer and Shoup; and, two criminal lawyers now plying their trade for fees after retiring as federal prosecutors.

At the trial, Dr. Parks had wondered what parity checks in relationship to the 12 on-the-beam and the 12 off-the-beam human emotions he had studied for furthering his spiritual development were occurring in the minds of the seven 00 and 01 minds that day in the federal courthouse. It was stuff too heady for a courtroom though, he decided.

While Dr. Parks testified to the Grand Jury, Pearbottom called Thom Botts aside and gave him a talking to. Pearbottom let him know it was against the rules of civil procedure for him to ever discuss anything said to the grand jury with Dr. Parks regarding his secret testimony that day.

"And I will see that you are put into a jail cell if I ever hear you have discussed items from the courtroom," Botts later repeated to Dr. Parks. "And I'm not even supposed to be telling you that, let alone what they asked me about," he said.

Pearbottom held the same aside didactic, albeit illegal and unethical, conversation with Dr. Park's son, also now Dr. Parks but that of the physician kind. The younger Dr. Parks, not easily intimidated, had immediately changed the conversation to army gun munitions and firing weapons comparable to the one being worn by Pearbottom in the electronically scrutinized federal courthouse built two years before with "high to epitome" electronic surveillance standards, the local press had commented.

The two state asbestos technicians, friends, red-faced, drinking buddies, chatted down the hall together. And former unemployed coalminer Pearbottom, the employee, EPA Criminal Enforcement person; and – oh, my, missing, the perpetrators who had chaired and signed for the state road commission committee to press federal charges, Joe Dunn, not present. And Mr. Reicht, missing.

Isn't it amazing, Dr. Parks thought to himself, that the two who took this action, who were dishonest to the US Justice Department, and then delegated to other bureaucrats the performance of their dirty work stemming from their own prejudiced resentments, were not required to be present at trial. Isn't it amazing, Dr. Parks' sponsor later commented to him on the matter: "And they're just doing their jobs."

"Oh, they are protected by the 11th Amendment to the Constitution. They were just doing their jobs. They are exempt from testimony," Dr. Parks lawyer said in reply later to the same comment.

But it seems everything that goes around comes around, sometimes sooner than later. According to a press report one month after the grand jury proceedings, Joe Dunn denied he was retiring from the state, even though a state engineering database carried the announcement, a newspaper reporter learned through a tip.

Yet, 30 days later, he "announced" to the same political reporter that, yes, Joe Dunn was "retiring" with intent to go to work for a consulting firm. Imagine that. Had he now been, in the words of Shakespeare, *hoisted to his own petard*?

And now a free agent, not protected by state lawyers, and, it is rumored, not as sober as one in recovery might want to be – in fact, was "repeating his history," according to the local rumors. Mr. Recovery, he once called himself, not available by telephone?

"I see," said Dr. Parks after calling a friend in the relatively small world of recovery in the Appalachian Mountains.

The criminal trial was finally scheduled and put on the docket after Dr. Parks had refused to "dogfall." That Old Virginia law term, Ben Wanton explained to him, was alliterative for when the fox hunter's dogs fall over a cliff, usually die or are too mangled to hunt, and all the men just quit the chase and go home for the night. The Justice Department wanted Dr. Parks to do that. Dr. Parks would have nothing of it. The pain would be too great.

Sponsors have final answers and the answer was no. That settled what could be described as a spiritual seeking process to do the next right thing. It would have meant suffering the loss of the $25,000 plus statutory interest to replace the credit card debt, remaining off the contract at an already estimated loss of $250,000, and essentially admitting guilt.

"This whole fiasco has made the state look guilty," partner Thom Botts would comment later to Dr. Parks. "Now if you press your $5 million suit, they may file civilly, just be forewarned."

Dr. Parks decided it was high time he went to speak with his sponsor. It had been a while since he had last sought the type of spiritual guidance for his earthly affairs, such as false criminal charges brought by a government he used to work for.

"Ed, the criminal trial itself is coming up in the Fall, and the woman at Justice has told my lawyer she is willing to settle. I would suppose what she is hinting at is that I could put the corporation out of business and that would make them happy. But on our part, the damages have been astronomical – not just in terms of money but physical pain from the injuries for hernia and back pain and the emotional pain of being mostly unemployed nearly three years, being fired from DED while on Workers Comp, no work on the contract, a nearly total consumption for three years of my energies, and more I don't need to tell you about," Dr.

Parks said.

"EagleClaw," Ed H said without his even asking the question, "you have no right to compromise your own truth and integrity in this matter. Don't ask. You are to go to a jury trial unless they settle for absolutely no less than one-half million dollars. Need I say more? You don't dog fall on the criminal proceedings, even with your freedom at risk."

"Enough said," Dr. Parks replied. "I'll be in touch by e-mail, buddy. And remember who loves you – there are lots of us, no doubt, and I'm just one of them."

He repeated the conversation openly with a local co-sponsor, who had become much closer to the case on a day-to-day basis. The conversations could have been pre-recorded and replayed. The truth is often repeated. No dog fall to surrender one's own truth to untruths, they both repeated.

They then smiled, hugged, spiritually loved one another as only two adult men close in the ways of 12-step program sponsorship can, and departed.

Chapter Six

Regaining Sanity

AFTER THE TWO federal bureaucrats, Pearbottom and the second office guest from the Federal Highways Administration, who was flown in so that the interview could be legally but secretly recorded, Dr. Parks surmised, he wondered again what was really behind their motives. Theirs was such a serious charge, criminal fraud for someone who had lived life not to make money, just a living, by way of 12 spiritually-based principles in life. Criminal means they want to put you in a prison cell. Civil means they want to punish you by taking, or in this case, keeping, your money, home, or all the above. He could begin to see that his future, meaning retirement, the golden years in which he hoped to author a novel while helping others in recovery – his life as he knew it – was being threatened. The threat was clear.

He arose that morning, showered, had one of his favorite Appalachian cuisine breakfasts of sausage gravy, biscuits and sauteed ramps for bodily vigor, then moved to his five morning meditations.

Hubert Humphrey with John F. Kennedy had once stumped the poverty-ridden ridges and hollows of Appalachee, visiting individually with many of the mixed blood and cultures Scots-Irish and Indian descendants. He said something EagleClaw would never forget: "Just be what you are and speak from the gut and heart. It's all a man has."

The words rang wisdom. He surmised he might have 17 years' preparation through spiritual growth which he would need to call on everyday in order to go through a re-birthing in life for the next 17 year cycle, like the locust and the jade tree, in order to blossom again.

His spiritual teachings had imparted to him that masculine spiritual recovery is a return to our guts and our heart.

He then returned to work at his home office, stepping from the home hallway, exiting past a required firewall, and picked up one of three two-inch thick technical reports he and Thom Botts had completed and submitted to the state, presuming they would be paid in 30 days as they had been for over five years now.

The last state asbestos tasking assignment had been relatively small by comparison to many highways projects he had directed in the past, always with full approval on completion by the client. It was small compared to many past contracts. What's the point? Could it be that someone else, such as Roger Pickett, close to the Governor's win last year and also the owner of another asbestos consulting firm, and an asbestos removal firm, wanted the work of the state contract?

Maybe, he thought, since Roger Pickett had contacted him last year after the election and suggested he would like to subcontract the work using his own employees for Dr. Parks' work assignments.

"Highways is the reward agency for politicians who win elections, you know" Roger had said to Dr. Parks, who had replied he would consider Pickett's proposition, but that for now there had been such a small amount of work that he and his business partner had performed the work handily.

He then wondered what the good old boys at EPA, rather than OSHA, had in mind, as the driver of the Federal Investigation. It wasn't driven by just technical enforcement, he knew. His private industry work for asbestos by federal and state rules, after all, was regulated by OSHA, not EPA. But it had been, of course, against EPA that he had served as an asbestos expert witness in Wheeling after they charged the innocent businessman there with improper disposal. EPA regulates disposal of asbestos, as well as in schools in the country. Neither of those work activities were presently involved in his state contract.

But even more distinctly, Dr. Parks remembered that before the court settlement three years ago of the Western Environmental case that he had been threatened in a telephone conversation apparently driven by alcohol consumption and its sister emotion resentment in a telephone call received in his Wheeling office from his former boss at Western Environmental, Rudy Shoup.

Shoup had announced "I will do everything in my power in the small world of environmental federal contracting in the future to destroy you and your small business." Dr. Parks had made a logbook entry of the pronouncement and had immediately gone out front to tell Thom Botts of the conversation since he had answered the phone before transferring the call to Dr. Parks.

Rudy had accused Dr. Parks of causing Western Environmental and Engineering to lose a former 23 year, $107 million dollar contract with EPA in part because he had resigned from that firm to set up his own minority-owned environmental consulting practice. Although Rudy was told expressly by Dr. Parks prior to the resignation face to face and was given full leeway for comments, Rudy advised him later he should have stayed on until after the new contract was won. But five years later, Western Environmental and Engineering had not honored his small firm's $2.4 million subcontract to Dr. Parks' Small Disadvantaged Business Section 8a firm. It would take a lawsuit to settle the matter. Next contract around, Western lost the opportunity to bid. They also settled out of court after Dr. Parks and his partner sued for the subcontract loss. The agreement stated that the amount was never to be disclosed outside the parties to the suit. Was Rudy still sick with resentment in his rumored alcoholism? It remained a non-asked question. It was a program of attraction not promotion. And until one concedes to his innermost self that he has a problem with any addiction, a cure is just not in the picture. But how far would he go with the threat in the future became the ques-

tion. It would require a complete seven-year cycle to have answers.
Dr. Parks often quoted Alfred North Whitehead out of his European cultural traditions. Old Alfred, the noted science educator, he recalled, had said "One learns best through the re-investigation of ideas." He related to that statement from his own life experiences. He also didn't always get everything the first time around and had to re-investigate and rethink issues in order to learn, to repeat lessons learned, and when the pain became great enough, to change.

Thinking back, Dr. Parks remembered again that he had served as the expert witness in Wheeling last year against the guy who brought the EPA action and lost and was embarrassed by the headlines. Marvin Reicht had teamed with Joe Dunn at the state Division of Highways, and thus two resentments against one fellow already served as a focal point of a prejudiced resentment by the two bureaucrats.

And the synergistic impact was being carried out against him, his children, his Indian-owned firm, and his business partner, by flagrant abuse of bureaucratic power plays through the court system in a culture where the intent is their "justice" through persecution by the government using its contractors. They had suspected he would just dog fall. He wouldn't and couldn't and still maintain his Step 1 spiritual principle of honesty, he knew. Honesty is not a replacement for acceptance when one has done nothing wrong and is being persecuted by vindictive bureaucrats out to make a name for themselves, add scoring points in their jobs, and the ultimate goal of "impressing the boss." He had already learned some lessons in life, such as these, and didn't need to relearn them. But there would be new lessons to learn, he knew.

Old Alfred had it right, of course, he had learned many times. He didn't always get everything right the first time, so as often as not he had to re-investigate and relearn and rethink many issues in life, and sometimes to react. Sometimes he did not. Today was different. He was no longer a doormat to be walked upon.

He had to always ask himself what role he had played in any resentment by others when –not if– it was recognized, and more importantly was the resentment in his mind or in the mind of others. Honesty, as always, was the first step and was crucial in that decision making process. He also had learned to ask is it real or is it just an old tape playing again in his head? This one wasn't.

The criminal suit against him and others was without any legal basis he could identify, in full honesty, as well as that of his business partner, his sponsors, and his lawyers. Yet his keep-it-simple answer to himself on the criminal matters as charged was this: "It ain't paranoia if it's real."

And the criminal charges were clearly both vindictive and real. They were written on paper called a subpoena to Federal District Court.

Over the next several months Dr. Parks utilized the time for performing some revenue-producing tasks for the firm; continued teaching part-time as an adjunct professor at the Jesuit University; and teaching part-time for the public school system. The term doctor means teacher. He enjoyed teaching.

But he increasingly stepped up his working with others in the 12-step recovery program, including doubling up on meetings for seeking spiritual growth – and to lower his own possibility of developing a prejudiced resentment against those who had given him good cause to develop it and to give a whole new definition to the French term *resentire*.

Resentments are the number one offender to those in recovery programs, he had been advised 17 years earlier by a sponsor, a lesson he didn't want to allow himself to forget. So he decided he would just pray for the sick bastards–pray that they would receive every good thing he desired. But in order to receive those good things in life –love, serenity, peace, he had to carry out some steps first – and they would someday, in some way, be required to carry out nothing less. That thinking works, he had experienced. It is the essence of an expression used very often around the rooms – let go and let God. It worked if he worked it, he knew.

He also knew that for those folks in any of the approximately 300 kinds of 12-step recovery programs in existence in America and throughout the world that the dichotomies and paradoxes of living life on life's terms comes to both literal and figurative meeting places at some point in life – as the computer signals 00 and 01 come together and require a parity check to move on to another energy form – in other words to send a message to a receiver.

He wondered what would lie ahead of the federal criminal fraud charges against him; his two children; and, his business partner Thom Botts, who had always had an unfounded fear of going to jail for some reason; and the corporation itself, which owned nothing more that a computer, a printer and a copier, all on their way to being phased out; and, $100,000 stock shares valued at $1 par.

Dr. Parks had personally purchased with a family loan the other environmental testing equipment utilized by the firm and much of it had expired beyond its value. His technical skills and knowledge were his selling points for hazardous materials testing and studies and producing technical reports, with contract labs providing the analyses.

He provided the technical reports of site conditions and quantities of hazardous wastes to be removed. Those were his marketable skills, not producing widgets he had learned to count in his business courses while completing his Ph.D. in Administration and Management with an emphasis on managing environmental programs. The degree had been earned through two years' hard work and research through an extension learning school at a California university accredited by the state department of education. It was in the early days of extension learning degrees, the British education method now widely accepted in the United States. But when Shoup heard of the degree program, even though the company paid the fees, he labelled the program a degree ordered from the back of a match cover. But he didn't have a masters degree to enter the Ph.D. program and perhaps that colored his thinking. Jealousy and envy come in many forms. But so does forgiveness and all the other 12 on-the-beam emotions, Dr. Parks had learned.

Thus, instead of widgets to be produced, Dr. Parks in a required *pro forma* counted his contract marketing skills, knowledge and abilities, SKA's the bureaucrats called them, for professional services contracts, skills he had learned in his Master of Science degree in Environmental Studies. Those were his widgets being counted and sold. And he had plenty goods in stock as well as an excellent professional reputation from former employers in industry and in federal government contracting program management for 27 years.

He could add to this timeline for his lawyer 14 years of his own environmental consulting success, whatever that term means. He had heard success defined as being able to respond appropriately to any event at the time it occurs.

But here in the meantime, it was just that – a mean time. Little to no work for the corporation, depression from the false federal charges, bills with interest for the company and for his household were demanding payment, and it would all get worse, he would learn.

He reviewed the scenario of the earlier field visit when the whole thing began that day in Logan:

The state employees, it was said, work with lots of personal opinions, but good old boys who have never collected a single asbestos sample, let alone had one analyzed, nor point-counted, and can't spell microscopy – all while drinking too much with the good old boys from the EPA, also with opinions, – it must have been a fun scenario at the local watering hole that day in Logan, named to honor the Indian Chief, after he left. He had located all the sampling points for them at their request. They didn't want to hear.

Do we know our asbestos from a hole in the ground begs the question for them, he thought. No answer was required. Returning to the office later, he had telephoned his former contract manager at the state DOH, an engineer he recognized would, regardless of the "technical issues," tell him the truth as he knew it if asked.

"Mike, what in the world are you guys studying that is taking so long to let us know what in the world is wrong with our work which we have been providing five continuous years' good professional technical services with nothing but compliments from you guys?" he asked.

Mike said, "Well, the Technical Section technicians decided after the environmental agencies complained of alleged differing sampling methodologies that they don't hold the same opinion as yours. So Joe Dunn decided to have your work re-surveyed. They did so, at a cost of $57,000 for your about $10,000 Logan job, only to have two of the three 'discrepancies' as Joe calls them, come out in your guys' favor. In other words, you guys found and confirmed through point-counting 5,000 square feet more positive asbestos wall plaster in one of the structures than what the Pittsburgh firm found. It's embarrassing to them, and I'm not sure I am supposed to be telling you this, but it's a matter of public record."

Mike the engineering supervisor for asbestos contracts spoke those volumes to Dr. Parks, who replied, "Thanks. That's amazing court evidence if I ever need it."

Dr. Parks asked what else. "Well," Mike replied, "the other is a discrepancy I don't understand fully and that is on the Huntington job. They couldn't find all the sample numbers on the walls. They re-surveyed and wrote sample numbers by our new proposed rules and for the filming where their new sampling holes are. They had photos before your sampling was done. We haven't required them until now, but they were good for the movie they also made of the re-survey work."

Dr. Parks could see the evolving case against his small business versus the United States with unlimited resources. Dunn refused to pay the $18,000 from the estimated $25,000 tasking assignment due his small business for work performed correctly under written contract and written tasking assignment, yet hired the Pittsburgh firm to re-survey the Logan job alone at $57,000 and the results made Dr. Parks' inspection look impressive. Dilemma time for the highways committee, no doubt.

"Mike," Dr. Parks replied, "We write indelible sample numbers on the containers as our contract requires and on the drawings and after the analytical results from the lab are returned to us – not on walls where we may make a dozen holes to see if it's all the same like-appearing material to be sampled, but send only three, five or seven samples to the lab, as required."

"Bob, I know that and I am not even technically trained in asbestos sample collections, but the tech over at Health, Gallahue, and the tech at DED, Wumble, think otherwise and they are doing everything they can, it seems, to look good to the EPA guy, who keeps complaining to Joe Dunn on your quality of work. He seems to have a real resentment against you and your firm for some reason."

"Thanks, Mike, and what is the other so-called discrepancy?" Dr. Parks asked. Mike said that under a sub-floor in one room that the kitchen cherry cabinets had been robbed out of the abandoned structure after the inspection and in the ripping out process that some nine-inch green floor tile had been uncovered.

"Mike – the state licensing law provides for that – I know, I wrote that rule for passage many years ago while I worked at the State Health Department. Under the federal NESHAPS rule – the same one that requires point-counting of samples I educated you guys about last year and the same rule I testified against EPA in Wheeling last year, we cannot just go in and rip out parts of structures because that may cause visible emissions for non-sampled material and that is a no-no. In other words, removal contractors are required by the state licensing law to be licensed inspectors also just for that reason – that if their workers uncover new suspect asbestos-containing material they will recognize it and have it analyzed, especially if we couldn't see it since we don't have x-ray vision."

"I know that too, Bob, from our earlier discussions with removal contractors for justifying add-on costs for those removal contractors, but I am just telling you that is a third discrepancy that Joe Dunn – and he's the driver here, is saying the matter cannot be resolved. We are re-writing our own technical rules for sampling and all you consultants will be contacted to review the proposed rules and give us your comments. The meeting is scheduled next month and you will get a notice. I believe they went out today for approval from Joe."

"Thanks, Mike. You have never had an uncomplimentary word for our work and I appreciate that. I hope your faith in us continues."

"Oh, it will, Bob, and I believe this matter is just 'a wind' on someone's part and that it will pass. I hope so. I haven't seen anything by way of justification to the complaints. They seem to be just opinions by the regulatory agency personnel. And I guess every state employee has his right to an opinion. But the tech over at DED won't issue a permit for removal to us as a result of the complaint by his guy at EPA in Wheeling, whoever that is."

"Won't issue a permit? Mike, our work does not require a permit, let alone one from WV-DED. What in the world is going on here? Who is this Leonard Wumble you are speaking of? He's just a bean counter recently put in that position I am told by Bill Adamson, Deputy Director at DED, so that they have some place to put him after he keeps raising hell outside the agency, but has civil service coverage.

"That is amazing to learn that. Wumble at DED and Paul Gallaghue at Health are friends and very much alike. Have you met them? They both are in their late 50's, gray-headed and red-faced, wear a white shirt and gray suit to work and both are asbestos technicians who are paid accordingly, and both like to act like experts with opinions that may or may not be just that – opinions.

"This information amazes me, Mike. I appreciate your honesty and candor, and I would like to get back to work soon. I haven't had a payday for months as a result of this action by Dunn and I may have to file a recovery lawsuit. But that's another day, and I hope to see you at the meeting you mentioned. Good day, buddy."

"Good day to you too, he replied."

Chapter Seven

So Don't Think

"Oh, I don't think so," his lawyer had replied when Dr. Parks explained his suspicion that a vendetta by two bureaucrats out of control with their power was potentially the driving force of the criminal charges. He was meeting again with Ben Wanton. "And even if they had such a prejudice against you just because they have known you for up to 17 years and in a 12-step recovery program or were jealous and envious of your highly technical work at EPA it doesn't mean they'd dare act on it," Wanton said. But Dr. Parks was there this time to discuss his civil suit for recovery of damages against the state and two individuals – Dunn and Reicht.

He had learned early in adulthood that the are four correct ways for answering known questions in his mixed cultural background of Western European and Native American cultures. All are honest beyond question but all are always situational.

The four ways to always honestly answer questions are 1)yes; 2)no; 3)I don't know, and 4)I don't think so. All four answers appeared from his biological hard drive computer in his head while speaking with and listening to his lawyer. Ben Wanton was recognized as a top-notch attorney who had been referred to him for this case against the almighty United States of America, whoever that is, or at least whom he might, with the aid of the two vindictive bureaucrats entrenched in their power, and without the aid of a lubricant, he thought, find out. But he hoped not.

Something more was beyond the present array of subpoenas for his two children, his business partner, his corporation and himself personally. He admitted he did not know what, however. Neither did his lawyer know.

"What about that supposed veil for why we have corporations," he asked Ben. "Isn't that called double jeopardy?"

"Oh, that theory doesn't apply with criminal charges," Ben had replied. They are out to get whatever they can and apparently they believe you have done something wrong if they can just figure out what it is."

"And what might that be?" Dr. Parks continued. "The charges are compositing already composited building materials, such as plaster, for goodness sakes, and it was positive beyond question. And we billed for five samples for 5,000 sq. ft. of surfacing mixed materials, all white to the naked eye. It was point-counted and still positive. It's not like we sent 25 samples as the non-technically trained in asbestos criminal investigator mistakenly said to me in my office.

"Our hours and rates are the same ones we have been using for years and were pre-approved before we ever went to the field, as they always are, so what's their beef, Ben?"

"I don't know but that's what we intend to find out either through discovery or cross-examination on the witness stand," Ben replied.

Ben Wanton had charged instead of his regular $30,000 fee for criminal defense a negotiated fee of $3,500 – a paltry sum by comparison. The act of the favor had come across through a friend who headed up the legal firm and was a friend of Dr. Parks for many years in their 12-step recovery program. George Straight of the law firm knew that Dr. Parks was telling the truth or it might kill him – physically, mentally and spiritually. No doubt in his mind, he had said, and agreed to get the case settled based on the facts and suppositions of the prejudiced resentments from the past of the two supervising bureaucrats. And the Justice Department bureaucrats needed "brownie points" for asbestos enforcement actions, win or lose, Ben had suggested in their first meeting. A press article that week confirmed the order of the US President George Bush to the Justice Department. Asbestos cases in the newspaper look like environmental enforcement to the public, after all, in their opinion. And consultants, rather than demolition contractors, are an easy target and usually don't defend themselves well, in their experience. The beans would nevertheless be counted.

In his 14 years that very week in a 12-step recovery program from "isms" from a fear-based European culture, as well as addictions not to be revealed at the level of press, radio or film for the individual, he wondered what "new" spiritually-based lessons he needed to learn in his third beginning "seven year cycle of spiritual growth – and decline." But little did he know that he would also pass the 17-year rebirthing process before he began to find out.

And decline, he emphasized to himself. No pain no gain. In that week of his 14th program birthday he had received four telephone calls that moved his life from forward and growing to reverse and pain. What questing and what level of sanity on behalf of two government bureaucrats had to be achieved for them to no longer practice their resentment, let alone maybe die or minimally get drunk at it, he wondered. But for others that was Creator's decision and action, if any, he decided. Maybe the sick bastard will have a heart attack or something, but that's not for me to know. My duty is to pray for the sick bastard – pray that he would receive all the good things in life I desire. What did he hold close and desire? Sobriety, spiritual growth, helping others and giving and getting love of the variety Creator allows between all mankind. He already had offered regularly as much as he could handle of the other kind of love, or at least it was rumored, he had heard from both female and male wags. It's called gossip and sometimes true, sometimes not so true, in his experience.

But he knew that was their problem in life, not his. His was to get through "it" whatever "it" might be – in this case a criminal "case" that he somehow knew would ultimately result in not just clearance, but hopefully also monetary rewards, and ultimately, spiritual rewards including patience and tolerance. But at what price?

And ultimately, before it was over in three to five years, maybe even seven years, he had been advised in a meeting with friends, he would regain sanity that only comes from "passing through the eye of a needle in life," it was suggested to him–and increased understanding through spiritual growth. It's required to survive and to 'keep green' he was advised, as in chlorophyl and growing spiritually. It was advice he didn't really want to hear, but sometimes we hear what we need to hear, not what we want to hear, they said. He heard. Staying green in life is to keep growing.

His friend, Dr. Gregg, also an expert witness, had said in the same meeting that "And those who live by the sword may die by the sword, but he who lays down the sword survives somehow and goes on to achieve experiential growth that we in the these rooms call spirituality. Some call it humility. That's different from humiliation for us," he added, then passed in discussion.

"We shall see, shan't we?" he mused to himself during the rest of the Mustard Seed Group meeting.

Dr. Parks said he had not been seeking all that in his life, but that if a circle of spiritual growth from false federal criminal fraud charges against him– putting him in a prison cell being the very simple goal of the criminal charges– then he knew he would have a strong circle of growth along the way. He recalled Nelson Mandela's story of 27 years in prison in South Africa before becoming president of his courntry. He didn't wish that on anyone, but he was not in charge, he realized.

His Native spirituality and that of all 12-step programs go hand in glove, he had learned, and offer the student a way to not only survive crises, but also to grow through the learning and painful process and also to regain sanity after time and then to also gain and regain being happy, joyous and free – and sometimes prosperous. Or, "free at last... free at last," Dr. King had said as a bottom line on such matters.

Both respected their own mountains to climb, no doubt.

But had he really bargained for all that in this defense process? Four ways to answer any question in a willing life of spiritual growth were the choices of answers available to him, he recollected. They remained four ways for four directions of life from the medicine wheel he kept hanging on his office wall used in sharing 4th step learning with sponsees.

Yes, he had acted within the definition of both responsibility to his Creator to be a willing instrument, and respect for self by not being a doormat to be walked upon; and, also in the words of his fellow West Virginian, Tecumseh. The Shawnee spiritual giant had said, "Show respect for all men but grovel to none."

It was time to see Ben Wanton again.

"It has been nice visiting with you today, EagleClaw, reviewing in detail the past case, but the reason I called you in today is not your potential suit for $5 million damages, but to announce that I spoke with Carol Jackson at the Justice Department yesterday while over there on another case and they have decided to file civil charges against you and the corporation under the False Claims Act.

"This time it's just civil charges because you're still demanding you get paid your $18,000 plus interest for the work you did and maybe embarrass them by filing a state court suit for damages. That's probably why they want to bring your *pro se* case over to federal court then remove it.

"That's the only reason too the judge has to bring it over because all the other charges are related in the chain of events that occurred and are separate and distinct charges as violations of the law, but have nothing to do with creating false documents or asbestos. It will show unreasonable favor to Jackson at Justice if Judge Goodrich tosses your suit, even though he can. It's like the proverbial male dog story, why does he lick his genitals? Because he can is the simplistic answer, but the correct answer is because he can't make a fist. But lets just see what happens. It may give us a case to reinvent our wheel if that happens, which it probably will."

"I told her you were planning to file the damages suit – just not how much and certainly nothing like $5 million. It will embarrass them, she says, after they didn't get to first base in the criminal indictment attempt. I again suggest you dog fall," the former federal prosecutor said.

Dr. Parks read his daily spiritual meditations that night then picked up the book of non-recovery literature beside the bed sent to him as a birthday gift from a sister in Dallas.

"Out of West Virginia comes the writer who is betrayed by his own intellectual efforts – John Nash has captured a Nobel Peace Prize with recovery from a disease of the mind that takes one from helplessness to hopelessness," the cover review said.

"Gosh, where did that come from?" he mused to himself.

John Nash chronicled leaving the Morgantown, WV area and had gone to Princeton, New Jersey, to carry out research for federal government-funded programs. His subject was a federal contract employee with an enemy – his own mind. He had a disease. He recovered. It was a great movie. Was history repeating itself, Dr. Parks had to ask himself. Another West Virginian had left for New Jersey, had written a wonderful novel about recovery, and once again out of the hills of West Virginia had come life-giving wisdom for others, his sister in Dallas had annotated on the review from the Dallas *Times*.

He remembered last Passover Seder with friends – Indians do all the holidays – he mused again, where only the stupid child fails to even ask any question. But the question was there in his mind: Could there be some level of paranoia/schizophrenia developing in his mind because of the continuing false charges?

Just asking the question, he thought, deserved some recognition of at least the possibility now and in the future.

Better talk with old sponse, he decided, recognizing the symptom of symptoms, and proceeded to pick up the telephone and call Columbus.

"Hi, Ed," he said. "I have something to bounce off you, just in case," and proceeded to do so.

"Recognizing the potential emotional symptoms is important," Ed said. "But the etiologies of the two diseases are very dis-similar. It is good you asked, he said, but there is no correlation. But since he knew to ask the question, he should then take some action. He had by calling him. Old sponse told him he had done the right thing just by calling and pronounced him safe, sound, and spiritually fit.

"Good night, and RWLY" they said to one another.

Dr. Parks thought about his own situation again from what the writer of *A Beautiful Mind* had recovered from, his mind, his schizophrenia, himself. At least he had remembered to ask the right question before he required an answer. The only wrong question is the unasked one, he had heard.

There had been a parallel in his own experience, he thought, with his 14 year and two 7 year cycles of growth, and now well into this third identifiable cycle of spiritual growth – and decline – out of his Native American spirituality. It had been an idea shared by his friend Louis Southworth with him many years before. It thus was not at all an original idea – just one shared among many cultures – and applicable in his own years in recovery, with growth periods of painstaking and growth and decline – sort of like life itself, he thought to himself. It was just living life on life's terms. But recognizing– and sharing– the terms was the real lesson here.

Birth, life, death, reincarnation, as the East Indians would call it, and not at all unlike what the Native American Indians also call it– cycles or circles of spiritual growth, decline and rebirth to live again until ultimately the Sprit in the body returns to Great Spirit, or God, or Jehovah, or whatever word one chooses to call that linkage of the sprit in the body he knew was there, with Great Spirit.

"And if one doesn't believe the body has a spirit, go down to the local funeral home and view the body of the deceased person whose Spirit has left the physical body," his sponsor once suggested. With that statement, acceptance, and seeking spiritual growth, had become life goals. It was not unlike the teachings of Herbert Spencer the philosopher, he began to understand. It was now 17 years ago that the term and concept of spirituality had been offered to him. About 17 years ago he could not define spirituality, but today he practiced it on a daily basis. He learned it best by the root derivation of the term – spirit and ritual. It included prayer and meditation; and, smudging from his Native culture, also a prayer and meditation process, and by observation of Nature. That summer the locusts would swarm his rose gardens and his mother's jade trees would bloom after 17 years domracy.

It was old Herbert Spencer, out of his European cultural traditions, who had said, "There is a principle which is a bar against all information, which is proof against all arguments, and which cannot fail to keep a man in everlasting ignorance–that principle is contempt prior to investigation."

It wasn't his place consciously to be didactic, he thought, but he couldn't help but think of Judge Goodrich practicing these principles in all his affairs during this painstaking period of his life. Did he say all?

While growing up, he had thought painstaking meant meticulous. He had learned to keep a dictionary beside his life-learning materials. Painstaking's root derivation had not changed, only his perception had been altered. Dictionaries do that for us. And using it had been suggested to him when he was told the word 'suggestion' is defined by Webster's as a subtle command.

And before recovery, he could not grasp a concept of what those other folks were talking about when they said the word spirituality. Now, he could write, discuss, even grow it himself.

That epiphany came to him the day he admitted he could not stop drinking beer on a daily basis after the first one by his own will 17 years earlier. The American Medical Association defines that recognized "ism" as a disease with its own etiology. They had done so in 1957 while he was 14 years old and growing up on a farm in the hills of West Virginia. It is addiction, defined as a physical craving resulting in a mental obsession combined with a physical allergy. The allergy causes the brain to release a chemical abbreviated as THIQ. And it's off to the races with the first drink of alcohol, or pill, or 300 other addictions recognized as the human condition. The cure is always spiritual, not physical or mental, he had learned.

His Native culture had taught him that all true knowledge comes from the inner self, that one just has to bring it forth to recognize it and then to practice it on a daily basis. It's more than just having in all cultures a conscience we are born with. It has been described by some as developing a Vital Sixth Sense. He knew. He had one.

Most real learning in his life had come following an epiphany of the educational variety of experience. His had come followed by a white light experience of the Bill Wilson variety and now 17 years successfully following a 12-step recovery program method. "It works, it really does," in his experience and he had seen and shared that experience with any who specifically asked. It is a program of attraction, not promotion.

And it keeps on working if you let it, by faith, not necessarily of the religious variety, but of the spiritual variety, and that too was his experience. Others' experience may be different, but he allowed for that. That was his experience. Your experience may be different, but the program allows for that too, he said often. One is not only allowed to define his own higher power there, but is also allowed to strike his own truth, he had learned.

And his Native spirituality had taught him the same

thing, especially during the last seven years since he had returned to practice that brand of spirituality in the hills of Appalachia.

Working with others was the key, most of whom were mixed-blood Indians, mostly of Cherokee, Shawnee and Blackfoot descent, usually mixed with various European and African American bloodlines. The work had become not only important but also at times life-saving for them, their families, and, of course, for himself. Bill Wilson and Dr. Bob Smith, he could see, had made that most amazing sociological discovery of the 20th Century – that one with an addiction may achieve recovery by helping another in recovery. That principle at times seemed too simple for the intellectual person to grasp. It worked for millions of people today around the world and it worked for Dr. Parks cum EagleClaw, too. It was all one, after all, like the Trinity. And it was just another example of the spiritual principle of acceptance.

Most of his sponsees were of English or Irish and Native American genetic descent. They were there because those Scots/Irish ancestors came to this part of the world, many to Virginia then Rockbridge County, Va., then on to the savannas in Greenbrier Co, Va., over the Midland Trail, US Route 60, the old Indian trade route, then into the Kanawha Valley.

Others had come to Pittsburgh or Wheeling then down the Spawaylathiepee, the Shawnee name for "the beautiful river," or Ohio in the Seneca language, to Tuendewee, or Pt. Pleasant, then up the Kanhawee River to the Indian towns there, the same way George Washington had, by keel boat and canoe. Kayaks then were still with the Indians in Alaska, unlike today. He and his son owned five kayaks now, one canoe, but no keelboats.

Those log floating boats could maneuver the shoals at Red House and other locations on the Kanawha before locks and dams were constructed. And they could haul provisions, such as survey equipment, food, and barrels of rum.

But after the Europeans claimed the land, and after the local Americans revolted against them, a new culture began developing in the mountains, one that became more fear-based than the one left behind. But the politics of freedom, that new culture's saving grace, survived and prospered.

Thus, Charles Robert Parks, born in a coal camp in West Virginia, had escaped the fear-based culture thrust upon him and his family by that later mountain culture. He had traveled much of the world, and had returned to his Native with a capital N roots insisting that his Indian bloodlines be given credence in his life– not just then but from thereon simply because it was real – real to an estimated 300,000 Indian descendants in West Virginia alone, many of whom still suffered also from one or more of the "White Man's Diseases."

Native Americans had used no alcohol, regarding it as a poison. Even by hazardous materials federal definition, it is classified as a poison. And on his English and Irish sides, the family could recognize genetically-based addiction all the way back in the genealogy to the 1200's to a Scottish uncle who drove himself crazy, it was said, trying to invent the perpetual motion machine. Sounded like he had the "ism" to him, Dr. Parks joked with family. Most of the Indian side of his bloodlines had zero tolerance, and therefore zero use, of alcohol. Some lessons of others have to be re-investigated, old Alfred North Whitehead had said. The same lesson had come true earlier in life for Bob EagleClaw Parks. But when the pain became great enough, like his Indian ancestors, he changed. And he kept changing. He had to.

He remembered that the British had hired out – he verbally used another term – the Seneca to settle Wheeling Island and the Ohio Valley and into Ravens Woods in western Virginia as a stronghold against the ferocious Shawnee, who later entrenched into Native Ohio towns with their capital called Chillicothe. It's the very definition of the term "capital city" in the Shawnee language.

One grandmother was Shawnee. Another was Cherokee

and Irish, the research would show in later years. One grandfather was full-blooded Cherokee, another Irish, another English, and so it went genetically and culturally.

He knew where he had come from and how he got here and who he was physically, mentally and spiritually. And he liked it, whatever "it" may be. It was called cumulatively, happy in life.

Realizing sleep was near, he thanked his Creator for another day of sobriety, good health and the ability to spirtually treat his disease of the mind and for acceptance that this too, whatever "it" might be, would also pass – one way or the other. He smiled silently and fell asleep in prayerful meditation, he like to call it.

Chapter Eight

Environmental Assessments

WALKING OUT TO THE office adjacent to his now four-year residence to operate his now part-time environmental consulting practice, EagleClaw glanced at an archeology Phase I Survey completed on a proposed coal mine site. His staff archeologist had mailed the copied report to the file the day before.

It was more than interesting, he thought, looking for clues of former Indian village sites or burial grounds on a future mountaintop coal mine removal site in a land once occupied by his ancestors. The relatives, possibly of his Indian great-grandmother or others, had lived in villages that had been surveyed away from Creator.

His ancestors believed Creator owned the land, the air, the water and all the earth, until the Europeans and their contractors did what they called surveying. They buried the lead plates and made talking leaves using ink from elderberries and wrote and recorded their opinions on paper pressed from hemp stalks. Could they survey the air they breathed or water they drank and own it also? They would someday in Eagleclaw's lifetime in the name of environmental protection.

He thought "what a concept" his ancestors must have smiled at – burying lead plates never supposed to be uncovered except for a parity check for ownership when contested in a law suit. And making laws for Creator in order to occupy land that his ancestors had occupied for thousands of years while practicing a culture which was traditionally organized and passed down generation to generation by storytelling and living one day at a time by the four seasons, in harmony with nature and Creator; and believing that all living things have a spirit that correlates to Great Spirit, the Spirit of the Universe.

The Native story of creation held that two brothers had been separated when the land masses now called continents had broken apart, but that the one lost brother would someday return from the East to rejoin his brothers and sisters here. He would return with his new family, and the tribes and families would be reunited. They were on Turtle Island, a huge land mass crisscrossed by trade routes from one end to the other. Tradesmen spoke a trade language understood far and wide, enough to get them through suspicious or even hostile villages anywhere on the big island.

The Lunar calendar used by most civilizations in the world outside European cultures was used by all tribes here. It is perfect and was the source of their name for their land mass – the turtle shell.

That calendar shell was in tune with all nature and was perfectly designed with 13 large rings representing the 13 full moons we have each year, with 28 little rings on the lower shell, the exact number of days of the lunar calendar per month and per year. Some men, but especially women, mentally and physically, relate to the 28 days per month each moon contains.

The turtle shell calendar needed no leap year to make up for the inexact non-lunar, Gregorian or Justinian calendar of the Europeans. The 28 days per year and 13 moons totalled 364, so there was no need for the one-fourth day adjustment every four years as with our present calendar. It was just a matter of respect for nature, the way it had always and still exists. It was accepted the way it was found. Some things never change.

But some cultures of people can change some things, including calendars, as varying European politicians did with their months so that some months were longer than others. Score one for Januarius. On the surface, he got the longest one. But the European culture is numerically pre-disposed to multipliers of 12's, like a dozen eggs. It is an easy multiplier and is logical when accepted by a whole culture. But the 13 moons messes up that system, so the politicians got to play with the days, and no doubt ego, then self-will, then other emotions became involved and the scientists who studied the earth, moon, stars didn't live long enough to calculate by mathematics outside the dozen and biscuit-based European culture. And what did those American Indians know anyway. They lived like savages off the land. And what did women know? It's all historically called the evolution of Western Civilization. It's just another example of the spiritual principle of acceptance. It's also history. If whole other cultures figured it out and used it, from the Chinese to the Mayans, why not the Europeans? Maybe they just didn't have turtle shells.

A comparison of names of the 28-day months shows amazing comparisons between all North American tribes. All called in the tribal language, for example, July, Green Corn Month, the month over wide longitudes and latitudes that roasting ears of corn ripen and are enjoyed. That always called for a celebration to show gratitude to Creator for physical nourishment. Corn was the staple food eaten all year by Native Americans, golden ears from the green stalk first, then dried, then parched, then ground, etc. and eaten in winter after soaking in lye, salt, sugars and other forms of preservatives.

But since European Americans had a real problem with the lunar concept for timekeeping, as well as their misnomer for what they called the Native's religion– spirit animals and ghosts and "savage" beliefs, they labelled them, that did not fit well with 18th century Christianity. They came here, after all, in nearly all instances, they said, to escape religious persecution. Thus, they weren't about to be open-minded about it all. And spirituality was not a recognized religious concept. The Holy Spirit was shunned as a concept by some protestant groups. But the Indians knew the concept well. The two just had different his-stories.

But the Indians could relate to Christianity, with its Trinity. It was more acceptance to the Natives than a dichotomy, as the difference in religion and spirituality was to the Europeans.

It somehow took a couple hundred years for those Europeans here, and many of the Indians, in America to realize one may have both. We're all interrelated, after all.

European culture was based on state leaders selected in succession by blood lines such as King George – blood that was a type unlike Native Americans. Native blood did not carry immunities to the European diseases. Native blood carried immunities to the common cold but not diphtheria, tetanus, whooping cough – all mass killers.

But the Native blood types, predominately O-negative and O-positive, are medically important today. Just ask any universal donor of Native decent possessing the O-negative blood type. Three years ago a Huntington, WV television station through its news program sought emergency donations of O-negative, or Native American, blood, they said, blood for a transfusion for a child there. The station was swamped with thousands of telephone calls from West Virginians and one day later announced please, no more calls. O-type blood genetically appears predominant in mixed-blood, indigeneous peoples, but often skips a generation of recipients, as do other genetic traits common to mixed-blood Native Americans, such as skin or hair color.

A true genetic change in humans, it is now known, requires about 50,000 years. The alcohol brought by the Europeans to America in the 1600's and on just didn't fit that genetic change timeline. Likewise, Native American's adapting to a genetic predisposition to alcoholism just doesn't fit that timeline, either. So someone or something would have to change. The culture doesn't have to, for normal folks, who can drink alcohol in most cultures, so it is left to the individual to change. And change he must if he has the disease of alcoholism and desires to live.

A culture can blame the victim, but that doesn't change anything. Perhaps the victim has an undiagnosed disease he doesn't know he has. And for that reason, jailing of those with the disease of alcoholism is precluded in American culture today – finally. That concept took 200 years to change, but change it did. Life is change.

Unlike Latin-derived names of diseases that killed millions of Native Americans, some were not yet even defined as diseases then, including alcoholism and addiction. For most Native Americans, it took only that first drink to bring onset of symptoms and to result in a whole new American chapter on the toxicology of alcoholism.

Historians estimate in the 1500's when DeSoto began the onslaught of Europeans coming to North America, 30 million Native peoples lived here. Today, the Native population of a much larger country, including Alaska, is less than 2% of the population, even though many mixed-bloods aren't counted.

The Native population of West Virginia increased itself exponentially 17% since the last census, in a state which regularly loses population. But that wasn't because Indians had more babies, it was because for the first time the state's mixed-blood population was allowed at census time to declare itself by categories. Most mixed-blood people didn't report differently than in the past, however, out of lack of "proof" and written records which say otherwise on their birth certificates.

But folks like Tiger Woods can now declare that he is one-fourth Indian, African-American, Caucasian and Asian.

Dr. Parks had taken his spiritually-based name EagleClaw seven years earlier in the now re-organized and state-recognized Indian tribe called Appalachian American Indians of West Virginia. Some 7,000 persons of Native descent who know who they are had joined and had re-adopted many of their Native customs. These customs at tribal events ranged from dress to spiritually-based naming ceremonies to regular cultural practices promoting their rebirthing a culture, including many powwows throughout the state. Powwows are spiritually-based events, homecomings, dating events, trade events, dancing, druming and singing – all the same sociological purposes cultures have always practiced. All God's children are welcomed. Just go there, he suggested to others who wanted to learn both culturally and spiritually.

As Dr. Parks continued teaching hazardous materials handling classes at chemical complexes and at local universities in the classrooms, he could often recognize the Appalachian Indian individuals with high cheek bones, Native American teeth and other physiological genetic traits.

His staff archeologist always looked for dental structures before arrowheads in burial or village sites as evidence that the bones belonged to Native Americans rather than Europeans. Native teeth have shovel-shaped, or squared, incisors, a gap between them, and the lower teeth curve inward at the gum.

And he often then asked at breaks what that individual's tribal lineage was. It was regularly Cherokee, they said, but sometimes if researched was Shawnee, or both, nearly always clarified with an addendum of German, Black Dutch, Black Irish or just Irish, but sometimes just European or African American.

Most who were asked readily said "My great- or my grandmother, and sometimes, grandfather, was a full-blooded Cherokee. We have her/his picture in the family Bible but were told to never tell."

That story is repeated time and again by Appalachian residents taught early in life by their grandmothers they were Christians, not Indians, that there was to be no talk of Indians who fought back, and that we are Black Irish, or Black Dutch, or anything to explain the olive skin coloring and straight black hair and high cheek bones or any genetic features which could expose their "racial" identity as other than the "white" listed on their birth certificates at the county courthouse from last century. It is often heard "she's just dark-complected – she was born that way." No doubt. It is nearly disturbing to ask the Indian question of the blonde mother of the "fallback" genetic child in the family with olive skin and Native teeth. That happens regularly because we can't yet in nature predict genetics in humans, only study them afterwards. DNA testing has given us the rest of the proof, however.

O-type blood was not to be discussed outside medical circles. It was a government indicator that would show in the world of science and medicine that some indigenous bloodline was present in the family history and that somewhere there was "an Indian in the woodpile" the Indians could say to each other.

"We don't practice spirits the way our ancestors did, and spirituality is a foreign concept anyway since we are and always have been Christians," his grandmother once said to Bobby Lee, EagleClaw's nickname as a child. In most Native American tribal cultures, one is allowed four names for four seasons and four directions in life. But in his English culture he had been assigned three names, then called another.

"Mawmaw, who was your mawmaw," he remembered once asking her as a child, "like you are to me?" Mawmaw and pawpaw are traditional Indian words for grandparents.

He was perplexed to hear her say she knew little about her. She had been "that other kind of Indian we don't talk about" and lived in the woods at the old home place in the Ohio Valley, a chink log house built by her Indian husband. Her grandmother had died while she was still a child, after moving with the tribe to Chilecothe for safety, her mother had told her.

Imagine that, he thought, not ever knowing your grandmother. What other kind of Indian, he wondered. He had heard her say it was alright to be Cherokee but if you said you were the others up north, the Shawnee, that was not alright.

The Shawnee had fought back against the European invaders. They were led by the Shawnee Prophet and his brother Tecumseh. He would hear Tecumseh quoted as a spiritual growth source in the hills the rest of his life, but not yet as a child in a secretive society. He learned to keep secrets early in life in that culture, but would someday learn that we human beings are "only as sick as our secrets."

In other words, even as a child he could figure out that his mawmaw's mawmaw had been driven from home and a whole culture of people with love in their hearts for each other, their family, had been driven off the land they had occupied for thousands of years. It was another America.

But he and his grandmother were back on the land after a generation of integration. They just had to deny who they were in part but could say safely they were Irish, which in part they were, or English or German or Black Dutch or whatever else they could identify to be white not Indian by attaching a label.

But secretly, he and the other grandchildren knew, she had privately smudged herself as a spiritual cleansing process the same way Native Americans openly do today throughout the country. But that was for her asthma, she had once replied when questioned why she used a feather fan to fan her hair and face with sweet smelling smudged sage in the closeted room off the bedrooms of her house.

And when the genealogical records were complete her one-half Cherokee bloodline was certified, albeit Shawnee in reality, and that her alcoholic Irish father years ago had moved into the old home place in the Ohio Valley, had bred a dozen children by her Indian mother, who was rejected by the children's father as a social outcast after she insisted on visiting Native American spirituality on the children as they became teenagers.

The Irish father insisted that only Christianity as he knew it be practiced in his house, and the children, one by one as they became teenagers, were farmed out to work and go to school at Red House. They were later relocated to a farmstead in the community where Eleanor Roosevelt once came to town to name her federal government socialistic enterprise for herself– Eleanor. It is now a small city with dual histories of Indians and surveyed by George Washington for King George and deeded, you guessed it, to his family, along with thousands of other acres called Washington's Lands in Augusta County. Later it became a huge Virginia Colony county. Today it remains in many respects a colony state. But this too shall pass if history, as in the past, repeats itself.

Too bad the American Revolutionary War ceded deeds of ownership from the English once the Americans came in to replace with diseases and rifles the first Americans, Dr. Parks thought. Thousands of acres of Appalachee were now owned by Pittsburgh coal corporations and many thousands of individuals with a history had it denied to them as citizens.

But truth always surfaces, even if it means denying one's own family heritage in a country where American heritage is taught as Manifest Destiny. But somehow today, manifest destiny fails the definition of spiritually-based principles. Some things do change, including whole attitudes, and sometimes cultures can even re-invent themselves. America is really very good at that this century. Creator has and will bless us for that ability to change. That statement is not a religious prediction, EagleClaw continued thinking. That is our real American history.

Dichotomies in American history are one thing, he thought, but outright denial of an entire group of millions of citizens denied their blood and cultural history is quite another, especially when that thinking was racially-based from the European Darwin teaching, he surmised.

He remembered that Darwin taught the culture here in *Origin of Species* in 1854 that there are four races by physiological and genetic characteristics. But Senior Environmental Scientist Dr. Parks could only figure both scientifically and spiritually there was only one race– the human race– but hundreds of ethnicities. He had in fact stopped using the term race, and wished that the U.S. Government would someday do the same, except as defining human beings.

He had come to believe that race is better defined by NASCAR than our government, so lets leave that to those more qualified. And with the advent of the Social Security numbering system and computers, who needs to be identified by the amount of tannin in the skin tissue? Identification by color doesn't work well anymore anyway with the mixes of people throughout the world. And in countries where he had travelled, the pronounced physiological differences of people classified by category, in West Africa, for example, change greatly on the same continent from, say, the Sudanese in Africa to the Temne in Sierra Leone. Computers with imbedded thumb prints have replaced the need to eyeball skin coloring of all God's children. And besides, prejudices, opinions, resentments and a hundred forms of fear are eliminated in the process.

The telephone rang, ending his meditative state, and a private firm had been hired, he was told, to collect about $6,000 state sales tax and she wanted to know if he was prepared to pay. Dr. Parks requested the name of the caller and corporation hired by the state to collect, then said he would speak with his bookkeeper and return a call. No doubt Pearbottom was at it again.

He knew that somehow, bad and good things in life seem to come in threes and he didn't want to allow potential paranoia to add to his monetary worries after he had performed $18,000 of work on the $25,000 state asbestos contract tasking order; had drawn the money down on plastic, as small business owners do; and, was now paying absurd interest rates on money used to perform state government work which Joe Dunn had refused to pay by a one-paragraph letter. The words, let alone the concept of due process, were not in the paragraph.

He had complained in writing again directly to the Governor's office only to receive no reply whatsoever. It seemed the governor had his hands full with other things. Little did he know the problem would continue three to five years, as projected, and threaten to kill not only his small business but also a way of life which was to become anathema to living life at the behest and satisfaction of two resentment-laden bureaucrats obsessed with their power and possessed with 11th Amendment protection as individuals.

Oh, there was recourse, he had been advised, but only through a four-step bureaucratic process different at the federal and state levels and one which would require several airline flights to Philadelphia. That regional "capital" is recognized for federal government purposes as the Mid-Atlantic Region of the United States – a foreign capitol to most people in the state where the national capitol is only 50 miles from the state's eastern borders, but not yet very accessible by roads not yet built, but roads Bob Byrd, historically, was working to have built.

It was possible, he thought, to take the George Washington Amtrak train via the Greenbrier Hotel to Washington and to disembark at the mall and walk to Bob Byrd's offices to complain of the bureaucratic abuse of power used against him and his small business. But that was just vivid imagination kicking in when an individual charged with criminal fraud for compositing composite asbestos materials as a federal criminal charge might just as well roll over as to attempt to explain a non-explainable asbestos technical issue to a clerk– let alone a US Senator. And elected officials are legally bound to have a hands-off attitude on contracts, even Bob Byrd, for federal government contract issues– enforcement labeled criminal against a fledgling environmental consultant practice owner in a state where coal is king and history is known but not yet written.

Or, if one becomes too unhappy or too unemployed there, the popular choice is to take the Hillbilly Highway, as about a third of the population, after all, has done in the past twenty-five years, south to North Carolina, or north, to Ohio, for work and a life.

History repeats itself, especially in West Virginia, he thought. The Shawnee fought back beginning with the battle of Pt. Pleasant, then moved to Ohio. They later were driven on during the Trail of Tears to points north, west and south, just as West Virginians are today.

Don't fight back is the real history lesson, as Tecumseh did after being born in the state near Clarksburg, he reported; or as did Blue Jacket, born near Richwood, and then moved on; or as Chief Logan did after fighting back, then moved to Ohio; or as Chief Pocatalico did without a fighting chance and was murdered; or like Chief Cornstalk, after sticking around being friendly to the government troops and their contractors, then being murdered and his body fed to hogs. Or, as his great-grandmother's Indian husband was, then sent along during the Trail of Tears roundup in the Ohio Valley with General Winfield Scott, only to be driven to Oklahoma Territory with his wife and children left behind at the West Virginia chink-log homestead. His homestead was later inhabited by the Irish Christian male alcoholic seeking furs and a "squaw"– a word now rejected in Native culture from the French language as a demeaning term for a part of a woman's anatomy. That was EagleClaw's greatgrandfather. His Irish name was McGrew, sometimes spelled McGraw. His wife was the Indian squaw. That's how many of us got here, he knew. And many others knew.

Those Europeans had come seeking food, furs, Native friends and looking to inhabit a piece of land in the woods for hunting and trapping while escaping the shanty in Ireland and starving from the potato famine.

Potatoes, like most good foods we Americans eat today, came from the Native Americans– not just white potatoes, but red and sweet potatoes, corn, squash, apples and dozens of other good foods, including one well valued by West Virginians today as well by even European chefs– ramps– foods growing here for at least 10,000 years and eaten readily by his ancestors before and after the arrival of the European ancestors looking to steal a continent one state at a time.

And later mixes of ethnicities with African-American free or runaway slaves occurred in all areas west of the Applachian Mountains. All tribes are known to have welcomed all ethnicities as "all God's Children" into their cultures and had adoption ceremonies waiting for them.

The outdoor drama *Blue Jacket* in Xenia, Ohio, tells that story, just as the drama *Tecumseh* tells much of the broader Shawnee history in Chilecothe. Other local Native histories include *Unto These Hills*, the Trail of Tears story of the Cherokee in North Carolina; *Solomon's Secret*, the Cherokee story of tears in Clay County, WV; *The Aracoma Story*, the Shawnee story of tears in Logan County, WV; and, several other similar quality productions in the Appalachian states where the Trail of Tears looked good politically to some but failed to achieve its full purpose and the people are still there in the form they are in today, calling themselves collectively Appalachian American Indians. They are the state-recognized tribe in West Virginia. Some things change well.

All the outdoor dramas are excellent amphitheatre portrayals of a largely unrecorded history of Appalachian Indians with scattered lives and even more scattered historical sources.

Chapter Nine

More to Come

YIANNI'S BOSS Harry Breeze had gone back upstairs after the four person meeting with Ben Wanton, Dr. Parks, Yianni and Breeze, announcing he had agreed with the criminal lawyer now wanting off the case and now bothering Dr. Parks to dog fall.

Neither Yianni's boss nor the criminal lawyer obviously could see a payday on the potential $5 million suit for a long time. They both had bigger fish to fry in cornmeal.

That afternoon Dr. Parks returned to his home and turned on the television. He saw a commercial for attracting a large number of people for a potential damages suit from a new medication that had gone awry and recognized truth in his own situation when he saw in the commercial Yianni's boss.

Breeze was now going after the large cache of potatoes. When one is hungry is when the mashed potatoes look the most enticing. And like his great-grandfather who came over from Ireland when the potatoes there became diseased, food and dollars somehow become much more important than social justice.

Nobody wants to hear *"don't stop thinking about tomorrow"* if the belly is growling today.

Ben Wanton left saying "good luck in the future" to Dr. Parks. He obviously had bigger foxes to chase with his $30,000 clients who pay by the hour, he had suggested earlier.

Yianni said he would retrieve the disk with his work over the past three months. His boss had said in their initial meeting that he "just couldn't believe" the Constitutional violations involved with Dr. Parks' case – not just lawyer talk – but sincerely expressed amazement, at the abrupt ending of the state contract and refusal by the state to pay without so much as even a notice, Dr. Parks remembered.

"Even Bob Byrd, the staunch defender of the Constitution, would be appalled," he also remembered Barrister Breeze saying. Talk is cheap to some lawyers he had met. But commitment without a quick payday is harder to come by was his experience.

Yianni downloaded the disk and asked Dr. Parks to step into the closed conference room. He looked with both his eyes deeply and stepped forward and gave Dr. Parks that full embrace. Both responded to the other respectfully, one of those rare times when two men empathize and don't need to say a lot of words. The hug lasted for that moment when two real men come together spiritually and with mental knowing that the other understands and feels empathy.

That pleasant memory had surprised Dr. Parks simply because he now had the inner knowledge that Yianni, after reading the documents Dr. Parks had hand-fed to him for weeks, were collective truth. It wasn't a term Dr. Parks used much in life, because it was just too big for most people to grasp. He then said "God's love" to him for the final time.

But Yianni had known, he knew, and he once again looked him in both eyes and allowed the knowingness of two kindred spirits to co-mingle in that moment of truth that says it all – 'I'm sorry" not being necessary– but one of offering the strength to carry on.

"The disk will get me started in filing my civil damages case in Kanawha Circuit Court *pro se*," he said. He took the disk home but had a little massage work left for two arenas of damages his former boss and friend Bill Adamson, Esq. had said to include. The work was completed in short order. He wasn't a lawyer and had never prepared a *pro se* case, but when something is the right thing to do, he had learned, Creator helps to provide the missing links. He didn't use the word luck anymore.

Yianni had done an expert job presenting the technical and legal case and Dr. Parks simply followed the model to include the two additional areas of damages Bill Adamson had said to be sure to include.

Next day he filed the case in Circuit Court, knowing it would likely be removed by Federal Rules of Civil Procedure by both state and federal listings to Federal Court by Jackson at the Justice Department, who had seemingly become emotionally ensconced with the cases against Dr. Parks– or was it instead, for, Pearbottom's cause?

He couldn't help but wonder what Carol Jackson's overly emotional involvement was with the case, or Nick Pearbottom, or others, let alone her last name, that county where Judge Goodrich also lives. Their family thing in federal and state politics was printed periodically by a newspaper political reporter without editorial comment: Goodrich, Bailey, Casto and Jackson– all "good" Jackson County names and families. Judge Goodrich's daughter worked for the governor, the state administration, which brought the suit through its Division of Highways against Dr. Parks and his small business. They were all associated with the Goodrich law firm, and the judge was Judge Goodrich. And the state case against Dr. Park's firm had by default become their case and *vis a vis* his case against them.

What a set-up, he mused. They were all not only linked, but were relatives intertwined with politics. What a fortress.

And a later tee-shirt by a famous New York distributor would tell the Goodrich family story again in a less complimentary way, of the recognized familial culture now ruling the land of Appalachee: *"It's all relative in West Virginia,"* the clothing article said. All sizes were quickly sold out after Governor Wisecoff objected to the cultural inference of the Appalachian culture. Some things never change, while change changes some.

The telephone rang and it was Dr. Parks' mother, who

said to turn on his television.

Some hijackers, she said, had stolen a plane and flown it into the World Trade Center. It's being covered live and they think there are other airplanes in the air headed toward New York and Washington and maybe Philadelphia or Pittsburgh and it's now over airspace in West Virginia near Morgantown.

When his mother called with a *suggestion* he reverted to the Webster's definition – a subtle command. And he had learned to react promptly. He watched the live coverage of an event that would forever change the course of America on that Nine Eleven date, and couldn't help but wonder why the federal government had employees like Marvin Reicht and Pearbottom spending every billable hour per day recently wasting with revenge over his asbestos expert witness truth against them while terrorists were destroying the world-recognized symbol of American domination of whole cultures. Maybe it wasn't for him to know, he thought.

His $5 million civil case for damages contained five arenas of damages against the state and Dunn and Reicht were named individually. Each charge, he knew, could be a law case unto itself:

(1). Count One: Breach of Contract: The WV-DOT, i.e. Joe Dunn, had without cause or due process, ended the work of the small business without so much as seeking a defense from his company. Due Process was not their thinking.

(2). Count Two: Tortuous Interference With a Business Relationship: The civil suit listed defendants Reicht and Dunn as the rightful culprits who had abused their power, resulting in provable damages to a government contractor private firm.

(3). Count Three: Discrimination of Civil Rights of the individual and the Small Disadvantaged Business: The corporation as a person had lost its prime contract, one that supposedly for the bureaucrats' records had been a minority-owned firm's setaside to meet federal guidelines in a state where minorities aren't supposed to exist – and if they do, they should be African-American or at least East Indian but at WV-DOT they preferably would be woman-owned and the 51% owner is married to a politician, preferably one in the state legislature or federal court system.

(4). Count Four: 'Blackballing' and discrimination in the State Merit System, precluding employment, as the direct result of the above actions for three successive years by government personnel. Plaintiff had a 100% score on the Environmental Resource Specialist employment category utilized widely by both DED and Health. Plaintiff was a former 17 year employee under the state merit system, with right of re-entry into that alleged system. But 14 interviews ago he had begun the process and three years later was still unemployed by the alleged merit system. The Wisecoff administration had hired or promoted 4,000 employees to fill or replace new or retiring employees during the period.

(5). Count Five: Plaintiff fired in violation of the WV Code and Administrative Rules while employed and injured on the job. There are no exceptions to the state code that say that no employee may be fired while receiving or is eligible to receive Worker Compensation benefits. Plaintiff received those benefits. Plaintiff was still under medical treatment months later for injuries sustained and witnessed as reported to his supervisor; DED's human resources personnel; and, his personal physician; emergency room physicians and surgeon who performed the surgery and oversaw rehabilitation for the next six months. Plaintiff will submit the medical records, already on file at the state Workers Compensation Commission.

Three law cases were now in progress: The criminal *cum* civil suit of the prejudiced resentments of the two bureaucrats charging Dr. Parks, his employees, his children and his corporation with "compositing asbestos samples" and "fraud" for billing for them as seen by the bureaucrats; Dr. Parks' *pro se* suit for $5 million damages; and, the Workers Compensation complaint filed separately in the State Court. A "bad faith" claim for the corporation was not close to being filed. And there would be more to come.

The State Circuit Court complaint ended "WHEREFORE, the Plaintiff, Charles Robert Parks, respectfully demands judgment against Defendants for compensatory and punitive damages totaling up to $1 million per count. Plaintiff also requests an award of attorney fees and costs incurred in prosecuting this claim, as well as any such other relief which the Court may deem appropriate.

Chapter Ten

High Time We Went

"HELLO, BOB, BEN WANTON here again. I would like for you to come into the office sometime and review some paper work on your case, particularly a letter report for the forced interview in your office that day between the local EPA enforcement person Pearbottom to his boss in Wheeling– I think you'll recognize a name or two from your earlier suspicions and the potential personal vendetta for your expert witness work there in the past. When can you come in?" Ben was admirably 'working' the criminal case but felt the damages suit would hinder his efforts in the future. He didn't want to drag out the matter beyond Dr. Parks' being re-instated in his former state position and not being indicted, he said.

Dr. Parks answered that afternoon and proceeded to wait, as lawyers cause one to do when a client expectation founded on fact not suspicion has been borne out by written documents from another source.

"Bob, I wanted to get this case closed by not allowing it to go to the grand jury, but the Justice Department lady, and I know her, Jackson, has already subpoenaed your son and he'll have to come in from medical school even though he had no relationship to the asbestos projects under scrutiny. And they want to question your business partner, because he prepared the reports and did the books," Ben said, asking again how soon that could occur.

"My goal again is to get your firm off the hook and you back in your job at the Division of Environmental Development with Workers Comp benefits paid after they fired you last year after you were on paid leave and covered for benefits. I know the director because he is a former federal district attorney in the Bob Byrd Courthouse where I was a federal prosecutor. I will talk with him personally and he will probably not want to let the word get out that you were fired three days after being hurt on the job, resulting in emergency surgery in this labor-sensitive state."

"Ben," Dr. Parks replied, "I am going to hold you to that. You have my gratitude. What is our timeline?"

"Well first we now have to see what the grand jury says and if they can't even come up with a ham sandwich, let alone an indictment for probable cause, we'll just have to see how things unfold."

"Good," Dr. Parks replied. "I need an income soon and I am hurting financially and have lost my small business' livelihood due to this federal investigation with no work on the state contract and debts for worked performed, then fired from the state position as a result of their calling the Governor's office complaining and this whole thing has to come to conclusion sometime. I'm hurting financially, but somehow Creator is providing the basic needs for me. My mother decided last week to distribute some small inheritance, not much, to my three sisters and me, but it helps tremendously that she has given me my dad's van after his death. I hope to receive some percentage for wages from Workers Comp even though the DED is protesting and even though I was having emergency inguinal hernia surgery at the time I was fired. Just doesn't seem right, does it?'

"No," Ben replied, "...but it's that political thing that to the victor goes the spoils, including calling the shots over and above the state Code here sometimes and nobody wants the governor of the great state of West Virginia to be embarrassed in any way before the next election. And besides, he has to wait for Bob Byrd to die off so he can take his place and nothing happens in his administration by mistake."

"We shall see, shan't we" Dr. Parks replied, "or in the words of his sponsor, nothing on God's earth ever happens by mistake...."

They both concluded their comments and Dr. Parks wondered "or does it" with the powerful v. the powerless – a good name for an historically accurate novel sometime, he thought.

"Bob, I began our appointment today with that realm of discussion and allowed you to repeat your thinking to me on purpose because I wanted to watch your facial expressions during discussions to verify what I believe I have been seeing in you. We lawyers are trained to recognize traits of truth, in this case, in clients, and being a federal prosecutor for 21 years until I retired from that position and took this job, I can usually tell by watching facial expressions when a person is truthful and is telling the whole truth. You have passed that acid test.

"But the real reason I asked you to come here is I spoke with the people at the federal courthouse yesterday, and I will put this into writing to you, that there will be no further criminal prosecution on the criminal case. They didn't get to first base with the grand jury last week. So they are 'declining prosecution,' as they say. It's that simple. I will be sending you a couple letters, one for your distribution, a simple one explaining no further action is necessary on the criminal charges, and a second one for the legal file with more detail."

Dr. Parks didn't much react to hearing truth that is compounded. One might have thought he would jump with joy, but the information he somehow already knew was coming, but remained suspicious. The entire matter was just beginning. His suspicions would be confirmed. The really important aspects of the attempted destruction of his life – no job, no work, bills for himself and the corporation, and more civil cases for the next two to five years, were still to come.

"And by the way while I was speaking with Jackson at the Justice Department office today she asked me if you intended to file counter charges for damages and of course I told her the truth, I just didn't tell her how much, and she said she had gotten way too involved for the judge's behalf in this case since the newspaper knows the whole truth, but that she may file civil charges on the same basis as the criminal charges if you intend to file for damages against the state."

Dr. Parks said "I suspected that, but isn't that double jeopardy as we were always taught in even our civics classes in high school as well as the constitutional law class I once took to complete my undergraduate history degree, Ben?"

"Well no, not in today's litigious world, like OJ, if one is criminal and one is civil. It's just like the OJ case, they may not get you on one case but they will wear you down and try to take your house, particularly if they have developed a resentment, in this case particularly if they have lost and if they need more billable hours as they do, after all, at the staff-laden Bob Byrd Federal Courthouse here. They have more staff here than what the four federal judges with four courtrooms with four staffs of clerks ands others than they know how to keep busy."

It wasn't the first time Dr. Parks would hear that story repeated.

"And Bob I have to tell you again that you should dog fall on this case just as I advised you to dog fall before and all just quit and go home or they will wear you down with their federal resources, and it seems like someone in Philadelphia is getting a few good laughs at all this."

"It may be your former employer who now works at EPA in Philadelphia and is personal friends with your Wheeling EPA perpetrators, shall we say. You can't win, Bob, even though you are owed thousands of dollars and lost a major contract as well as a state job at DED and your retirement and professional reputation and of course your income are at stake. They must have something on you or they wouldn't continue. I used to work there and they must have something to bring civil charges, and their pride is at stake since they have not proven anything wrong."

"Ben, you asked me to dog fall before the grand jury met

and I refused because I had done absolutely nothing wrong except to tell the truth in Wheeling in Federal Court in a client case that EPA had not performed it's own required testing in that case. And that was not wrong for me to do. EPA's Reicht lost, and they don't want my telling more truths in the future when their own people are not technically trained, but instead are being driven in their jobs in this case on personal resentments."

"Bob," Ben replied, "my case with you is finished. You will need to hire another attorney firm to represent you on the civil matters. My contract was for the Federal Investigation which is now closed, and I suggest you seek another attorney firm for your civil defense. I will pack up and send to you my file and I need to move along to make some money in life, frankly, and my standard fee is $30,000. I know it can't be met by you with no resources left. I have nothing more to say to you presently, it has been good working with you at the behest of my boss as a result of his knowing you through that certain 12-step program, but I am here to make money. I'll be in touch for your picking up your file."

Two days later Dr. Parks again met with Harry Breeze, who said upon coming to the conference table, "Now Bob, Ben has suggested to me that you dog fall in the federal case and that would preclude your filing damages owed to you and the corporation by the state, including claiming legal fees. I believe now what will happen is that by Federal Rules of Civil Procedure #13 by both federal and state rules is that your state court claim would be removed to federal court and thrown out by Judge Goodrich. He understood the system.

"Harry, I refused in the name of honesty at the suggestion of my sponsor and in simple decency to dog fall before, why now? No, I won't. I have been substantially damaged in many way to the tune of about a few hundred thousand dollars, including the contract loss and the state job loss and being fired while on Workers Comp and four other counts.

"To simply say those two vengeful bureaucrats can get

away with this act of a prejudiced resentment on their part is absurd. They have a personal vendetta going, one for losing to my expert witnessing in Wheeling, and another due to a personal matter that Joe Dunn has a personal vengeance for a perceived control issue dating back 17 years to my sponsor who ran against him for a district election and who resents that several of us whom he knows today began a 12-step group in the valley for gay, bi, lesbian and transgendered men and women in recovery. He opposed that organization as an out-of-date conservative with one small group up in Edgework and refused to let the schedule of meetings be printed to include that meeting."

Once again, the truth always surfaces, he thought. He had just blurted out the truth, as he knew it."

"Can you believe that an individual could be that sick while claiming membership in a spiritually-based 12 step recovery program?" his sponsor had asked, along with many other members, at the time the event was unfolding.

"And now that the truth is out on that resentment, Harry, I cannot help but continue my case for collecting damages. And besides, the truth of this matter, whatever happens, needs to go over to Judge Goodrich. Now I know I want to file my damages suit just so that the Judge will be forced to see the chain of events of damages in my life resulting from this prejudiced resentment."

"I have no moral choice here but to do the next right thing," Dr. Parks said. I know the case will be transferred from state court to Federal District Court but sometimes the truth just has to be told regardless of the consequences– or no consequences," Dr. Parks added while walking to the entrance door.

He was leaving to play racquetball with son Gabriel, as scheduled.

Chapter Eleven

Three Joys

"Dad, I just gave you a quick call on your cell phone to see if the two grandkids could join you and Gabriel at the Y while you play racquetball. They love the children's room there and it's a good time for their socialization and they get to see their grandfather in the interim. You seem so preoccupied lately. They don't get to see you as much as they continue to grow up. They're in first and second grades now and probably haven't seen you over three times this summer. I will bring them to your house to meet you and I can pick them up afterwards or you could drive them home, whichever you want to do," his daughter America said quickly.

Truth in all forms always came through others, but especially through his children, he recognized. But none of his three children had suggested the dog fall method of justice as being acceptable. Getting through it was their suggested alternative.

Spending mostly time at home to himself, his life had become ensconced in the legal enforcement defense even though no crime had been committed. But a committee in his head had instead required an imaginary defense over which he had no choice but to respond.

He had still been dealing, after one and one-half years, with a jail cell attempt by the two bureaucrats. But were they attempting now to take his house he was still paying for? The same fraud law they would be using for civil charges provided for potential exponential volumes of dollars if convicted on any basis by a jury if it was one which bought into the current political climate expressed by others as

"Now is not a time to be questioning our government" in light of the 9-11 fallout. Was that the next item he would have to defend? He had already lost his business as a vital entity; had suffered physical, mental and emotional harm; his primary company contract; a state job for retirement; and owed debts he could not pay.

But he had invaluable things left– his three children, two grandchildren, family of sisters, hundreds of friends and a dozen sponsees who believed, trusted, and loved him for the person he was. It was worth a gratitude list, minimally.

But would they suffer too for the person he was becoming with or without his choices of PMS– physical, mental, spiritual– pain; and for what some might call professional embarrassment; and, others, 'complications' of the mind visited upon him without his opinion mattering much. Had the two bureaucrats known fully what they were doing outside their personal vengeance; or could they even perceive; or maybe they would never know. They knew.

"I'm not responsible for what other people think," he surmised, and returned to the telephone conversation with his younger daughter America.

"Yes, honey, I will get the grandkids at my house then deliver them to yours tonight after racquetball. And thanks for the opportunity. I have been hungry to see them lately. See you here about 5:30, ok?"

"Love you, dad, and I guess I will see you then at your house. Bye. And remember to fasten your seatbelt."

She had been using that phrase to say "I love you" since she was 14 years old.

Dughter America was now 27 years old with two children, married to a guy her dad admired and cared for, and the family had just moved into a nice new house they constructed overlooking Lake Chaweva.

He recalled that he had made a decision three years earlier to move from Wheeling, three and a half hours away, to Charleston, when his first granddaughter Joyous Star, was born to America. The birth was an encouragement to finally after 11 years move from that town he had learned to not particularly care for. But he had a new company, new start, new well paying contracts with private industry, who paid their bills well in his experience, and it was just time to move back to where family was. And some year in the future he would need to finish his state retirement years and plans.

His real joys were his children, Jenny in Sitka, Gabriel the physician, and America, the mother of his other joys in life, his granddaughter, whom he had offered the Native name Joyous Star; and earlier grandson Eagle, who selected his own Native name at four years old. All were in relatively happy spaces in life. That fact and the move from Wheeling freed him up in some ways now to become, he surmised, the person his Creator had always intended him to be, not that he had not been living that way for 17 years in recovery – happy, healthy and free to be and the long version of freebird, as he sometimes referred himself.

He had found a way to move back home where his children and grandchildren were, bought a home with $20,000 cash he had saved, began remodelling, planting shrubs and a rose garden. He had a banner first year in business and had a decent second year in business for the new corporation. And son Gabriel, waiting on acceptance to medical school, moved in and helped with the remodeling, renovated the upstairs into his own living quarters, built a patio in the sun, and the two resumed their racquetball. But Gabriel would leave in the Fall in more good times for medical school. He would do well, and learn to kayak on the beautiful Greenbrier river. And dad would too. And dad would get to go visit him there, buy groceries, spread a little joy, and Gabriel would graduate and move back to dad's house for two more years for hospital rounds, rotations and racquetball. They were glad to be living together once again.

But other things would happen, including two deaths in the family of a parent and grandparent, both of whom had lived relatively happily until old age, the law case against Western Environmental would be settled, the house paid off, and life's occurrences would continue, as they do. It was living life on life's terms.

But that very week of his 14th year recovery program birthday he had not expected the four telephone calls that would send that whole life from forward to reverse. The four conversations alleged he was a criminal for compositing composite wall plaster sampled for asbestos; that he was being fired from his new state job in order to not embarrass Governor Wisecoff just in case the criminal threat was proven true in the future; that his company's professional liability carrier denied lawyer coverage on a criminal charge; and, that he required emergency surgery as the result of the job injuries suffered three days before being fired by the state DED.

"Bye, baby, see you and the grandkids at 5:30," he had said to daughter America and hung up the phone. He decided it was time to make that gratitude list and to seriously consider finding a local sponsor to add to the quality but long distance sponsorship he had continued to receive for the past 14 years. Some things in life are not to be subtracted but instead added.

His gratitude list was topped by his continuing recovery, his loving family, his health which would recover in the future, and all the good things that come along in life if we are painstaking through any phase of our development, whatever that phase may be.

And life was lived in phases, in cycles and circles of pain, growth and recovery and then joy, in his experience.

He could now delineate 17 year periods like the first when he left home to go to college and "make something of himself," as his European culture encouraged. Seven years later he would marry and spend the next 17 years there on a beautiful farm in Appalachee.

At 34 years old, he saw a cycle of young man growth completed and begin to change, but later a passage into professional growth but then decline into depression and addiction and required recovery. The next year he stopped caring about a lot of things, and at age 43 he changed because he had to.

At 50 years he had seen the advent of children growing to adulthood and successful in life, children with whom he had shared his two seven year, now 14 year recovery spiritual growth cycles. At 51 he had a successful small business with 13 employees and himself but was tied into legal contracts with a large firm where two individuals who became vengeful and combined their synergistic negative energies against his minority-owned SBA 8-a firm, but who then lost their own huge contract, and thus job positions, as a direct result of their sustained resentment-laden actions.

But the following birthday would find him back home with family and children and all the good things life has to offer if he accepted them. But he had more growing to be accomplished. And all he had to do was keep showing up.

"Pawpaw Bob, we love going to the Y with you. Can we go every week?" his granddaughter Joyous Star said, her brother Eagle joining in on the fun.

"We'll see, baby doll." He realized he had not seen much of his own grandchildren, his own children, or much of anyone else now for well over a year with the concentration and preoccupation with the federal criminal charges, loss of business, loss of job, and personal pain from the job injures requiring surgery.

He was at the beginning of one of those seven year cycles in recovery, the third such new beginning. The pain was to be taken in order to get the joy. And, whatever it was, it too would pass, one way or the other, his sponsor had always told him with an audible and experienced laugh from the stomach and heart.

Now at 58 years old the job injuries didn't want to heal quickly. Inguinal hernia and a prolonged back injury had been sustained simultaneously while moving a loaded 300 lb. metal file under instruction from the boss while working at DED.

Even though hospitalized for surgery on an emergency basis to prevent gangrene from setting in for the inguinal hernia surgery, all of which was duly reported to human resources and his boss at home the day of the accident, and off work on suggested and approved in writing earned sick leave, nevertheless, he had been fired from the DED job three days after the injuries and emergency hospitalization.

He was an at-will employee in an at-will state, he was reminded by his DED boss Bill Adamson, Esq., who was also their chief legal counsel. Bill had received instructions on the firing from the DED director who was appointed by the governor. Wisecoff would have no embarrassment to his administration with the next state election coming up, his boss had informed him while handing him his letter. And Dr. Parks as an at-will employee had absolutely no recourse to the firing, even though he was injured, he was reminded.

Dr. Parks returned to his vehicle on his way to the hospital that morning. The effective date of the firing was three days after the injury. The two had met in the designated parking lot at his boss's request on auspices of signing off on the sick leave forms, which he did for that day and the next, but then handed him also a letter with the simple statement that he as an at-will employee was discharged and added again that there was absolutely no recourse available. Dr. Parks looked him deeply in the eyes. He saw an individual who was not well.

According to his boss Bill, "Seven or eight people, including the head of the state Democratic Party, Steve Black, had telephoned the governor's office, as well as several government bureaucrats," ...including at EPA in Wheeling and DED in Charleston." They had called complaining that a 'potential federal criminal' was working at DED.

The governor's office staff had told the DED director, his boss said, "to preclude any future embarrassment to the governor by not having him working there anymore." That governor, the local jokes had it, had become a left-handed e-mail keyboard operator. It was a clear case of the left hand being preoccupied and not knowing what the right hand was doing. Men do those things in life.

Dr. Parks was an at-will employee but was hired as a returning state employee with 30 days sick leave, other benefits, and past good references on file for quality accomplishments throughout 17 years of earlier employment during the years in the state merit system. He had won many recognition awards and had served as president of two state-wide employee organizations and was well respected by his peers and supervisors.

In later e-mails to him at home, his boss Bill had said even though he was of course aware of the potential Federal Investigation at the time of hiring, and following four extensive interviews with him and other personnel at DED, that he too was now suffering repercussions for having hired him. He said in another e-mail to Dr. Parks that he now blamed him for the loss of one of his two positions at DED – Chief Legal Council. He remained the assistant DED Director for about another month, then the press carried a story of his history there and his exiting.

The press release from the DED was his story. One sometimes has to read between the lines for even reputable newspapers when history repeats itself.

At DED and other state agencies, top personnel in the state often get two paychecks for two jobs performed simultaneously. Bill had not only been the top lawyer at DED but also received a paycheck as the Deputy Secretary.

Likewise, the division director was both the Secretary in the Governor's Cabinet for the Environment, the Development and Education Secretariat to the governor, but also the Director of the Division of Environmental Development. The dual political pay slots commanded allegiance in times of political turmoil, one might say.

It's a West Virginia story, he had been told, although one

no doubt repeated in other states. But it is also one that speaks of power and politics and the age-old story of the powerful delivering to the not powerful. The state's history is one continuous trend of that truth, from the time the politicians sold the people down the river by allowing the rich mineral rights of the state to be purchased by out-of-state corporations for the coal, oil and natural gas, to today, with having the United States' lowest per capita income. Some things never change, it has been said. People in the state used to say "Thank God for Mississippi" when that state had the lowest per capita income and West Virginia was 49th. But things change once in a while. Mississippians now use the phrase in reverse.

West Virginia is one beautiful state, blue-green most of the year except for the southwestern coal counties, which show perpetual grayness in the winter, but turn pink with redbud and rhododendron in Spring and green lush foliage and white sunshine in Summer. Pink green and white are Creator's colors given freely to a topographically beautiful state.

Its beautiful rivers run from placid, like the Ohio and the Great Kanawha; to whitewater, like the New and the Gauley, to some of each, like the Greenbrier and Monongahela. Its fishing rivers, like the Bluestone and Great Cacapon, fed his ancestors fish since time immemorial.

It's mountains are majestic and contain snow ski lifts not found in comparison until one reaches the western states. Its people are beautiful, cultured in many cultures, are loving and hold innate intelligence on par with all people. They are Native and Christian and Buddhist and Unitarian and are at all spiritual levels of development. It's just all on the individual, not the collective population. It truly is almost Heaven and has a magnetic attraction with its mountains and rivers comparable to few other locations on several continents EagleClaw had visited. Its natural mineral wealth is comparable to Alaska and Texas but composited into 24,000 square miles, the size of a single park, Denali, in

Alaska, or a similar sized park in Texas. But it's all relative. And the owners, the citizens, don't own it, like the Natives didn't own it, and can't yet conceive in their hand-to-mouth culture that they don't own the place. They are tenants, and the wealth daily goes out to other places, but unfortunately very little returns as payment or parity check. Like its rivers, the natural wealth is drained off to somewhere else. Bob Byrd has performed unspoken wonders to return some of the wealth, but it's yet a long time coming. But like Nelson Mandela's spending 27 years in a dank prison, then becoming president of his country, things can change. Change changes some, it has been said.

After Dr. Parks' work injury and repair surgery and back physical therapy, lifting more than 17 lbs was now a no-no, the Workers' Comp doctor's studies had reported. Pain in his left testicle resulted from lifting much more, and that "message" of pain was enough that he could no longer lift 70-100 pounds of environmental testing equipment he owned, let alone operate. All men know that pain, and some women, and that it results in a parity check physiologically of a churning stomach. It is to be avoided at all costs. That lifting was often required for hazardous materials field testing, such as the soil gas survey equipment. It was history.

He had been put out of his profession of the past 17 years, Senior Environmental Scientist, by one lifting mis-que, one quick accident following instruction on the job at a state and federally funded agency which had no help available for heavy lifting of office furniture. He had been told three prior times by the building supervisor while seeking assistance in the new location that "we just don't have anybody for that purpose. Get someone to help you out of the hallway."

But he could perform administrative work such as the job of Small Business Ombudsman, a federally required position under the Clean Water Act, the one he was fired from, just in case he was guilty of compositing composite asbestos samples. Not even an indictment, or ham sandwich, had been achieved by the two bureaucrats with Ms. Jackson in the drivers seat. But do the right thing? "Say what," they said. Instead, civil charges were being instigated and Thom Botts' prediction had come true. Thom at 17 years growth in the ways of Indians in recovery also had fine-tuned his vital Sixth Sense. It is there if we let it be.

After checking in at the YMCA with the grandkids he began warming up and stretching for the aerobic exercise which he could still perform and, which, in fact, helped with the healing process, his physician had noted to him. Son Gabriel appeared at the racquetball court. As usual, dad lost the set, but took one game. Some things do change.

"Dad, I'm glad you can still play. I have a lot of stress at times, low level, at the hospital, and I'm glad we can still sweat and laugh together, as you say, that being what this game is all about." Dr. Gabriel said.

"Well, son, I remember when you were 15 with long hair and doing what 15 year old boys do and every Sunday morning I would drag you out to the racquetball court and I would stay just ahead of you enough to not discourage you from coming back, even though I wasn't always sure you really wanted to play, but at least it was time we could spend together. There are not always a lot of things outside fishing and with us also racquetball that a father and a 15 year old son can actually enjoy doing together sometimes."

"And as you went through college it was always a chance to visit with you, but once you went off to medical school and played an A level player sometimes two hours a day for stress relief, you ran off and left me with your skills on the court."

"Remember when I used to turn around after we played and say Gabriel, you're getting better. Keep coming back?"

Gabriel smiled, and answered "Yes, dad."

"Do you want to add something more, dad?"

"Yes, today I note that you now turn around after we play and say, "Dad, you're getting better. Keep coming back"

"Gratitude, gratitude," Dr. Parks said to Dr. Parks, and silently to the big guy upstairs who was probably listening.

But a Ph.D., compared to a Doctor of Osteopathy today from a medical school now honored around the country by some even more than a Doctor of Medicine degree - a physician - was no comparison to his Ph.D. doctorate, just the same word. But the senior one remembered too he always wanted to remain both a teacher, when applicable, and a student, which is always applicable if any humility at all in life is to be attained. And humility is the key – in all of life, he had learned, to serenity. And serenity was his goal each day in life and both Dr. Parks had it, whatever "it" may be with serenity, most days, most of the time.

Sometimes 'like father like son' can be a very good thing, if we work at it, they both had found.

Dr. Parks served an excellent fast and low back corner curved serve shot, missed by the younger Dr. Parks. And as happens in most of life, his mind then continued off in some other direction as the serving, sweating and smiling of the game continued, along with the thinking:

-It is amazing, the power – and the dichotomy – of the same word, spoken the same, but taken in a wholly different context, such as "doctor."

-And if you don't want to take my word for it, just ask a bureaucrat who would like to have one but isn't willing to perform the work for it.

-Enough is enough. I need to get those two lawyers moving on the $5 million damage suit and nail those two bureaucrats who perpetrated their prejudiced resentment on me, my children, my business partner, my corporation, my life for the past two years and I'm no way close to settlement.

For the first time in months he allowed himself to feel the emotion anger. He took the game, but not the set. Recognizing that emotion, he would then go to the Men's Meeting at the church and discuss terminal uniqueness and the feelings that allow men to opt out of patterns of growth in life.

He wasn't about to be close to opting out of anything in his life at this point. And he wasn't about to opt into terminal uniqueness that would change his way of thinking. It was not an option and he adjusted his thinking by taking that action.

Almost finished, a knock at the door signaled court time was up.

"Good sweat and laughter and good set" Keep coming back," Dr. Parks said to Dr. Parks, heading to the sauna and shower.

The following week Dr. Parks for his consulting practice had new business cards printed, returning to Bob Eagle-Claw Parks, Ph.D. from the European Christian name of C. Robert Parks, Ph.D. presently on the card.

It was not about a change of identity or anything else so esoteric, but instead just saying to those who needed to know more definitively who he was, he surmised.

"Please don't put quotes on my Native name on the card, whatever you do," he had said to the printer employee.

"EagleClaw is my spiritually-based Indian name. It is as real in our culture as my Christian name is on my birth certificate."

When West Virginia had become a state in 1863, only "white" or "colored" were choices for that *wasicu* birth certificate, he remembered, but just because one thinks something, doesn't mean he has to speak it to another, he had been taught. "...and it is not to be quoted like a nickname," he found himself repeating in his mind, but not to the printer employee.

"Just the way the name is written there, please."

"I see," said the printer technician. "It will be just like you have it written here, sir. And by the way, I am Eagle-Eyes. I'm Cherokee and an Appalachian Indian."

"Oh, I see. Well bless your heart," he said to the blue-eyed, red-headed young lady.

"We can't always tell by looking now can we?" she replied with a smile brighter than her eyes. "And may Creator bless you, too."

"Will we be billing this to your American Express, sir?"

"Yes" he replied, still wondering if he was coming across on the card name change as defensive, or just honest, argumentative, or just making a point, he asked himself. What's your point, he then wondered. The answer that came was this: I am still willing to grow along spiritual lines, whether the source be my Native spirituality, program spirituality, or "all" our spiritual sources, he concluded to himself.

So be it, he reasoned to himself. Just another lesson in acceptance, and life is full of them. It's all in what's in a name, he concluded. Another lesson learned, and he was on his way home to check e-mail and telephone messages.

The phone rang and he answered to the joyful sound of his older daughter Jenny's voice from Sitka. "Hi, dad, its me, Jen, I haven't heard from you in such a long while. I miss you and I've been here a year already."

He remembered a year had gone by for her being there and he had been all-consumed with the prejudiced resentment and resulting uncontrolled legal attempts of two resentful bureaucrats who may never be brought to justice and the whole scenario taking up most of his life.

"Dad, maybe you're imprisoned by those two vengeful people. They may be achieving their goal with or without you. I got your short e-mail saying the criminal charges had actually been dropped."

"I know, honey, I'm sorry I haven't corresponded much with you, but I have good news. I am coming to visit with you and your brother Gabriel and fiancé Linda are coming, too. Can you accommodate us for a week and the other week we fly over to Anchorage and go to Denali?"

"Sure," she said, "... and I will start working on the travel arrangements here and get us a rental car and a cabin at Talkeetna if that's ok, dad."

"Sure, honey, and the dates in my e-mail will work since there are no more court appearances scheduled presently, but my criminal lawyer has told me to find yet another firm to represent us for the civil damages but I haven't found one even after a long search and several interviews. So the time frame of July should be just great. How will the salmon and halibut fishing be then?"

"Just great, dad, and I will line up a fishing trip for Father's Day and we will catch some big ones. The boat captain and his wife are my friends now and I know he has Father's Day available since most fishermen here stay home on Father's Day. And this one is on me for Father's Day since I know things are tight with you.

"Thank you honey, yes, they are, and Gabriel is paying his and Linda's share and I am using frequent flyer points for my airline ticket and it will all work out. See you in July."

"Bye, dad. I love you."

The trip went as planned, Dr. Parks remembering that after two years and a long physical healing process that life was to be enjoyed, that he had not invited the legal troubles into his life, but that they were there to deal with anyway, and that someday, he hoped, justice would occur with or without him, the US Justice Department, the EPA, the DED; or any of the other devils coming his way in life. Maybe there was a greater purpose behind it all that he could not see.

"Jenny, I have really enjoyed the Father's Day trip. I will smoke the fish I am taking home and thank you for a wonderful trip to Alaska and seeing you again. As soon as two more years go by and the remaining school debts are paid off and you finish delivering a few hundred Native American babies for the Public Health Service here, I will be glad to have you home," Dad said, boarding the plane home.

Native peoples smoke fish. It's just a truism, his Native friend Adam had said recently. Adam is Cherokee. He knew. And EagleClaw's salmon and halibut were headed home to Appalachee to be smoked in the Little Chief smoker after brining and maple syrup curing. And they would be shared and relished by sponsees, family and other native and Native peoples back home.

"Dad, I love you and have a safe trip back to Charleston. See you next spring at Gabriel and Linda's wedding and write and call more often." "I will, honey. I promise to do better. Goodbye till next week. I'll call or e-mail when I get home."

"Have a good flight home, dad. I love you too."

Chapter Twelve

Spiritual Growth is Always Preceded by What? Pain?

THE OFFICE TELEPHONE rang and Dr. Parks answered in his usual manner since the chase by the two out-of-control bureaucrats began, by simply saying his name. He figured anyone calling the company at this point knew his name since business for the corporation was practically non-existent.

He had used his thinking ability and his own personal resources, such as they were under the circumstances, to pay personally the overhead for the corporation. He knew he had to keep the company alive until at least all the court cases were settled. Some lessons in life need to be learned just once. He had learned that one when he was forced to close his first conulting practice after Western Environmental & Engineering starved out the small business on the Superfund $2.4 million contract by not sharing the work, but with his having to maintain technical staff on call and sophisticated hazardous materials monitoring equipment with little or no work for it, let alone pay for overhead costs.

The overhead costs for the second corporation were now running about $20,000 a year. But they somehow got paid mostly out of his personal checking account then direct-expensed to the company in hopes someday things financially would again balance for both the ledgers and scales of justice. Hope remained one of his on-the-beam emotions.

Interest only on the drawdowns for the highways work

and the telephone bills and legal fees had become the uppermost overhead costs for the corporation. His primary contract had been ended by simply not being renewed by the state division of highways, and very little contract work for environmental technical services was now available in a state run by coal "whores" as the local press now referred to the state governor and those who now worked for him at DED. The state agency performed most of the environmental work in the state for others. They were more than regulatory, they also provided services called testing and planning. He concentrated on what he could – helping others through sponsorship. It was about the most he could do under the trying circumstances of having his small business destroyed, his life interrupted, fired for the first time ever, and charged criminally then not-so-civilly by environmental personnel whom he had challenged for a client in court, seeing through their vindictiveness even then.

Of those countless program sponsees he had worked with 17 years, he could always see a trend in the individual when he was ready to go back out to his former lifestyle, repeating his history, he called it. A clear trend would become apparent in the personality of the individual characterized by conning, whoring, lying, then using.

Conning picks up where honesty ends. Whoring occurs when one abuses the emotions of another person for his own gratification. That's the broader Webster's definition, not the exercise of trading a $20 bill for whatever, although that applies also. Lying to oneself about all the above then occurs, and the last event is simply the result.

Dr. Parks for 30 years had known the governor on a first name basis and had donated the $1,000 maximum personal amount to his last campaign. He remembered on several occasions passing the new governor in the Pittsburgh Airport during and after his campaign, always saying hello in a personal manner.

Gov. Wisecoff had once written a letter of reference for Dr. Parks, lauding his "protecting public health and the environment" efforts while the governor was then a Congressman, a prior state legislator. But when it came hiring time after the election for Dr. Parks' efforts to qualify for a state job, his goal for completing a state retirement after getting his three kids through college and other schools, and 17 years' earlier good work for the state, his letters of application fell on deaf ears. Instead, he was hired by a personal acquaintance, Bill Adamson.

But several weeks later the subpoenas were received, the grand jury met and the subpoenaed staff by deposition told simple truths that the prosecutor did not enjoy, such as the fact that the required five, not 25, asbestos samples had been collected from the plaster, that the small business only cleared 60 cents for shipping and reporting costs per sample analyzed – much less than that of other firms working on the same contract. But not much else was repeated from behind closed doors, as the EPA person made clear in fearful instruction stated both out-of-line and intimidatingly in the courthouse hallway earlier to both Dr. Parks' son and business partner Thom Botts.

Nothing was repeated, as instructed, they later told Dr. Parks. Dr. Parks had overheard the very conversations, looking busy talking with his lawyer down the hallway, so he knew anyway. The phone rang again, interrupting his thoughts.

"Bob, this is Ben and I am sending you that letter I promised, to verify that the Federal Investigation is closed and that there is and never was any basis for a federal criminal investigation charge. In fact, I am sending you those two letters, one for our eyes only and one which you may use if you so choose to collect for billing for the work you performed.

"It has been nice working with you and I am sorry you had to spend your last dollar of Workers Comp injury award money for the corporation to pay our firm. But it was money well spent. And I spoke with my boss George who makes the staff assignments here. He told me what he said he told you that Joe Dunn is his program sponsor and that we won't represent you because he is his program sponsor and that he doesn't want any program resentments developing between them and that that is a conflict of interest, so we won't for sure be representing you in the civil trial. Have a nice day." The call ended about as quickly as it came.

He returned to his thinking again. He had expected no reward from the new governor, but he did know he was well qualified after educating himself in the broad environmental and administrative fields of government work for administering any number of programs, especially environmental and public health, for the state.

No reply to his letters was ever received despite follow-up phone calls to staff and to the governor. Following the dismissal in writing of the federal criminal fraud charges, Dr. Parks had written a letter directly to the governor asking for payment again of the $18,000 work performed plus statutory interest for his technical work submitted and used by other contractors.

Just as his letters of application did not receive replies, neither did his request for paying his corporation's bills receive replies.

He again called the governor's office asking for payment now that the criminal trial had ended in his favor. "We don't get involved in contracts," the woman had replied. "But aren't you the administrative end of state government," he asked? "Yes, but you will have to talk with the highways division director's secretary. I can give you that number, sir."

He already had it, he replied, and thanked her for her comments, then asked:

"And isn't the highways director appointed by the governor?"

"Yes, of course, but you must speak with them. They have already said the court system is in charge now and refuse to pay, even though no indictment was handed up by the jury. I'm sorry, but I can't help you with contracts," she closed.

Later, the prosecutor handling the earlier criminal case at the Justice Department, Carol Jackson, complained in writing to Judge Goodrich that "a letter writing campaign" had been instituted by Dr. Parks after he requested payment from the state after no criminal indictment came down. She had also reported to Ben Wanton that the Federal Investigation had ended. But she changed her mind, it seems. It was her prerogative, after all. But can one say lack of work, malice, or other purposes? But the question would answer itself in a few short weeks when CID Pearbottom appeared at Dr. Parks' office door with more supoenas.

"The State of West Virginia will work to put you out of business if you are a small business." He had heard that quote in his travels around the state many times but dismissed the statement as somewhere between false, resentment-laden opinion and a broad and generalized distant comment by the individuals repeating it. Little did he know, however, the experience behind the statement was based on truth – and experience – not until his own ox was gored by those resentment-laden bureaucrats who had somehow held onto power through successive administrations and who were rumored often to have accepted state bribes and free trips given by large business firms, most corporately held in Pittsburgh, New York or Richmond.

Small business is big business in West Virginia, the US Small Business Administration had lauded the year before in promotional campaigns for its own importance as a federal and state agency. The truth, as it always does, however, surfaced over a long period of time. The agency is promoted by lending institutions who receive government-guaranteed loan status and make money on the individual as well as the small business even with the known fact that a documented 95% of new small businesses working with the agency fail in one to five years, and that the remaining 1-4 % fail over the next five years. The last 1% aren't tracked, they say.

Hello, he answered the phone again to yet another telemarketer firm the governor had helped establish in the name of economic development. He and other politicians had created 7,000 new jobs in the state, they said, most from telemarketers hiring folks at minimum wage who weren't quite ready to leave family in the state yet.

And more coal was mined that year than at anytime in history, but the industry was mechanized for mountaintop removal and longwall underground mining. People were now just a commodity and ample workers were available throughout the state. Hugh mining machines were tax deductible and no health or retirement plans were obligated. The governor had already raised $1.4 million in his campaign coffers for the next election. EagleClaw's vital Sixth Sense made him wonder if someday in some way those mostly lawyer and coal business donations would have to be returned. That's the rule when one doesn't run again for elective office, he had heard.

Dr. Parks and his business partner Thom Botts 10 years ago had shepherded their first US-SBA-guaranteed business into that final 1-4% for seven years in Wheeling and had even achieved US-SBA 8(a) Status – a carrot lauded to lead to success in the nation's largest industry, federal contracting. Yet the last three years were spent facing criminal and civil charges from resentful bureaucrats there. Life has its dichotomies, he supposed.

Their last federal subcontract win for $2.4 Million, however, had somehow escaped Congressional intent of earlier political climates in the country after the word "goal" was inserted into federal small business legislation. And the prime contractors, including Western Engineering and Environmental, had learned early on that unmet goals in federal contracting meant no worse than a proverbial slap on the wrist to the large firm, but death to the small business. With investments of often five years time and untold dollars to win the right to subcontract, the question for the small business owner becomes whether the untold dollars for that time will ever even be replaced. His experience became the answer. The answer only begs the question, in his experience.

Western Engineering would later replace the environmental part of its corporate name after discerning from government bureaucrats that "we are environmental, not you contractors" in this country. Feelings and opinions are taken personally by bureaucrats, they all would learn.

The two entrepreneurs at seven years operation chose a Chapter 7 USC Bankruptcy for the corporation with $6 million subcontracts in their files with large environmental and engineering federal contractors. The old adage that a contract is worth only the paper it is written on unless both parties choose to comply is true with government contracts.

And what large federal contractor chooses to comply with sharing $6 million in pass-through currency when its profit margin may be that same amount? Sure, some African-American firms especially in the DC area are put out for show as small federal contractors, but the fact remains that only .05% of federal contracts go to minority-owned firms in the United States.

So who in government is willing to stand up for more than an imaginary "goal" for an Appalachian Indian-owned firm which meets all other federal guidelines? No one Dr. Parks had located came forward, including US-SBA officials.

His firm had received about $30,000 work over a year and a half on the $2.4 million Western E&E subcontract– or about one-half a salary of one technical firm employee with overhead per year. After the five-year bidding process Dr. Parks estimated that $144,000– the original amount of his small business loan– had been expended in time costs for winning the subcontract with Western Engineering as the team prime bidder.

"Those are unrecoverable costs in the admin-multiplier," he had been told by federal regulators making choices of what a small business may bill for costs, even though the small business' admin-multiplier was less than one third of that billed every day for overhead by the large prime contractor business.

Following the Chapter 7, USC action, the next day Dr. Parks and his partner had organized a new corporation– this time dismissing readily most federal contract activity for the small business as pie in the sky. But private industry, he knew, needed his services. They had, after all, paid for costs of bidding federal subcontracts as well as bid costs through overhead for a few small prime contracts for the past seven years. All the private industry contracts were satisfactorily completed, and all were paid. Government work was different in a harsh, economic way.

The first year of the new corporation, in a new location in the Methodist Building in Wheeling– 20 feet across the hall from the EPA Criminal Enforcement Office– a record banner year was achieved by concentrating on private industry work.

Most new work was located in the Charleston area, however, with some residual work in the "rust belt" of the Ohio Valley. Even there, however, technical services were thought mostly to come from Pittsburgh– not from small businesses locally owned, even if the personnel used to manage federal Superfund Programs for US-EPA and other federal and state agencies.

But the small jobs paid the rent, and the larger industry jobs allowed for some level of success for the new firm. And at a personal level, his three children were about through their first college degrees, and a first grandchild was close.

Also continued as a revenue-producing account by the new firm was the state division of highways asbestos building inspection contract. Adding up the work meant a logical move to Charleston and the expansion of that existing field office for the new corporation for both the business and the personal side of the ledgers in his life. Both should balance, he surmised. He called the moving vans and times were getting better.

The move was a good business decision, the results showed after the first year, and a legal action was filed to recover damages from Western Engineering for failing to honor the designated contract award to Dr. Parks' firm. The federal contract conditions specifically spelled out the small minority-owned business was to receive $1.4 million worth of work and an additional $1 million was available by FAR Rules for allowing the small firm to perform additional development work. The $2.4 total allocation sounded good and looked good on paper– unless a prejudiced resentment by individuals such as Rudy Shoup and team member Mike Springer was involved– and unlimited EPA tax dollars are available to them for telephone and travel and other choice activities.

Rudy is a 'short-in-stature' New Yorker who early in life resisted his admittedly neurotic culture in that city and decided to seek his fortune in Texas. His highest academic honor in life to date was finishing a BA degree in biology, which, with his bravado and height-enhancing cowboy boots. parlayed him into an environmental biologist contract position. He had changed his religious affiliation from Jewish to Catholic as a part of his personal makeover, and "paid his dues" he repeated often, by survey sampling in hot personal protective equipment, PPE, the white plastic 'moon' suits and much more, at a landfill survey site in often hot Texas heat.

His dues paid, he returned to the northeast with his vocal bravado-laden resume, a slight Texas accent in tow, but still couldn't pronounce the New England-lacking 'r's.' And as luck happened, he landed a section manager job in the fast-evolving new federal environmental contract field in the 1980's with Western Engineering & Environmental in Philadelphia.

Folks in government in the regional capitol of Philadelphia are easily impressed by business types who speak authoritatively on the telephone and make staccato pronouncements, preferably with a deep masculine-sounding voice, while often also discussing contract conditions that the government bureaucrats can hardly remember to put into contract bids. The *Federal Register* was delivered daily to his desk before bagels and smoked fish with cream cheese were served in the office.

And folks in Philadelphia, often from homes across the Delaware River in New Jersey in a town seldom identified except by an exit number, are awe-struck by folks from the rest of the country– about anywhere in the country. They grow up thinking Philadelphia is the regional capitol and that Washington is an administrative center, and that New York and Florida is the rest of what there is. Parochialism lives everywhere with many folks.

And if the accent is New York with Texas, the Philadelphia folks are again star-struck that a cosmopolinity not of their knowledge has just cast a spell over them and they are at your command.

In other words, provincial, or the fear thereof, takes on a whole new definition to many citizens of Philadelphia. They only recognize the world as being between New York City along I-95 to Washington then Florida and Texas and everywhere else is somewhere out of reach, except of course, New Jersey.

And West Virginia and the people who live out there are completely anathema culturally to their fellow Americans who live in Philly and South Jersey. They know it's out there somewhere, but one just can't get there from here and it is another country somewhere west of Virginia but in the South, they think but aren't sure. But they think Indians still live there in the mountains and dig coal and probably smoke fish for a living. Maybe their fish is smoked somewhere out there, maybe. They don't know where their fish is smoked.

But, as the Philadelphia federal contractors learned early on in the environmental cleanup years of US history, there's money to be made out in them-thar hills via cleanup of large Superfund sites with Potentially Responsible Parties with corporate names including Monsanto, Union Carbide, Kodak and no doubt other deep pockets.

If only those sites can be identified as containing hazardous wastes, then there's gold in those hills.

And there must be a plethora of them in that Indian valley with the strange sounding, wrong-accented spelling that begins with a K and contains 30 continuous miles of chemical plants. And that doesn't even include the Ohio and other valleys with other Indian names and more chemical manufacturing wastes from the past. What a super opportunity, the federal contractors surmised, if we can just assess those environments and open government accounts under the Superfund program.

Hiring someone from the area with technical histories would also be helpful, it was surmised, and that got Dr. Parks hired away from a meager $23,000 per year job with state government at a time when three children were coming up for college.

Born into a coal camp culture but educated to a maximum available Master of Science degree at home, Dr. Parks, who was not then Dr. Parks, was offered a doubling of his salary and stock options and the opportunity to complete a Ph.D. by Western Engineering if only he'd choose to move to Philadelphia, then return to the Kanawha Valley to work most of the time. That was in 1988.

The promises in his life of a real American job were there for the taking, he saw, and a life change had occurred, allowing him to now pay his bills on time and help his three children go to college– not like his own experience, working at a supermarket part-time to pay for his education, but instead actually assisting his children to attend college in a normal fashion, with time to study, make good grades, and then get on with their lives.

The choice was the only one to be made, and he resigned in good graces the alleged security of a state government job and the movers came and life in Philadelphia was enjoyable. Flying into West Virginia, except sometimes driving to

Wheeling, visiting regularly with the children who after the divorce lived with their newly remarried mom, things got better quicker. It was a year into recovery back then, and the promises were coming true.

The three children grew from early teenagers, went to college and graduated. Two went to medical schools and now deliver babies for others, and the third now raises her own babies.

That's how it was and here's how it is now: Life as he knew it– small business operator and technical environmental scientist and homeowner and respected family and community member, somehow just didn't jive with the charges of criminal fraud by the United States, whoever that was– with all its power and people and bureaucrats like Marvin Reicht and Joe Dunn.

The two bureaucrats had teamed in an effort to destroy, or at least put into a jail cell– the individual who had at least somewhat succeeded somewhere between the West Virginia coal camp and now a grandfather– with honesty, humility and continuing spiritual growth as his primary goals in life, not to mention the primacy of sobriety in all, he repeated all, his affairs, even this one. Especially this one.

Acceptance as a spiritual principle is a requirement for spiritual growth, he had found, but that does not mean one is a doormat to be walked upon by two sick bastards, his sponsor had said; or as a former newspaper boss Ned Chilton used to say "those with power abusing the powerless."

Powerlessness isn't the word the newspaper publisher Chilton used for schoolchildren and families reading his text. Chilton used for his employees a much more alliterative verb not suitable in that context. He used the other word for what the powerful do unto the powerless here. He was an honest, wealthy man who very unfortunately died playing racquetball at the YMCA at age 65. EagleClaw was now 60.

But it's just another phase of our history here, presently called West Virginia, formerly known by other names.

Change should be welcomed, it has been said. And that history, now that the state has one beyond the American Civil War, will continue to repeat itself by trends and cycles and circles of life, birth, death, rebirth and pain and growth no doubt into its own future. And it may even be hoisted to its own petard. It is still a wealthy state. Maybe it just inherited its poverty this time around to feel pain necessary to spiritual growth.

The state wealthy in natural resources doesn't offer many excuses for the poverty of its citizens outside its own history.

It is a state with an addiction to coal, recently likened by a Pax citizen to the mother abused and beaten by her culturally and perhaps physiologically challenged husband. He suffers to her spousal abuse, common in the Appalachian redneck belt. She stays because she loves him. She should leave him. He might get well, or die of an addiction. Neither is really in charge, but neither knows it, yet. They all have a long road to recovery.

That thought was authored and published in the state's leading newspaper by Daniel Wright. He's right, of course. Wright was EagleClaw's grandparents and mother's maiden name. It is also the family name of the state's tribal Indian chief, who is mixed-blood Cherokee and African-American.

Names don't specify character traits, however. Dan Wright of Pax is right, while other Wrights are wrong. Marvin Reight was wrong. Or as lawyers are fond of saying, my right may be your wrong.

Chapter Thirteen

Making Amends

ON THE TELEPHONE he heard a distant-sounding voice from his past. Dr. Parks wasn't really sure he recognized the caller's voice. The tonality was illusive. Was it Rudy Shoup or was it Joe Dunn, maybe?

"This is Joe Dunn and I called you in order to make arrangements to come to where you are to apologize and make amends for taking an action that I could rationalize and justify in my mind at the time– you know– the legal action on behalf of the EPA cocky bastard who used the asbestos technicians to stir up the criticism of your work and end your contract. I rationalized and justified in my mind what I was doing was just my job but I was just conning myself."

"Yes, Joe. How may I help you?" Dr. Parks replied with a tonality of inquisitiveness from training in that spiritually based recovery program which teaches one that sometimes the mental health issues of addiction are best achieved through asking more questions, but not expecting forgiveness.

The process is called making amends for emotional wrongs or harm done and especially emotional pain caused others, no matter the justification or rationalization. The amends are to be made promptly– but what addictive personality does anything promptly becomes the question.

"Joe, I am a little taken aback at the nature of this call, but yes certainly we can get together soon. By the way, I have had a question my sponsor suggested I ask you next time, and not wanting to approach you after the trial, I will ask it now if you don't mind. It may sound a little didactic at first, so I apologize in advance if that is the case, but is it true that you were, *hoisted to your own petard* at the division of highways and that's why you no longer work there as a highways engineer?"

There was that kind of deafening silence on the other end of the line that is best described an a black hole without any type of receptors even in existence to send back a parity check or any other type of confirmatory response.

"Bob," he paused but labored the enunciation, "I prefer to say that I retired after 34 years of dedication to the efforts to build roads that now crisscross the state and that I retired only after an announcement from the governor's office which served as a political indicator to me."

"I understand, Joe. I read the two key articles by the political columnist Fanny Silers in *the Valley Gazette*, beginning with your denial that you were retiring even though the state Engineer's Dataline had carried the announcement as a surprise to you, and then the second column where you confirmed that you were after all retiring in order to work for a highways consultant. Is that correct?" Dr. Parks asked.

"Yes," Joe replied, "but the nature of my call to you is to apologize to you after the trial that things are not always as they seem and that I was, in fact, nursing a prejudiced resentment, as you labeled it in the courtroom with your lawyer's help.

"I really have nursed that resentment for 17 years since you and your partner Thom Botts started the only group that was allowed to get by us for gays and lesbians and whatever those other mixes are in people in recovery. My sponsor and I avowed that no such group would ever exist here in the middle of the geographical area we cover for the program and then you showed up as the general service rep and your sponsor vouched for the group and then he ran against me as the recognized group leader.

"We viewed it as a violation of our Fifth Tradition, that we are singular in purpose and those outsiders could come to our meetings if they felt like it. It was just more than we could almost bear and then you two moved to Philadelphia where we thought you belonged. Later. seven years ago, in fact, your own environmental consulting firm won favor with our staff for your quality technical work and excellent pricing for your asbestos work at a time we didn't know our asbestos from a hole in the ground.

"And when I realized only years later, in fact, when you moved your operations from Wheeling to Charleston, and I began seeing you at meetings and you said your whole name, that you were the same person and still not only sober but now Dr. Parks and under an annual half million contract where I had signed the contracts, I really felt mislead in my own history."

"I just couldn't resolve in my own mind with my tasking orders each time to your company seeing those volumes of our dollars, even though I know you only got paid an hourly salary less than mine, even though you were the company owner but working as a scientist in nasty old buildings scheduled to be torn down as soon as you inspected them–if not before, by vandals or prime contractors in a hurry to remove the structures whether friable asbestos was present or not."

Volumes had just been spoken. Silence and a deep breath were evident.

"Joe" Dr. Parks said slowly, "have you been sober all this time or are you, shall we say, going through a process with a Step 9 instead of the normal daily inventory in a Step 10?"

"You know the answer to that already, I believe. Does one re-do a Step 9 and make certain telephone calls if there is not a renewing purpose called recovery behind the actions in your and my program, Bob?"

"No, Joe. There isn't. I am sorry to hear that. It could have been me through some of this long process. But I too have to be into forgiveness as a spiritual principle or I recognize the potential consequences in my own life. I have not kept coming back for 17 years by fighting circular battles.

Instead, I have learned circular spiritual lessons, which is what they all are, according to both my Native spirituality and my program spirituality. I mean, after all, I did not do this thing myself and who am to reinvent the rules?

"Yes, I will be happy to meet with you soon and chit-chat about what happened, but I will have to share with you some of the outstanding damages to my life during this period, but, always remember and never forget, Joe, that all I or you have to do is to be willing, just willing," he said with emphasis, "to both ask for forgiveness and to also give it out and up when the appropriate time comes, else we perish, right?"

"Right, Bob" he said. "When can we do this"

"How about tomorrow morning after Mustard Seed meeting. Can we meet there?"

"Uh, well of course, I suppose. I have never gone there."

Dr. Parks said the meeting might provide a healthy prelude to the discussion.

"Say, Joe, aren't there some reparations, repairs, and what is that third r-word, restitution, we use for scenarios like this where the issues are bigger than both of us?" he asked.

Joe said he would give it some thought, but didn't know what he could do as far as any financial reparations, since he no longer worked for the state.

"Perhaps the answers will come if we ask for them, maybe?" he replied quizzically.

"Maybe, Bob. We'll see." Joe said.

"By the way, Joe, are you still with the new consulting firm?"

"No," he replied. "I was out on the road doing too much traveling and had to meet with some large federal contract employees who said their prime contractors were unhappy with some of our work and we had to appease them by entertaining them in clubs and one night one of them asked me to file a legal action that had amazing similarities to your case, and, lo and behold, I somehow agreed, and to make a long story short I found myself conning, whoring, lying and using on a quick downhill slide almost before I realized what a real roller-coaster ride I was on for the new company."

"And before I knew it, I was enjoying the ride, so to speak, enhancing my mood as a cover-up for what I knew I was doing wrong from a personal standpoint, and *bam!* and then it happened."

"One led to many and the roller-coaster ride was over soon and they let me go in a short period of time. You know the story, and then there was that guilt and remorse and finally I ended up in the hospital with a hazy mind at best, and being a professional level employee it all ended just like that without the gory details. And here I am, calling you after starting over and working through a process and jumping ahead for some reason to a Step 8 list with you because I know I have to if I am to, let us say, survive."

After a shorter than instant silence, Dr. Parks replied "Bless you" and we'll see where the discussion takes us tomorrow. Goodbye."

Chapter Fourteen

What Price Justice?

"He no longer works for EPA, he had a heart attack after some trial he lost in Charleston he really wanted to win. It was his second loss of a trial in the last two attempts, someone said. He had to retire on disability. He went to Philly for a staff meeting and was writing up a report of the trial loss when he said he wasn't feeling himself from being so upset, so he drove himself back to Wheeling while he was having a major heart attack, and that's a five to six hour drive and horrible if the weather is bad on the Pennsylvania Turnpike. He said he just wanted to be home. It did major damage to the lower part of the heart, I heard. I guess he was in denial and didn't want to talk with anyone, but it was too late by the time he came back to Wheeling after that drive. So he no longer is the Criminal Investigator Division person. Some fellow in Charleston has been doing his work, I heard. So how are the three kids doing? I heard they finished their degrees and your son Gabriel is a physician now. Congratulations, I know you helped all your kids a lot all those years while one year all three were in college the same year. That must have been tough. We were all admiring you here, especially with your completing your own Ph.D. God bless you and them."

It was a mouthful to say the least to hear all that said as he simply stood and listened and smiled demurely. The truth always surfaces.

He had come to Wheeling again to place a claim for a mechanics lien on a city-owned property after his employees had performed $53,000 environmental project management work for worker protection for lead, asbestos, PCB, TCE and PAH removal work over seven years earlier. The lien had not been perfected with a hearing, he explained, but a property transfer for the lessee was about to take place and lessees are potentially responsible parties under the federal law CERCLA, so they had to clear out the potential liability by assigning the potential for any potable water back siphonage to the City of Wheeling, where it belonged, since they owned the property. A release of lien to the lessee was being negotiated, so he wouldn't sign the release until he and his partner were paid. They had filed the lien as individuals.

The City of Wheeling, or at least the stodgy old self-willed City Attorney Paul Boose, had refused payment for extra work tasked on the earlier contract to his environmental technical services firm. Then Challis Flint, the federal programs coordinator, refused to have remediated the trichloro-ethylene and polyaromatic hydrocarbons found by the drum load buried in soil beneath the concrete floor of the basement of the federally-funded project. The soil had PVC plastic potable water lines owned by the city running beneath the basement floor. At flood stage, or under negative pressure, the drinking water lines could backsiphon. Solvents surrounding PVC drinking water lines is not a good idea in the public health arena, at flood stage, or a fire down the street, or any time at all.

The city had promised to at least negotiate with Dr. Parks' firm and another contractor at the time, both of whom had gone unpaid. Both had filed a lien on the property title. The negotiation didn't happen.

A private bar owner was now occupying the structure and had insisted that federal guidelines for his lending institution be met before signing a new lease. He had moved there from another state and knew the federal rules. The four-story historically restored structure had a record of hazardous wastes of spent solvents, dangerous to the public health when located next to a glued plastic line carrying drinking water for the city and running through the middle of the wastes generated years earlier, still in place under concrete in a flood zone. The TCE solvents were also PCB-laden solvents. They had been used to clean electrical motors at the machine shop in the past. The capacitors contained PCB's at high levels in their cooling and lubricant oil, and the hazardous waste was drummed on site, spilled on the absorbent wooden floors in the late 18th Century building, then were poured down the drain, whichever came first.

The chemical wastes were expensive at best to dispose, so employees stored the drumloads of hazardous wastes in the basement until the business closed. The building should have been a Superfund site, but bureaucrats are protected by the 11th Amendment, after all. And besides, they were all local friends, the business owner and the city officials.

There they leaked, and conveniently soaked, into the ground under busted concrete for as long as the soil would absorb it, which is never forever for petroleum hydrocarbons, even in sandy river bottom soils like that geologic strata of the Ohio River Valley in Wheeling.

Dr. Parks' Certified Industrial Hygienist and his Industrial Engineer had reported the hazardous wastes collection in writing. The mess had not been cleaned up after the federal programs coordinator McCarty belligerently informed Dr. Parks that "federal environmental law does not apply in Wheeling, WV and you and your firm had better learn that right off, DOCTOR Parks," he had emphasized.

Their photo-ionization air monitoring instrumentation had gone off the scale when the volatile organic compounds had been measured real-time by the CIH, the industrial engineer and by Senior Scientist Dr. Parks when the site was environmentally surveyed. He had never seen a reading of that magnitude even at the burning of an on-site lab full of mixed chemicals at a huge Superfund site in the Kanawha Valley.

But here today was supposedly a check in the amount of

$74,000 –$53,000 plus interest, for taking the pain of nonpayment and for being patient with the very real possibility that one would never be paid for technical work performed by requirements of CERCLA and RCRA. Failure to report to officials could have resulted in disbarment as a federal contractor in the future, he knew. The FAR said so. Federal Acquisition Regulations? How far was the only question asked, however. EPA-Wheeling had investigated – by air monitoring above the newly and quickly poured concrete floor. "No problem here Ma," one might say.

Nevertheless, and through no fault of his own, he thought, the right thing was occurring with or without him. And his actions, except for a lot of past worrying – if his employees would be paid, and government tax departments, whomever they may be, would be paid – it all had been useless worrying. If one worries, why pray, he had heard. He was not in charge here, he realized.

Worse still, he had once envisioned the tax bill in the state's computer would be more than the present payoff, a fact he had witnessed once before, and then demanded a review of the records, again requiring a tax attorney. But the business ended the fiasco with a 10% settlement. Justice, that Step 9 goal, isn't always on time, he thought. Step 9. Justice. Wonder what that high-flying concept really means in our culture today with government contracting? He asked himself, believing that probably that really no answer would come. It didn't.

City contract attorney Paul Boose had died, he learned, of brain cancer at 39 years old. He had only appeared older than his years. As the attorney for the city, he had refused to accept a standard federal contract from the local environmental firm written along suggested federal guidelines, but had come to Dr. Parks before his death, head shaven, to explain that he knew the city actually owed the money to Dr. Parks' firm, but the contract terms were so poorly drafted he knew they would be thrown out by a judge if the issue went to court.

Instead, a mechanics lien was filed by Dr. Parks and his partner. It had expired beyond the two year statute of limitations, but the known threat of TCE beneath the basement floor was rumored public knowledge in the small city. There is no statute of limitations for threats to the public health. Even the Romans knew that as they mined and used asbestos and lead. Their asbestos workers always died 20 years later of horrible deaths and the statesmen who drank acid wine from leaching lead goblets couldn't get it up anymore. They knew it wasn't just the alcohol in their wine–it was also lead in the goblet but, none in their pencils.

"If the beer at the Artisan Center ever tastes like dry cleaner fluid," it had been said around town, "don't drink it because it is back-siphoning from beneath the basement." All the former employees at the site knew the story. They had reported it while the building was being historically restored after an evacuation was called from the fumes emanating from the basement. The asbestos envelope was so contaminated during the removal that workers began passing out and gasping for air after the concrete floor was fractured. It was quickly patched for installation of an elevator shaft. Dr. Parks had personally supervised the Level B investigation. A clean-up was too costly for the limited Bob Byrd funds available, he was told. He was also told they were only getting paid by the initial contract, not additional hazardous materials work. And thus the lien was filed after they were told their work was complete and don't come back for dinner, please.

Back-siphonage laws have existed in the United States for 70 years and the elimination of possible sources is covered in the law, but after all, "federal environmental law does not apply in Wheeling, WV," it has been said. The philosophy was even pronounced as an acronm at the office as FELDNA-WWVA.

And besides, the center was a favorite project funded by Bob Byrd, and funds did not include an environmental cleanup of hazardous wastes. Challis Flint had said so earlier.

Poly-chlorinated-bi-phenols, or PCB's, asbestos and lead had been removed from the site purchased by the city administration without an environmental survey. But when workers complained of light-headedness and testing was performed, many drums of the former machining and motor cleaning solvents in the building basement were then hauled to a farm in Pennsylvania, then some returned out of enforcement fear, and then some more taken to an unknown location by a construction subcontractor.

Federal environmental law, including the Resource Conservation Recovery Act (RCRA) really doesn't apply in Wheeling, WV. Don't even ask.

An EPA contractor survey team from Western Engineering later visited the site after a worker protection complaint was filed and –yes– air monitoring above the newly poured concrete floor showed zero levels of volatile organic compounds. Now let's see, FELDNA-WWVA is the acronym that federal regulatory bureaucrats now love there.

It had been an interesting return visit by Dr. Parks to pick up a long overdue check in the land where the acronym FELDNA-WWVA was spoken, the land of the white skull.

And speaking of WWVA, the Wheeling AM radio station still heard from the northern Canadian provinces to the US Virgin Islands, its Jamboree USA was still packing in the tour buses to the town named for the Indian word Land of the White Skulls. Plastic replicas of Indian skulls supposedly found by early European settlers remain on display at the Artisan Center as a reminder of those who disagree with Native culture and the way of life in WWVA.

The Western European culture there, with language spoken in a slight Southern Belle accent, is still practiced by the white folk in Wheeling, at least by those of German and Northern European descent. They retain the Great White Way. But it's a cultural thing, not a racial thing, they tell us. Their annual debutante ball is about coming out in the old cultural sense.

The Wheeling Symphony, directed until recently by Maestra Rachel Worby for 17 years, is located in the smallest city in the country with a professional orchestra. Keeping up cultural appearances is expensive in the small city, but some things are worth it, while others aren't.

The Victorian Era city has many histories, beginning with driving out the ferocious Shawnee, to Chief Cornplanter and Daughter Winona and her boyfriend George Washington, and later a hidden agenda by Mingo Chief John Logan, whose family was murdered after partying with the European Virginians with strong liquor. Virginians have a strong history in Wheeling. It was at one time one of Virginia's largest cities. It was Wheeling, Va, then. Today it is West Virginia's third largest city but declining rapidly. It is a city said to be cursed by John Logan and the Mingo Tribe. To live there is to believe the curse is true.

Chief Logan was out on a Fall hunting party while near Wheeling his sisters' baby fetus was cut from her stomach and scalped in earlier years. The Virginians used a lot of alcohol, and of course shared it with the Indians, then challenged them to a shooting contest. The Indians shot first, and then were shot. It's a true story. It's all in the town's history.

Near Wheeling a thousand Native American skeletal structures were later found along Wheeling Creek, gleaming in the sun after the Virginians came down Wheeling Creek to the Ohio River in earlier years. Bones and teeth are still plowed up by farmers. The full report is kept filed in the Ohio County Public Library in the county history room in the basement. No one much reads there though. But some do research there. Many Native-blooded people still live in Wheeling. They just don't powwow much.

But Chief Logan's family doesn't live there anymore. Dr. Parks doesn't, either, but he still teaches hazardous materials handling classes there. Some things change and change changes others, it has been said. Chief Logan moved to Yellow Creek, Ohio and died a violent death at his log cabin west of there, shot in self-defense by his brother-in-law. The domestic violence with Logan's wife had gotten out of hand after a domestic violence altercation. He thought he had killed her accidentally while drunk, but only knocked her out. In Indian culture to kill someone was to be killed by their family. It's the old testament Jewish law parallel. But Logan didn't know she was still alive, so when the brother-in-law came to visit his cabin in the woods, he presumed the worst. Logan shot, brother-in-law shot, and Chief Logan was dead. Another historic tragedy in Indian country involving alcohol had begun with the coming of the Europeans to America. It is far from over. Logan's famous speech after the Wheeling incident earlier in life is recorded in brass in front of his statue at the Mingo County Courthouse. EagleClaw and the tribal drum reenacted John Logan's life tragedy and the speech at the statue restoration earlier in their tribal experiences. It was broadcast live in Logan and Mingo Counties and it was a good thing. The statue and speech are worth a visit there. It is our real Applachian history – our American history.

Logan's story is one of revenge after befriending the white man, then dying of alcoholism. The second West Virginia county, Mingo, was also named after him and his tribe.

Many of the state's counties are named for their Indian histories, such as Pocahontas and Kanawha and a dozen other counties. Most of its rivers retain the Native names, such as Pocatalico, Kanawha, Monongahela, Guyandot, Ohio and others. And many of the people, about one seventh of the people in the state, retain their bloodlines. And some retain their Native spirituality and are still there in the form they are in today.

In Wheeling, the Mafia controlled much commerce until recent years, when the guys pretty much killed each other off when there was barely enough left to fight over. The speakeasies had been damaged by legalized liquor by the drink, and are now gay bars; the meat racks down by the

YWCA have been replaced by adult book stores; and, the economy of downtown has left for shopping malls 10 miles either direction in Ohio and Pennsylvania.

By 1959, the airport had gone to Pittsburgh International, and the old timers still owned the asbestos-infested empty buildings throughout the city. The old money was still there but in banks and not being re-circulated. Downtown was just that – down.

But the coming out debutante balls with Southern gowns, the symphony, some of the old money from industrial steel and coal days, and even some of the people, remain to ply the cultures remaining. But, the rest of America zooms past it all on I-70, which, if one is not careful, forces the driver off the highway both before and after the Wheeling tunnel into a lost loop of the decaying and vacant downtown.

Dr. Parks headed to the city building to pick up the long overdue check and remembered the ethnicities who had built the city and admired how some small businesses run by Germans, Poles, Italians, Lebanese and other groups of immigrants were still in business somehow. They still sell wonderful things hard to come by in the rest of Appalachee including varieties of feta cheese, wonderful fish sandwiches at the Wheeling Fish Market, pita breads, olives and oils, and ethnic white pizzas.

Those Europeans had come to mine coal and make steel, nails, and glass three generations back and were still present in the form they were in today – mixed blood types, mixed skin colors, mixed names of origin and mixed in survival methods in the rust belt city left behind in its own history. The city had been a former state capital of a state where history repeats itself and cultures live and die until they recover by rebirthing themselves. That hasn't happened yet in Wheeling. WWVA, the famous radio station for going on 100 years, has even moved across the river to Ohio.

But some things do change, and on the outskirts of town Dr. Parks recalled that a wonderful Jesuit University and a flagship city park admired throughout the country existed for the gaining of knowledge and recreation of body, mind and spirit.

"This too shall pass – one way or the other," he cajoled, "but not so long as Bob Byrd lives in Congress. God bless him. It's about our turn in West Virginia America and WWVA," he mused to himself.

And, of course, Wheeling was home to a field office of US-EPA, and the US Justice Department, and Northern District of West Virginia Federal Court, where he had a famous experience or two as an expert witness telling the truth in the land of the white skull. And it was the state bureaucratic home for the Catholic Church, the Scottish Rite and other European cultural traditions still trying to eek out a living from a culture gone south.

Once larger than its nearest city Pittsburgh, it didn't adapt well to change, clinging to its history instead. History was held fastly to the heart in Wheeling, too close one supposes. When it died, it just couldn't seem to rebirth itself as Pittsburgh did. The old rust belt industrial sites are still there and still not cleaned up because FELDNA-WWVA is not spoken there. Don't even ask.

Many Native Americans and other Americans had lived and died and left this land of the white skull used to instill fear into newcomers. Dr. Parks realized that he was just one of the humility-laden Indians who had left by choice, he remembered. Or was it by Creator's Will? It was probably some of both, since the change occurred comfortably like a gentle wind, he surmised as a clear indicator of acceptance of Creator's Will in his life. Others' experience for determining Creator's Will in their lives may be different, but we allow for that here, he reminded.

He had learned a lot in the city of white skulls. He had started his own business, something he only used to drink and dream about – the American Dream – and he had completed his Ph.D. while there, mostly by extension learning and self-study and the proper use of the will, he had observed, along with a few other life-long learning lessons.

But the largest lesson he learned was that he didn't know much compared to the knowledge that surrounded him in libraries from Alexandria to the wonderful one in WWVA. He learned that all life is wholistic and integrated. One must always learn and share the whole pie, but always respect the integrated parts and how they relate to each other, like people and spirits and cultures existing side by side and changing like the wind. It is difficult to see cultural changes but easier to look back at them as trends in history.

And he had learned in Wheeling that he had no control over any of it. His primary responsibility was to help others and in that process to grow spiritually, whatever life and Creator sent his way. In the end, he knew, he would be reborn of that process and that he would keep coming back for more – and get it.

Chapter Fifteen

Bye, Bob, Bye

"BOB, I WOULD LIKE to see you at my office soon so we can discuss strategy for recovery for the five-part civil damages case you had removed from Federal Court and tossed after Carol Jackson realized, probably, the implications to the governor's office, particularly since you have shared information with James Haute at the newspaper.

He was speaking with Al Halberts, Esq., who had agreed to represent him for three areas of work: the civil defense following the criminal charge dissolution; his five-part damages suit against the state; and, the "bad faith" claim against the firm's professional liability insurance company for not providing legal services for sampling methods charges.

Halberts began like most lawyers marketing his services, saying how we are going to do this and that, then petering down the cases to compromises representative of all the worst lawyer jokes that go around the culture year after year. Some things never change.

"Wonder why the newspaper didn't print anything when your *pro se* case was filed in state court? You know some reporter took note, unless they were just plain dumb. I mean, suing the state for $5 million isn't just an everyday occurrence. It's news," Hal asked.

Dr. Parks replied not necessarily that they were dumb, maybe instead it was a new young reporter on that beat – just not well trained, since that too had once been a part of his experience.

"You know, Al, while I was 19 to 21 years old I was a reporter at the Valley *Gazette*. I was young and could write news style, but those weren't always good qualifications for replacing wisdom for writing responsibly for a well respected newspaper.

"Ned Chilton, the publisher, admired my work at times, but I was young, hung, and dumb is the truth of the matter. I was also finishing a college degree, abusing a couple substances, in school full-time, in my first marriage to a lady I could not wear out, but that's another story, and, well, I was inexperienced and when I reviewed public records I have to admit I didn't always know what I was looking for. What was news and what wasn't I didn't always know, and what was conning or not, and we always had local politicians and marketing individuals thrusting so-called "news' at us.

"But I do know the correct answer to your question. Jim Haute said "probably that's just what they're hoping for" when I asked him about a newspaper article on the whole complicated mess of my firm and my being charged with criminal fraud by an agency I used to work for.

"Or at least that government agency's former contractor, whom I had sued and settled with; and, agency personnel I had gone up against in federal court as an expert witness and they lost a professionally embarrassing case which also showed their personal vindictive motives as individuals," he finished. Isn't the parallel interesting with their clear vindictiveness in my cases, Al?"

"I understand, Bob, so when do we begin getting some paperwork, a few sheets for each count to start with, from your files, for filing for damages on the $5 million charges we contracted with you to pursue?"

"How about starting tomorrow. I'll need a little time to get the required paperwork together in a succinct form for you but it is high time we went, as Joe Cocker would say.

"Or, 'Turn the Page" as Bob Seger would say." Al answered.

"Tuesday I will be by and we'll get started topically on all five arenas of work. See you then."

"Thanks, Bob. And don't forget this month's $400 check

if you can arrange it."

"Thanks, Al. See you then."

Dr. Parks had taken an extra day, thinking after all, three years of emotional pain at the pleasure of two vindictive bureaucrats – one drunk again in his addiction, he had heard yesterday from a friend in the program, and one drunk on his own ego but upset in public after waiting three hours holding restaurant seats at the Pittsburgh airport for his national US-EPA boss, then leaving just before she arrived to go to the bar and not be seen again.

Reicht's reserved seats there had been taken, strangely, instead by a guy representing himself as the governor of West Virginia and a female state employee with a northern European accent. They had drinks for two hours and instructed the maitre'd to not say anything to anyone, regardless of who they were, or to let their presence in the enclosed booth be known.

A sizeable tip guaranteed their privacy and the national EPA director was re-stationed with an explanation of a mix-up in seating following a late plane arrival. Her aide must have been displaced in the mix-up, she and company surmised. They decided to stay in Pittsburgh the night since they had been non-plused by their last hotel arrangements near the Region III field office in Wheeling.

"Governor, your plane for your flight to Portugal is arriving. I'll be happy to bring your check now. Shall I make it out to Governor or to Bob, Sir? "Neither," he replied. "I'll just pay by state voucher, thanks."

"Yes, sir. right away." It was their third overnight to Portugal.

It was a country Dr. Parks had felt by his own Sixth Sense attracted to for years, but couldn't figure out why, except maybe some of his West Virginia ancestors had come from there to Appalachee estimated about the 1400's and settled in a city now called Charleston.

They were documented inhabitants, about 1,000 of them, called Melungens. Many of their descendants still live in pockets throughout the state in areas such as Calhoun County, along with other Indians as they were mistakenly called, both terms common by acceptable use but inaccurate and wrong terms after all these hundreds of years. Wrong "facts" often get repeated as truth in life, he had learned. Native American and Indians and Melungens made a hit list of wrong facts in the state's history, he had found. But that's history and he was sticking with his story.

Dr. Parks had returned from a vacation flight long overdue for visiting friends and practicing his remaining but "acceptable addictions" out of the 1960's expression – *sex, racquetball and rock 'n roll, but not necessarily in that order*, in Las Vegas. He was walking down C Corridor in the Pittsburgh airport when he spotted Governor Bob.

Both had lived in their younger days in Roane County, one Bob EagleClaw as a county health department sanitarian and somewhere between a gentleman farmer and a hippie farmer, but nevertheless a farmer.

The other Bob had become a Congressman and then had run for governor and won. Each Bob had known the other Bob by first names and more.

Farmer Bob had said many times he still had enough Indian in his blood, psyche and spirit that he just couldn't keep his hands out of the dirt, that growing things –a big vegetable garden, bees, cattle, horses, trees, hay, children, whatever, was his forte in life. The other Bob, a lawyer, made laws. He too had once been a Roane County farmer. They were more alike than not, but the comparisons ended there. Farmer Bob had learned to observe, not compare, in all life.

His path crossed sometimes with the other Bob at Legislative functions for promoting new legislation, or while the politician and lawyer Bob danced a mountain jig in parades in the county seat, especially near election time.

Governor Bob appeared to hold clear Indian genetics and had lived on Indian Creek Road. EagleClaw wondered if he truly even knew who he was or where he had come from, and if he knew, was he in denial.

Their proverbial paths crossed at other times in uncanny ways at times at somewhat uncanny locations – at an upscale restaurant downtown run by a gay black man also a friend of both Bob's – Dr. Bob's while in college, and Governor Bob's at the wine bar or the Middle Eastern salad bar and later the four star chef at the Governors's Mansion for successive governors, including governor Bob's.

And, yes, there had been more uncanny crossings of the two Bobs in the small city in earlier years.

Lawyer Bob while younger stayed at a livable but questionable at best small hotel in downtown, the one next to the adult book store on that street. Farmer Bob sometimes went to town and had a couple drinks downtown before returning to the farm–yes, that bar around the corner from the hotel and the adult bookstore.

And sometimes their paths would cross in those directions, also.

But as time went by, Bob the politician went to Washington, Bob the farmer farmed and did what farmers do. And sometimes their paths would cross at the Pittsburgh airport per chance as farmer and state employee Bob was on his way to or from the regional capitol in Philadelphia to seek or pick up funds for constructing new public health centers in Appalachee or to meet with federal funding engineering regulators or the like. Bob the politician was usually flying from Washington to Pittsburgh to get back home for the weekend to Appalachee, entered mostly via US Air from Pittsburgh from the north or not at all.

During the last gubernatorial election campaign, Dr. Bob, mostly unemployed due to a certain prejudiced resentment resulting in the loss of his and his small business's livelihood, nevertheless, responded to a direct telephone request from politician Bob's staff to donate $1,000 to his long-term acquaintance friend's campaign. It took a while, but between short term jobs, Dr. Bob put together the maximum personal donation money out of some level of allegiance and an honest desire not to be rewarded but respectfully in hopes of working a state-appointed job in the future for the governor with his Ph.D., Master of Science, a clean record of past achievements, and a just-as-honest desire to offer his substantial technical and management expertise to the state in the new administration in some environmental or public health protection capacity in order to, rightfully so, finish his state retirement plan.

But as letters of application and résumés and a couple visits to campaign headquarters and some telephone calls went unanswered, Dr. Bob found it amazing that a politician after winning could simply forget his constituency–one person at a time.

Department heads with no seeming talent or experience in their subject matter were announced one after another, however.

A nursing home chain owner was appointed to head up the department of health, never mind that the state Code required either a Ph.D. in a health field or an M.D. or D.O. degree could be substituted – but one in political science? It was a telling experience, but you'll have that here and everywhere.

And the environmental department? Why, a lawyer, of course. Never mind environmental technical expertise and its applications. It was development that mattered, not technical skills. And who but a lawyer might understand those illusive federal laws called CERCLA, RCRA and mountaintop mining rules to eliminate the mountains for development of Walmarts, which had become the state's number one employer and growing.

After one year, no state job was looming, so Dr. Parks went to see the civil service system director to see what he might not be doing right. So let's look at some lesser positions such as a toxicologist, or maybe environmental resources staff position. No? Well, how about the merit system, where a 100 percentile score was achieved by the applicant – the highest in the state at the time for applicable positions in a couple categories at both Health and DED.

Interviews, yes, yes, of course. They're required for the merit system if one is in the top five percentile ratings and sends in an application from the public database. And every new hire must be approved by the Governor's office staff, and he keeps a list, you know. But the job – oh, well, we only have to hire from the minimum score – not the person best qualified for the job, he was told by the Personnel Division director.

That spells the person on staff wanting a raise and is a friend of the hiring officer. What's this merit system you speak of?

Oh, that's our management system to hire people already working for us and promote them so that they don't become demoralized as state employees. We can do that, you know. So even though you educated yourself well, have the experience, all the correct technical qualifications and may even be able to do the job, we hire in-house, and that means our friends, our smoking buddies, our drinking buddies, and, oh, yes, the new appointees friends and party affiliates if they are well known to us.

And what is this merit system you speak of? It's just one of our traditions – a time honored story here but also in many states, others would add.

Following dismissal in Federal Court of the criminal fraud charges brought in the name of the state Division of Highways, a long-term acquaintance of Dr. Parks and his boss, who had accepted a $500 donation from him during the campaign as well as from several environmental and engineering consultants at a Polka Dot Golf Course fundraiser, had introduced the future gubernatorial candidate to Dr. Parks after dinner there. That had been four years earlier.

"Hi, Bob," both said to each other. "It's been awhile, hasn't it?" they said to each other. "Maybe the next time we're together we'll have more time."

Dr. Parks answered the telephone after closing a deal on

an archeology project at a planned and permitted mountaintop coal removal site on one of many Indian Ridges in the state. By some act of serendipity it was Phil Fitzgibbons, his staff archeologist returning his earlier call.

But no arrowheads or burials there, his archeologist had said. "No self-respecting Indian would have ever lived on the top of that pointed mountain ridge, five to 11 feet wide at best. It's a clearance."

"I have mixed emotions on our work for mountaintop removal, Phil, but at least we are out there beforehand to salvage Native American sites where they do show up. I guess that's better than not doing it, or like before, when the sites or burial mounds were simply bulldozed over the mountainside without anyone viewing it to save them."

"By the way, see the *Daily Mail* today, Bob?"

"No, why, Phil?"

"Your governor down there–that Bob. *The New York Times* misspelled his name as Wiseoff, I think, but it seems he got caught getting a little on the side with a female state employee at the development office and then her husband, or her ex, I suppose, is highly resentful and called the press about a divorce and announced he's running for governor just to embarrass Bob. "

"Then someone sent an unidentified e-mail, no one knows who. Oh, well, at least this time it's a woman scandal, I guess. Bob, isn't he the one the DED bureaucrats didn't want to embarrass just in case you were some alleged federal criminal by the DOH and EPA silly charges that didn't even bring an indictment?" Phil asked. Some questions don't need answering.

Phil lives in Pittsburgh and is a professor of archeology and paleontology at the Franciscan University of Steubenville, Ohio. He had been a company associate, like several other professionals in their respective fields, for years and worked as a subcontractor producing quality Phase I Cultural Resources studies for Dr. Parks' environmental consulting firm.

All of them, including the QA/QC chemistry associate, Dr. Wayne Grey Owl Appleton, had been subpoenaed to the civil trial to say the firm and its owner produced false documents – either about themselves or studies they produced.

"Bring the resentful sick bureaucrats on," more than one of them had said.

Phil had heard the news on CNN before Dr. Parks heard it in Charleston.

"Oh, ok. No, I hadn't heard. I'll check it out. But I'm from the government and your check is in the mail, Phil, and I am here to help you, and what's that other one firemen quote? See you Phil, and thanks again till next site."

"Oh, by the way, the State of Virginia is coming up on a 400 year quad centennial, or whatever that's called, and some Indians there are trying to get state recognition of their local tribe that's been there for thousands of years, kept the early Virginians from starving when their ancestors arrived and all that, but the state legislature has refused to grant legal tribal status out of fear they want to establish casinos, even though their state recognition documents clearly state they preclude casino gambling," Phil added.

"But still they have been refused recognition unlike what you folks have in West Virginia and it seems like the proposed legislation dies in some committee every year. Isn't that amazing that can happen in this country 400 years later? You might want to look up the article in *The New York Times*. That's where I saw it. Well, I have to run to teach a class. Let me know if we get that archeology bid here in Steubenville."

He said he would.

"And say hello to governor Bob if and when you see him. Bye, Bob."

"Bye."

Chapter Seventeen

Patience and Tolerance as a Code

"Now let me see if I am getting this right: Bob Wisecoff's administration allowed, through his division of highways, federal criminal fraud charges to be brought against you, your two children, Gabriel and America; your business partner Thom Botts; and, the corporation, for having done nothing wrong you or Ben Wanton can identify? And the driver for the case for the US Justice Department in Charleston for a couple EPA-Wheeling vindictive bureaucrats that you were an expert witness against and they lost the case? Amazing."

Over the now four years waiting, it was a conversation repeated several times over by way of explanation, often to the question, "How's Business" from associates and friends.

Afterwards the criminal charges were "declined prosecution" due to no evidence whatsoever of wrongdoing, except serving as an asbestos expert witness in federal district court against an EPA enforcement officer known as a guntoting jock walking through downtown Wheeling. Folks there supposed he was looking for an asbestos to shoot.

Dr. Parks was in Wheeling once again to teach classes at the Jesuit University. It was his seventh year teaching there. The long-awaited date for the civil trial was scheduleld in three weeks, and Halberts had prepared a supoena to the trial for Martin Reicht. It was to be delivered at his office in the Methodist Building on a Friday afternoon and classes at the university were to be taught Saturday. He rang the electronic surveillance buzzer, but no one answered. Reicht was not there, though, for whatever reason.

Dr. Parks went looking for him to deliver the subpoena, but learned instead that he had a major heart attack between the criminal trial and the twice-scheduled and twice cancelled civil trial. Perhaps he how understood why the earlier trial dates had been rescheduled by the judge for no apparent reason. It seemed someone just didn't want a trial to occur after Dr. Parks filed extensive reports on his own in the federal court record, and provided full factual data on all charges as well as the factual history in the case against him. Truth always surfaces, even in the land where it's all relative.

The workers compensation judge, the following week, ruled with a bench memo that Dr. Parks had not followed an administrative rule for appeal within 10 days of the DED firing. He did not address the constitutionality of the rule for a state employee versus that for a private industry employee. He saw his state retirement and work of four years evaporate, temporarily, at least, before his eyes. This was a powerful political parochial machine.

It was clearly time for an overdue visit with old sponse in Columbus and a couple days break from the circular thinking for Dr. Parks. And a weekend out of town would be good R&R for him, he decided.

"And you expect me to worry about the governor getting caught getting a little nookie on the side? That's not my issue with him at all. I made up my mind about that guy months ago– I have been conned by a man I have known for 30 years, given money to, campaigned for, and have at such levels that now seem revolting to this self-respecting man– let me just think about all this to you, sponse.

"Maybe that is the problem – thinking again," sponse advised. It was what he needed to hear, or course, and he knew it.

"And now you say your Higher Power through you thinks my Higher Power through me should write one of my newspaper op-ed page articles and give it to *the Valley Gazette*?

"And point out you say that here is the governor who has admitted wrongdoing with a state employee, for gosh sakes, she's getting a divorce because of it, and you want me to pray for the sorry guys and for the ex-wife and the children of this other Bob I have known for 30 years? I see. I'll think about it, sponse. I will be in touch and thanks for the weekend.

EagleClaw proceeded home along US Route 35, the Shawnee Highway from one end of that former nation, its trade route running from the Kanawha River border with the Cherokee at Charleston and ending at Xenia, land of Blue Jacket, and near the former border with the Miami Tribe, the English translation, or Maumee, the French understanding of the indigenous peoples.

Some Miami Indians had migrated along the Shawnee Highway to the Kanawha Valley and settled a couple hundred years ago on Cabin Creek. The first white cabin dweller from Virginia who built the cabin was later murdered by those local Indians, it is written. That story would repeat itself for the next 100 years in different locations in Appalachee. And Tecumseh would ride through, asking all Shawnee to move to unite in Chilecothe, and many did, and then integration somehow took care of the remainder of the population left here. Another hundred years later a Civil War changed the American Revolution history of Appalachee, and the whole country, and then industrialization and coal mining became the area's history. And then the interstate highways were built and America encroached, one-third of the population left the places of their births, and the balance remain today. Perhaps those left can rebirth themselves someday. EagleClaw had a nice drive home through Chilecothe to the Kanawha Valley along the Shawnee highway called US Route 35.

After returning home from Columbus, the local headlines the next day gave him a whole new concept, humorously, for a whole new kind of 12- step program:

"*Wisecoff tight-lipped on affair*"

'Our family is together,' governor says in first outing since first admitting affair. *The Valley Gazette*, page 1. Admitting Affair. Adult Admission. Is that something like the First Step of Recovery? We admitted we? Or is that a Triple A? Adult Admissions Anonymous?

Dr. Parks said he really didn't care what the governor did on a personal level, but he did care what he had callously done to destroy his small business which formerly employed seven people in a state where unemployment rates are below those of Mississippi.

And now his state work was going to a Pittsburgh firm, where employees were flown in or drove in over long hourly distances at what had to be twice the amount of dollars the three in-state small businesses received on the same contract.

He now understood why it cost the large firm $57,000 to re-survey his $10,000 job in Logan which Joe Dunn had ordered. It was just one more piece of misleading information for the trial. And that was his experience.

But self-righteous humor, even of the political variety, was not his forte. But once again he found himself moving right along and turning the newspaper page, as Bob Seger would say, and the Scorpio Horoscope was next: Today is an 8. As a result of a recent confrontation, you will become very wealthy. Hmm. Well now, let's look at that one, and the humor continued in his mind.

"It has been my experience, and that is all I can base my decisions on, whether for good or bad, that once in a while I get just the very opposite of my horoscope prognostication. Hmm. Damned if you do, damned if you don't. Look before you leap, yet he who hesitates is lost. I know. I don't know. When you know you don't know, you know. I know I don't know, but I think so.

"But my best thinking got me here. I give up. Someone knows, guess who? I know he knows and maybe he'll let me know. Maybe if I'll just pray and meditate the answer will come. After all, those who scoff at prayer and meditation

are those who just haven't tried enough, it has been said. Perhaps I should just listen."
And so his meditative state began.
"Nothing, absolutely nothing, happens on God's Earth by mistake. There are no coincidences. There is no other choice. The truth always surfaces, and the truth shall set you free. Freedom from bondage and free at last, free at last.
Then a client called to say he needed some paperwork to complete a tasking assignment bid from last week.
"You will have it in the mail shortly and thank you," Dr. Parks said.
No matter the large financial losses resulting from the prejudiced resentments of the two bureaucrats and legal cases of the past four years, he was always taken care of financially during this long period and checks arrived in the mail regularly, it seemed.
He had even paid off his house during the ordeal. Even some small miracles should be recognized and shared, he had said to the group at the continuing Wednesday night St. John's meeting, the *Live and Let Live Group*, the very one serving as a mustard seed of resentment for Joe Dunn and his sponsor the past 17 years ago. Life has its dichotomies.
"And sometimes we just have to get through what we are going through to get to where we're going," sponsor Ed H had said.
On Monday the board of education called to ask him to man the library at a Pocatalico school. He had done so on an as-needed basis many times in the past two years. It paid the rent, so to speak, and was the most positive thing he knew to do during these trying times. And besides, he enjoyed teaching those little ones who reminded him of his real joy in life, his two grandchildren. And that school library had a sizeable collection of books of Appalachian history, including "*The Bloody Indian Battles in West Virginia*" and other collector items he used for browsing while at work there.

And God helps those who help themselves, no matter what. And besides that, it was about a $100 a day he didn't have before and he had met a couple new lady friends who desired to operate is body in its healthy state and to maybe direct his mind following direction of physical body. Not a bad deal, and besides, one wanted to hire his physical expertise for some "remodeling and other chores at home" for the summer but only after taking him to her beach house for a week after school was out. And good things come to he who fills in the blank spaces.

He had invited her to her first Passover Seder to meet family and some friends and said he would give it all some thought. Let's just give time time, he had said in their last conversation, but found himself very busy over the next couple weeks with all manner of things from racquetball to kayaking with son Gabriel to other forms of rock 'n roll and living life on life's terms. He had many friends.

All good things come to he who waits – with patience and tolerance.

The time now passed four years in the continuing ordeal.

Chapter Eighteen

Waiting On the Civil Case

BARRISTER AL HALBERTS had called Dr. Parks on the first Sunday in May at home to "just say a friendly hello" since he had not returned his calls for about a month for answering such questions as whether the court schedule for submission of deposition information was on schedule. The schedule had been adjusted by him this time with Jackson at Justice to accommodate Al's schedule, he was advised.

Since the scheduled date had passed during the past week, Dr. Parks thought he'd better at least telephone Al and ask. A new schedule had been arranged and the civil trial wouldn't be conducted until the Fall, Al said. Little did the defendant know a year later he would repeat the cycle.

That's good enough, he had replied to Al, and it just might be enough time to write a novel he had in mind dealing with interwoven themes of bureaucratic abuse of personal powers and resentments while protected by the "balance of government power" or maybe a book of Appalachian Indian history he had wanted to write; or, a third possible theme of individuals in recovery from a fear-based religion, or culture, or addiction, or themselves, or all the above, maybe.

"What a concept" Al had replied. "Do it, Dr. Bob." And later, another friend, Dr. Stout, had replied "But I am looking forward to the DVD version of the book." Friends will be friends.

But getting beyond the chit-chat with his lawyer for the civil case, he had other more important questions for the lawyer, such as now that his $5 million civil case had been removed from state court to federal court and was now thrown out by Judge Goodrich, when could it be re-filed in the state court of claims?

Al had told Dr. Parks in their last meeting two months ago he wanted him to concentrate not so much on the scheduled civil trial for damages against the government, but instead on a new trial in state court to collect the damages visited on Dr. Parks and his firm and his family. Coins and mouths have two sides.

Al had said to Dr. Parks that for every wrong committed against one there is a righting action. He hoped Al was right and had to believe so as his attorney to whom he was paying $400 a month after scraping it together from his part-time teaching salary. The two had reached an agreement after talking that Dr. Parks would pay the monthly fee and it would be returned from the court case winnings of the civil case and the lawyer would receive a contingency fee of one third.

He hoped the contract was minimally worth the paper it was written on. "We shall see, shan't we?" echoed in his mind.

Dr. Parks asked for the written contract as he had learned to do, and was handed a hand-written agreement by Al stating the above terms and that he would remain on the cases involved as per an earlier written request to lawyers "so long as the cases required."

The cases required at this point action and energy for defending the federal civil case against Dr. Parks and his firm; the state court of claims case brought by Dr. Parks individually for $5 million damages; and, the "bad faith" suit against his professional liability firm after the insurance carrier denied coverage they excused as criminal charges, then rendered their same opinion on civil charges.

The insurance carrier had refused to represent him and his firm on the criminal fraud charges, even though the issues were clearly errors and emissions claims on behalf of the vindictive EPA bureaucrats for compositing composite building materials, then billing, fraudulently, of course, for those allegedly composited materials.

He was also charged with submitting false documents under the False Claims Act, such as a false Ph.D. degree claim, false credentialing for a well qualified staff, and several other false charges by the bureaucrats. They were charging him and the firm with charges they were guilty of in the prosecutiion, it appeared to Dr. Parks.

Pearbottom used the letters C.I. for criminal investigator after his name on EPA documents. When one has no letters, any old letters will do, one supposes. After all, what other letters would he use? Coal Miner, after all, just doesn't get it in the federal bureaucratic culture.

Failure of an insurance firm, even in West Virginia, to represent its insured client in the state can result in treble damages when convicted, the state code says.

Dr. Parks had immediately discussed the charges after the first subpoenas were received and had delivered the material to his local insurance agent.

"You are clearly covered for representation with your policy" the local agent representative said. "I'll fax it to New York and they will have to decide coverage, however."

About five days later a fax was received denying representation to the firm in a 19-page compendium of legalese language put together and sent by a middle man consultant and his female friend in Alabama. Dr. Parks had been paying from $2,600 to $10,000 a year for the Errors and Omissions coverage, depending on volume of business, for 14 years. Legal coverage was not applicable, they had said.

The state asbestos contract had required the E&O policy to perform on the state contract. Yet the one time in 14 years it was needed, the coverage was denied to the tune of 19 pages of reasons in a pre-printed format sent not by the company but instead by a two-person home office subcontractor located in Alabama.

Dr. Parks' acquaintance Bill Adamson, Esq. had drafted and put on disk the planned lawsuit and made it available to Dr. Parks. But Al seemed to have little interest in that suit or the disk until the civil charges were over, he said on questioning as to why he had not filed charges. Collusion was not an issue for him, he added.

Al worked on his own as a subcontractor, it appeared, at a firm which had a direct relationship to coal companies in the state. Al had been referred to Dr. Parks by his daughter America on a chance referral and, after speaking or attempting to speak with a dozen other lawyers to explain that his former criminal lawyer Ben Wanton had said he had completed his legal tasking, he had been somewhere between turned down to looked askance at by other lawyers for four months while trying to find new representation.

The long explanations and beliefs and opinions did nothing to convince the lawyers each time that there just must be something wrong here; or, that they didn't "speak asbestos"; or, they were just too busy. Ben Wanton should still be his lawyer, they said.

Al, however, was immediatelly friendly and receptive to Dr. Parks on first meeting and agreed to take all three cases. "We'll win," he had said. "We'll see, shan't we" Dr. Parks had replied to the lawyer. It would cost $400 a month, refundable on a win, and one-third contingency. Two cases should produce settlements and the civil charge case was there to be defended and won, he said initially.

He promised on second meeting that he would redress the actions of the Justice Department lawyer who seemed to be more than aggressive in representing the state and federal bureaucrats, including C.I. Pearbottom, whose EPA office was located in the same Bob Byrd Federal Building as Carol Jackson's office. The building is filled with government representing government.

But many things in life are not always what they appear to be, he had learned many times over in his 59 years.

Dr. Parks sometimes wrote op-ed page articles for the state's primary newspaper, and its editor James Haute had said to Dr. Parks that probably that was one of the feds' goals– hoping to get an asbestos story into print. They didn't.

The field office of US-EPA in Wheeling regularly produced canned press releases of its real or imaginary enforcement activities in the state. They have a full-time person to do nothing but issue press releases, a Terry Gone. Some were printed, most often they were not, the editor said.

That qualifier had been good news to receive from an editor of a major newspaper known for its agenda of being pro-environment, but not pro-abuse by the powerful doing unto the powerless. It was their history from its first publisher through today.

Haute had said to Dr. Parks that his newspaper disregarded most of EPA's canned heat since the day an EPA employee working in the state claimed in federal court that his non-existent college diploma had been chewed up by his dog and that was why he couldn't prove he had one, lying in federal court on the matter.

The Gazette carried and repeated that false claim by the EPA former employee for years, and the falsehood remains a source of humor at the newspaper and in the minds of environmentalist trying to do the right thing to this day, not just in West Virginia, but throughout Region III of EPA. But it's not repeated with much humor in the regional capitol in Philadelphia or in the federal capitol in Washington.

"I had a college degree but the dog chewed it up so I had to throw it away," they joke when referring to that former EPA On-Scene Coordinator who worked in West Virginia in Region III. The court joke delayed a Minden PCB cleanup for several years. He resigned, but his reputation preceeded him. He and a friend left EPA to work in private industry, using work experience as a reference. He later worked in legal enforcement. His friend returned and is now a section chief with EPA in the regional capitol, Philadelphia.

EPA-Wheeling's Pearbottom no doubt had the awful and continually embarrassing conversation of that EPA employee's history of a false claim for that college degree in mind when he tried to prove that Dr. Parks did not possess a Ph.D., "...except from some African country database," Pearbottom had actually said to him and Ben Wanton at the federal courthouse prior to the criminal trial. That primary hope of evening an imaginary score by Pearbottom faded after a deposition showed Dr. Park's Ph.D. to have come from a State of California accredited institution.

Dr. Parks had produced a copy in deposition in the Western Environmental case and a State of California Assistant Attorney General had verified under oath that the degree was valid and accredited by the California Department of Education upon issuance. But facts aren't always facts to some.

That would have seemed to end the discussion matter except for Pearbottom's spending untold man days charged to the government taxpayers researching the matter under his own conviction but failing to uncover the public deposition until it was brought forth for discussion by Dr. Parks himself at federal court.

But Pearbottom seemed beyond embarrassment when the truth was handed to him in the Bob Byrd Federal Courthouse. It really didn't matter, he said, because they had films of Parks sampling on a state asbestos contract activity where he had failed to measure positive asbestos wrapping on HVAC materials in a house in Huntington because the pipes were covered by walls. He had heard facts don't always make the difference, he replied to Pearbottom.

For a formerly reputable federal agency for whom Dr. Parks had worked seven years performing quality technical work for assessing and cleaning up Superfund sites, he was somewhere between dismayed and astounded that the same agency in Region III in the Enforcement Section had such employees performing such useless tasks as this one, and others, he had observed, particularly for Pearbottom's more than vindictive boss in Wheeling. It was history now.

In recent years, 1.4 million people in the United States had slipped into poverty. Seven of them used to receive paychecks from Dr. Parks' small business. And 10 million Americans had their identity stolen, at a cost of $57 million. It has been said that bureaucrats themselves may be the future downfall of the American democracy. But now is just not the time to criticize the government, he had been forewarned by his lawyer, retired from the federal court system but now seeking cases for defense against it.

Rather than cleaning up sites contaminated with dioxin throughout the Kanawha Valley still spilling the known contamination into the Kanawha River, here were bureaucrats trying to get unjustified press coverage for enforcement in an environmental arena and to get a raise from their boss, Charlie Kay in Philadelphia.

Dr. Parks also knew Charlie Kay personally from seven years past work experience in Philadelphia and Wheeling.

The last time they were together at an alleged training meeting in Florida in January set up by Rudy Shoup and charged to EPA contract Superfund monies, Parks and Mr. Kay had dinner together after visiting several area Orlando theme parks. "What a nice place for a Winter meeting," they thought.

Kay was visibly upset at Parks because he had scheduled a day's annual leave on the trip and arrived one day early in order to visit Orlando theme parks. Kay and his personal friend at Western Environmental, the contract holder, had charged travel time that day to billable hours.

It would create a discrepancy in billing for them should someone higher-up compare time sheets, they said to Parks, who had toured parks other than the one the three planned to visit together. Rationalization and justification in the human condition can be difficult discrepancies to bureaucrats at all levels of government, he had observed.

The two bosses, one enforcement, one contractor, then went to the theme park together the next day, registration day, they said. They had pre-registered. Whatever.

"It all works if you let it," Parks had replied to them. Parks said he just didn't feel morally right visiting theme parks on contract billable meeting hours, so he had gone on his own annual leave time.

The others, including his boss Mike Springer and friend and former co-worker at the Philadelphia EPA office Charlie Kay could determine their own schedules, he politely said to them, while he attended scheduled meetings.

"Fine," they had replied, "but who are the ones you are trying to impress. If not us, then who?" Mr. Kay had asked.

"No one," Parks had replied. "It's just a matter of honesty at a personal level in all our affairs" he added, and said that he didn't feel right being dishonest about federal contract billable hours that subconsciously he would remember, even if the bosses conveniently forgot. Some things change things, he knew.

He noted each week when he submitted his time sheet that there was a printed notation on the top right hand corner that said misbilling was a federal offense.

The other two had looked at each other and smiled gingerly, then Springer said the two would go to the theme park without Parks and they would meet him next evening for dinner.

It happened that way. The meal conversation was pleasant and light and it came time for ordering dessert.

Parks said he wanted the key lime pie. Kay said he really wanted to order it too, he had not seen it on a menu in Philadelphia and regarded it as a Florida regional food anomaly–lime juice in pie? he said.

"Hey, its wonderful, try it. It's a little expensive, yes, but worth it. Kay declined and Springer ordered as his dessert another Samuel Adams. The key lime pie arrived topped with whipped cream, was the correct color of high yellow not green key lime juice, and Parks took the fist bite.

As his taste buds exploded as only key lime pie can do for the discerning, or at least still hungry diner, Parks smiled and said, "That's the best key lime pie I have had since I was last in Key West."

Kay waved his fork in front of his face in a twisting motion and said he should have ordered a piece but was simply to too tight to pay the $4 cost.

"Try mine," Parks said, leaving the dessert plate in place.

Kay scooted back in his chair. "It's too slender and I will just let you have yours and I'll order a piece next time."

"I'll send your wife the recipe and she can bake you one. It's the recipe the Greenbrier Hotel in West Virginia uses and it's actually better than any key lime pie I have had in Key West or elsewhere in Florida."

"My wife doesn't cook much of anything," Kay replied.

"Ok," Parks replied not knowing what to say at that point.

"Well if you want the recipe let me know since you'll not typically see this pie offered in restaurants in Philadelphia, so let me know," Parks said, looking demurely at other patrons to hopefully taper off the topic of discussion going nowhere.

No resentment building with this fellow, head of criminal enforcement in Region III, he thought to himself.

Next day Kay told Parks at social hour that he was "jealous" that Parks could order the pie, that it was a foreign concept to him. Parks suspected some form of personal resentment in the comment, but dismissed the guessed-at emotion behind the message being sent and smiled and walked on by not wanting to resume that discussion again.

He had other more important things to do, including completing and e-mailing a pollution report to his Wheeling EPA contractor office.

Parks left the training session meetings as they adjourned at 3 pm for "open discussion" while the truth was the time allowed those who chose to go to the open bar set up for the meeting.

As a person in recovery, he could be comfortable in those environments only about an hour, or until people became visibly intoxicated, then it was time for him to leave. No explanation was required, he believed. He just excused himself. Some things in life don't need to change.

In recovery then for only two years, he didn't openly

avoid such social activities, but didn't hang around unnecessarily. Instead, he changed into swimshorts and went to the pool.

In mid-Florida in January at 80 degrees, he decided, he could use a little more tan in his skin. With his Indian genetics, since childhood, he could tan noticeably and quickly in an hour per day if he only had access to the sun.

He had gone to the pool instead of the bar for two days about that time and Kay and Shoup said they were already a little jealous that his tan was already readily noticeable.

"It's my Indian blood genetics," Parks had replied. If I just get out in it the sun tans me easily." Springer replied that if Parks ever had his own business he would quality for minority-owned status with federal regulations for contracts.

Parks said he was somewhat aware of that but didn't quite understand the process and wasn't sure how much it mattered anyway since he didn't have plans to have his own business in the foreseeable future, but might someday.

The next morning Parks consciously chose to eat breakfast with "the big boss" Rudy Shoup and asked him if he could share his table.

"Of course," Shoup had replied.

"Rudy, can you explain to me how one becomes a minority-owned business subcontractor, such as on the our Superfund contract?"

Shoup said first you have to be a very civil Christian East Indian who has immigrated here with the family jewels hidden so that your personal net worth is declared at less than $250,000, or be African-American and willing to be installed as president of a corporation that is set up and directed by others who have an interest in the prime federal contract.

"Is that tongue-in-cheek or reality, Rudy" Parks asked.

"It's real but not what you will read in the Federal Register. Our two minority firms on this contract– the East Indian firm and the African-American-owned firm– are headed by former Western Environmental employees instilled, shall we say, in those companies, and the stock shares are

51% held by them but undeclared amounts of 9 percent each are, for example, held by my three sons for providing for their college expenses someday. That's just an example, you understand."

"I see – is that standard in the industry for federal contract and subcontract firms or is that a management decision – and I use the term euphemistically – just for our particular contract." he asked

"It's legal and, in our case, required, of others if they want to do business with us. We also have former employees, you will note, from corporate headquarters strategically placed in those firms as managers. Dr. Sanghavi sits in his office on the Beltway but our man there Raymond Parr calls the shots.

"He bills to the subcontract we provided to them and he and I talk everyday. Likewise, at the other firm. You can see that no longer than what you have worked for us interviewing and hiring new employees for them on the contract, no doubt.

"Their contract slots are filled by us and sent to them to fill slots for billable hours position.

"We call it the team approach. It lets the new employees know they are working for us even though their paychecks are issued by the subcontractor corporations.

"By the way, Parks, you have been doing an excellent job of interviewing and hiring good quality technical employees in the short period of time you have been here since we asked you to perform that function in addition to your environmental scientist site assessment duties.

"What is your method of success that thus far has been very pleasing to us as well as our client EPA over in Philadelphia?

"Well," Parks replied, "I really only look for three qualities in an individual before making a recommendation for hiring to Mr. Springer. People are credentialed already before getting accepted for an interview, of course, so that leaves me the freedom while interviewing for reviewing and determining the following three things: are they honest, upfront, and share information?

"Those qualities are often difficult to discern, but I seem to have a knack for knowing the correct answers before I finish the interview, although I sometimes call them back for a second discussion and interview.

"Do you recognize those personal qualities because you too already possess them?" Shoup asked.

"In all humility, I had never really thought about it, but I suppose you may be right and that makes it easier to make the decision based on what I hear, see and observe during the interview, I suppose," Parks replied.

"You know Mike Springer is downright jealous of your uncanny ability to hire good people who please the client for the team for no longer than what you have been on board with us."

No, Parks replied. He didn't. But he bit his tongue to not say what he did recognize about Mike Springer as the boss with a South Jersey culturally based personality, it seemed – that a constant sense of urgency was a very basic part of his personality make-up.

He just assigned it to the culture there and admitted he didn't know or care much for that culture and that he couldn't change it anyway, so he accepted it as it was. It was not his culture, but he just observed, not compared, since he couldn't change it.

He had too many other things on his mind with the two job functions he was now performing on the contract and also constantly being called out to sites to sample hazardous material organics and metals, not to mention constant demand for his asbestos sampling capabilities.

He was the only scientist of 43 on staff who could properly sample for asbestos, and it was often found in thousands of cubic yards on old industrial clean-up sites throughout the region.

It had astounded him the first few weeks on the job that EPA personnel were highly concerned about metals in soils on these sites but had no clue that the pipe lagging falling out of the sky from overhead pipe wrapping was asbestos-containing material.

"Its pipe lagging," they would comment. "We are here to find hazardous materials and CERCLA doesn't define asbestos as a hazardous waste," he had been told.

"Yes, but, it is defined as a hazardous waste by other federal environmental laws, so just because we are funded under CERCLA doesn't mean that it's not a threat to human health and the environment, especially to us workers here, does it? We know it is a killer and here we are as contract employees with the stuff falling on our hardhats. It is friable – that means we are breathing it – while we're out here on sites looking for spent solvents while breathing asbestos fibers – a known carcinogen," he had said to the EPA on-scene supervisor the first week on the job.

"Perhaps we should simply sample the stuff and see," he suggested. "Only the laboratory can tell us." Parks knew by looking from years of past experience most of the samples would come back positive from the laboratory. They did.

"But we're not funded for asbestos removal. Our enforcement section makes private firms do that. We're consultants and our removal contractor is not qualified for asbestos removal and we can't pay for it anyway" the On-Scene Coordinator still objected.

The OSC's primary technical qualification for his job had been experience in the streams response unit to spills before going to work at EPA to direct contractor operations for the Technical Assistance Team for Superfund sites.

He was often too drunk or hung over to get to the site in the mornings. He was far from the only one often so impaired.

Two weeks later Parks was asked to survey the site and found about 10 metric tons of asbestos-containing material in roofs, gaskets, thousands of feet of pipe lagging, on huge old storage tanks as insulation, and many other sources, including the abandoned laboratory on the site.

The cost eventually was nearly $1.5 million of the $23 million cost to remove the "emergency" threat at that site. Another $31 million has been spent to date on remedial efforts at the same site. Asbestos sampling costs in the environment here can be very relative, depending on whose ox is getting gored, Dr. Parks remembered.

And the federal contractors loved it there in Appalachee. Wouldn't you?

But the dioxins, the no-word at the site, never to be repeated, they were told, remains on the site buried by a clay-lined pond landfill cover to this day.

The water table from the area still drains into the Kanawha River, used for drinking and recreation downstream. But the Superfund site is only one of many known dioxin-emitting sites in the valley where the Native American ancestors buried their dead in both honorarium mounds as well in level cemeteries.

Some of those level burial grounds are now used for growing corn or for manufacturing chemicals for other Western cultural practices deemed more important than former burial sites.

But such is life and death in the Western world.

Some things never change, while change changes some.

Chapter Nineteen

The Challenge

THE PHONE RANG in the consulting practice office and it was administrative manager and business partner Thom Botts. He was now doing much better after three years in his state job, leaving the consulting practice after business had declined and no money was available from the part-time work for salaries, let alone benefits.

His salary had more than doubled to $34,000 a year. He had now surpassed by $5,000 per year his former salary for the firm, with full benefits now accruing. He life scales were now balancing.

He had to date five heart and arterial correction surgeries by the age of 37 and knew he had to have health insurance in the future to live.

For five months he lived hand to mouth paying a COBRA co-pay and then the money from savings completely dried up. He lived at no rent at Dr. Parks' home.

It took the five months to test, interview and be hired by the state agency, but the day had finally come to start a new job with benefits at an annual rate of pay of a whopping $15,000 a year in the state job performing computer functions for the collection of overdue child support payments from deadbeat dads.

Even before getting things right in a recovery program, Dr. Parks too had personal experience with that arena of life. He had no sympathy for either those dads or moms who refused to help pay expenses for feeding and clothing their children who may or may not live with them or their former spouses or partners. It was just a moral thing from both his cultures. He had done so earlier in life, then college expenses began and Creator provided well.

And so had Thom Botts done the next right thing. His child support arrears, from nine non-recovery years, however, were still mounting with interest. But he had agreed with the mom and with a lawyer in the program that he would pay from that day forward and add future year amounts for college expenses through a masters degree for the daughter.

The agreement was accepted verbally and reduced to writing by the lawyer friend in the program. However, it was adhered to 13 years, but had not been recorded at the county courthouse of the then residence of the mother and child. Thus it was later held invalid by an agency he was now going to work for. Life has its dichotomies.

At a hearing on the matter, an administrative law judge allowed that he now owed $44,000 in back pay. He wondered if he should challenge the agency. It would be interesting, he decided, but he was not allowed resentments or they would take him back to a life and death issue from the past– back to his addiction of choice, thus ultimately illness instead of spiritually based recovery would be the winner instead of the individual in recovery. He gave time time. He would win the battle but lose the Pyrrhic victory, an historical lesson Native Americans have had to learn time and again.

It was a tough decision. He knew he didn't know all the answers but that the correct answers would come in some form if he just continued growing spiritually and attending meetings and picking up the simple set of spiritual tools provided to him by his recovery program.

That all unfolded when, seven years later, and now a management person for the child support enforcement agency, he paid a final sum to complete his monetary duties to the mother of his daughter.

The amount, paid for years, and a final settlement amount in the thousands, was now paid. And history often repeats itself on a personal and family and state and national level.

It's just another circle of information, EagleClaw decided, based on his Native American cultural view of all life. It's all in circles in history and repeats itself. Just the dates and facts change.

Life is change, after all, he had learned in many ways which he could now describe as physical, mental and spiritual —- just like the dis-ease that so often afflicts humans with addictions until they have to get into recovery and to change – or die of it. Those were the two choices.

The telephone rang and it was daughter Jenny in Sitka just checking in. She asked if he had told the story of his walk on the beach last July during his visit – *the challenge*, as she had called it. He laughed and said he had in fact repeated that story several times. Native cultures stay alive by the art of storytelling.

He had survived *the challenge* while walking alone on a beach across the bay from Sitka with its dozen or so Alaska tour ships in the harbor. He had walked through the rain forest down to the shore while watching eagles and ravens play in huge old fallen hemlock logs.

Several eagle feathers had wafted out of the trees and landed at his feet. Native American spirituality assigns special spiritual medicine qualities to eagle, raven, hawk and other spiritually-used symbols given in nature by predator birds.

Moving around the beach in the 50 degree Summer coolness of Alaska with snow-covered high mountains in the background, he noticed nine full bottles of Australian lager remaining in an unkempt arrangement in the sand.

The brown glass was covered with cool-looking condensate reminiscent of many bottles of beer he had consumed between 37 and 43 years old. After seven years of hard drinking and reaching an emotional bottom in life, he had to make a decision to literally live or die.

He had asked for help because he could not on his own

not drink beer except work hours after a first one. The help came immediately in the form of a "white light" experience – one which he could not talk about, even to old sponse, at the time, fearing he would think he was crazy– which of course he was from the effects his addiction. But he became willing to try to get better through a 12-step program. It was a program for life, not just quitting.

On that Alaskan cool day, the temptation was there, he thought, and no one would ever know – or would they?

Yes, they would know when he could not stop again – or he could die first, whichever came first. The thought was enough to cause him to say thanks, but no thanks, look up, and move on along the beach.

He had later told the story at a meeting in Sitka, returned with Jenny to that craggy beach two days later on her day off, and all were gone. But there was more to tell. Moving around the beach and locating a headstone of John Brown, Sitka's John Brown, not Harper's Ferry's John Brown, more temptation reared its head.

At exact eye level on a 200-year-old spruce log left over from probably a hundred years ago when the Sitka area was first timbered, was an unopened pint of Kentucky Bourbon Whiskey, nicely chilled, a thick black plastic seal cap around its bottleneck.

"Now that would get a party going," he thought of the party that must have been held at the deserted beach the night before. And bourbon on a 50 degree day chased by Australian Lager – wow, what a day, and no one would be the wiser – unless he died from the extended slip. How wise?

EagleClaw had gotten his spiritually-based name from keeping his head in the clouds closer to a Higher Power while keeping his feet on the ground. It was now his responsitibity to share those lessons learned this time around. Some lessons should only have to be learned once.

At his feet were nine frosted full bottles of lager. He actually reached down to touch one with his forefinger to feel if it was as cool as it appeared to the naked eye and, in his subconscious mind, romanced the first swallow.

They were a perfect temperature and he wiped the frost from the dark brown glass with his forefinger and the glass was then golden brown. His feet on the ground, bending over, he glanced at the effervescent liquid inside the pint wide-mouth bottle that had that golden brown liquid appearance very familiar to him.

Some things never change, but he had. He then raised consciously his head to the clearing blue and white overcast sky, and said, "Yes, but I would know. And someone else would." He continued to look up. "Unless I died, of course, before I got back to my home, and family, and kids and grandkids and sponse and mother and the civil trial and ...and my program."

He smiled a smile of love, respect and gratitude and remembered there was a noon meeting with local Indians, Russians and Americans, the three cultures alive and well in Sitka.

The cruise ships now unloading passengers in Sitka had caused a slight traffic backup, but he arrived at the Russian Orthodox Church only a few minutes late. A local eagle tribal member had brought smoked salmon and a local raven tribal member had brought chewy frybread as a treat for others at the noon meeting. The two made a perfect lunch.

For the first time there EagleClaw shared immediately his "challenge" story. The group laughed, one cried, one young man left presently, and those remaining shared frybread, smoked salmon and a universal spirituality.

He realized once again that quite often Native peoples had it right to start with spiritually, and that organized religion had often interrupted a path of spiritual growth in an effort to save others from their own cultures. And life has its dichotomies, it has been said.

In these meetings, three cultures blended beautifully without challenge while individuals spoke the spiritually-based language of the heart always prevalent in 12-step program meetings– meetings filled with "all God's children" of many ethnicities who come together to share and help each other recover from a disease of addiction foreign to all – did he say all – their indigenous spiritual growth patterns.

"Yes, Jenny, I have told *the challenge* story here several times. It always gets a good laugh and that miracle-without-asking gets repeated time and again just like all the other miracles that occur in our lives through continued love and tolerance– our Code, so to speak."

"It's a good story, dad, and one I will never forget. Talk with you again soon and thanks again for keeping in touch more this year than last. You're getting better, I can tell. Keeping coming back. Love you, dad. Bye"

The telephone rang again. It was daughter America, asking if dad had written more work on his book of Appalachian Indian History featuring all the chiefs born in the state. She had helped proofread the first few chapters and was ready for more work.

"Baby," as he still called her at 27 years old – with her express permission – I just can't seem to concentrate and settle down with the other horrendous things which have occurred in my life with or without me. But I do have a cover jacket concept for long photos or caricatures of Red Jacket, Blue Jacket, Pocatalico, Cornstalk, and Tecumseh on the cover. Did I forget anyone? Then I think about Cornplanter and Logan, who were not born here like the others but were significant cultural heroes in our history, and where to place them, and well, it's confusing me. Any ideas?

"No dad, but I'm sure the answer will come when the time is right. Maybe someday you will have a Summer off and can write that history book and I have another suggestion for a book you could write. It would be individual stories about all the people you have helped down through the years in the program and what they're doing now, like Dr. Jeff and his looking for quarters for his next six-pack and riding his bike to meetings because he didn't have a car but is a physician today 14 years later, or Scott now raising his children, or John in Wheeling who conquered both agoraphobia and alcoholism and dual addiction with a little help from you. It's just an idea. Maybe someday."

"Baby, maybe someday I will be inspired to write those stories for others, but for now it's about all I can handle to write my lawyers notes on the three or seven or whatever lawsuits necessary to straighten out the continuing damages visited on us by the two vindictive bureaucrats."

"We shall see, shan't we" he replied, lowering the discussion to a close. And how are my two babies and are we still going to the park this evening for a weiner roast and let them play on the rides?"

"We sure are dad. They look forward to it every week and seeing Pawpaw Bob and laughing with him as he swings them on the swingsets and teeter totters. We wouldn't miss it for the world, and don't forget the mustard this time, dad."

"Love you, baby. See you this evening at the park."

Checking his e-mail for the first time in a week, he had a note from former DED boss Bill Adamson. He had bought a vehicle from Dr. Parks, making payments each month and was ready for a title transfer. He had been hospitalized following resigning under pressure from DED, he said, but was now back living at his mother's home. He had repeated his history, it was evident. Some things don't change until we change.

Dr. Parks flashed on daughter America's book suggestion which he gradually dismissed without verbal comment and now had a higher respect for anonymity at the level of press, radio and film. Had Bill Adamson been included in the book as a successful lawyer and government administrator in such a book, where would he fit now?

And what would the public reaction be if they learned he would likely have died of drowning on his own vomit had a visitor not shown up at the hospital at "an opportune time" while he was alone and strapped to his bed unconscious following his last spree and a vehicle accident?

No, it was not material of a book. It was their stories and history but Dr. Parks' stories were not material for a book lauding success in a program that is individual only and always good for one day at a time.

And besides, that book had already been written in a finer form by others and now is outsold only by the Bible each year. It's a big book. But the idea was a great one but already ensconced in a great book of the Western world in a much more miraculous form. He was grateful that his children now shared their own sourced ideas with dad. They were close that way.

That was one of the promises-come-true in their relationships with both their mother and their dad that was the direct result of their having shared for about 17 years their spiritually-based recovery with their children in an honest, open-minded and willing way.

And the benefits of that love of their children and parents were coming back to them in the form of loving rewards. And not so parenthetically, it had helped produce three wonderful. healthy, offspring who were doing things like delivering babies in Alaska and Appalachee or raising same in same. We are all products of our cultures. And cultures and people can change for the good, if we get our selves out of the way and let it, whatever "it" may be.

Life was good and getting better despite the pain of the two-year threat of prison and one-year and adding civil fine time visited upon Dr. Parks by the two bureaucrats with their prejudiced resentments.

He was now vacillating on a scale for the two that ranged from the four-letter "f" word, fear, and the other "f" word in his repertoire, forgiveness.

He was trying to stay presently in the middle of that scale in his life. No matter, though, a bigger design was in place in all their lives and he knew and had learned over and again that he did not control the scale – or much else in the universe outside his own personal reaction to that which came his way.

He was responsible for being an instrument, and the music of the spheres in his life were playing on. That music had a rock 'n roll beat with solid group backup choral sounds orchestrated with strings and included a Native American tribal drum sound from a drum out of the woods provided by mother nature.

EagleClaw had grown up being musically trained in European culture and had spent many years playing in orchestras in the public school system. The practice continued through military training while in college band and ROTC.

He knew the West Virginia Symphony or the Wheeling Symphony required 27 specific instruments to produce replicas of music of the spheres from European cultures.

But he also knew a symphony of music in Native American culture was produced once the drum was "awakened" after being hollowed out from a large tree in the woods, stretched with dried animal skins, singers added who sang thousand year old songs using "vocables" from no distinct Indian language, and a symphony of music of the spheres, the source of all music, is produced in that process.

And despite all the seemingly "bad stuff" which had occurred in the previous three years, although not of his own making or design, during that third in the seven-year cycle of growth, his life had become, he could surmise, its own symphony.

And once more he had come to realize that pain is simply a necessary precursor of spiritual growth. And that is really about all that is required in this lifetime this time around to be happy. Pain and faith and courage and willingness are the keys, "but these are indispensable," old Herbert Spencer out of the European cultural tradition had said. Some Europeans, some Native cultural heroes, and some people, have it right.

And if one cannot accept that concept as a spiritual axiom, then ask Mahatma Ghandi or Mother Teresa or Nelson

Mandela or, failing that, maybe Bill Miller, or failing that, maybe, EagleClaw, who will say to you all true knowledge comes from the innerself. One has to simply seek it.

Chapter Twenty

The Governor Will See You Now

AFTER THE CRIMINAL charges were dismissed and the federal reinvestigation showed no evidence whatsoever of wrongdoing, written statements had been filed clearing his name and that of his company and family, he thought, but the vendetta was far from over. Dr. Parks proceeded with his five count, $1 million per count civil suit for damages. Carol Jackson had teamed with Pearbottom to avenge the heart attack suffered by his boss "and good friend" Marvin Reicht, then the very same charges against the asbestos expert witness were refiled in Southern West Virginia Federal District Court. The charges surrounded the work of the "set-up" in Logan and Huntington.

Strangely, however, the charges did not focus on the third part of the project crowded in by a zealous bureaucrat through a lady friend at the tasking assignment desk at the West Virginia Divison of Highways. Bureaucrats sometimes take their own actions for friends. The sister assignor for projects had added the third project, EagleClaw had been advised, for her friend for the Huntington-Melissa Road project. On the Logan and Huntington projects, the properties, carefully photographed by the avengers prior to demolition, and prior to inspection, EagleClaw suspected, had all been demolished. But, still standing were the structures for the third set of parcels, strangely, not charged in the civil case, the Huntington-Melissa Road project. They were photographed before the trial.

And a jury could go there and see that the technical documents matched inspections – thus exposing the false charges that the properties had not been inspected at all after Carol Jackson simply ran out of material for the prosecution. Something just didn't fit in her scheme promoted for Pearbottom. What didn't fit in the prosecution plan were the remaining properties still standing for the unfunded-for-demolition Huntington-Melissa Road project. All had been assigned under the renewed contract in the initial $25,000 tasking assignment. It was more than interesting. It was more than deceitful, also.

After the criminal trial ended in a jury's decision to not bring false charges, Dr. Parks had then sent another letter and went by to schedule an appointment to hopefully now get paid for work performed under written contract and tasking orders with the governor.

He again expected to be given an appointment time with an aide, but asked to see the governor himself, noting that he had known him personally for 30 years and had donated $1,000 to his campaign, the only time he had even hinted at use of some form of political loyalty. He wasn't sure how he felt about it, but his small business, his income, his professional reputation and future retirement plan were at stake now. The laborer was worthy of his hire, perhaps.

The scheduler, who had identified herself as Dede Mascia-Smith, said the governor was very busy on his personal computer but she would ask him about the issues.

They had met once before, he thought, while she served as liaison for Congressional affairs and Wisecoff was a US Representative, he believed but wasn't sure. She typed in an e-mail with an instant message, she said. He was too busy.

Parks explained his situation once again – that he believed his non-payment on a state contract had resulted from a prejudiced resentment of two bureaucrats, that they had personally vindictively encouraged the WV Division of Highways to file federal criminal fraud charges, but that nothing had been found wrong, and that his small business now needed it's $18,000 plus interest for work satisfactorily performed, and the firm needed to be placed back on the contract.

She nervously explained again that "We don't get involved in contracts, and the governor is on his way to Portugal today and I won't be able to review this matter with him for several weeks. I'm sorry," she said.

On two occasions in successive weeks, Dr. Parks telephoned messages, wrote another letter to the division of highways, but received no response.

Thom Botts had returned from a free cruise ship vacation won by a sponsee at his workplace based on sales. He dropped by the company office to catch up on a certain computer discussion– one might say confrontation– at Dr. Park's request.

"While I was out of town I heard something on the national news in Mexico that the governor had a long-term sexual affair with a state employee, what's that all about?"

"You haven't heard?" Parks replied. "Apparently the woman's husband spilled the beans over a divorce and the governor admitted Tuesday in a written press release it was all true. She's a state employee in the development office and they traveled to Portugal several times and other places together. Bob's wife is very distraught and the kids must be suffering something awful. They still go to public school, I think here in Spring Hill, and so it must be awful for the whole family to know that your father, the governor, can't keep his pants zipped. But you and I have known that for years, haven't we?"

"No wonder he didn't have time to deal with state contract issues. He had other issues. Oh, well as our Native culture teaches us "everything, absolutely everything that goes around comes around."

"It all applies," Tom added, "...whether it's sex, racquetball or rock 'n roll, we've heard it all before."

"Here's the full story from the *Associated Press*. It is the most singularly well written newspaper article I have ever read, frankly. Read it. It's by Lary Messina. He's the one who has all our press releases you lost with your hacker Marc out of the corporate computers. And by the way, you still owe me an honest explanation of that tragedy, but first read this story. It's interesting that Wisecoff kept the secret for a full month typed and ready to give to any reporter who asked, but none knew to ask.

"What fear the guy must have experienced carrying that around and keeping that secret that several staff already knew about. I knew it too, or at least suspicioned it from seeing the two at the Pittsburgh Airport when he refused to acknowledge me or who I was when we passed in Corridor C on his way to Portugal for the third trip with her.

"He looked more sheepish than that night we both saw each other than the first time 30 years ago at the adult book store downtown. He had that same look on his face, in fact.

"And it certainly adds credence to that little saying we hear around the rooms, by James See, "A whiskey glass, a woman's past, and my program's grass."

"Anyway, here's the full article. Read it. It's a corollary to Deep Throat if I ever heard one. It's about the most definitive article by any reporter I've ever read," handing the clipped article to Thom Botts, with the headline folded back.

> For nearly a month Gov. Bob Wisecoff rarely appeared in public without a folded piece of paper in his pocket. Although not quite on par with the nuclear codes that accompany the president, its contents proved pivotal.
>
> The paper contained a statement in which Wisecoff acknowledged a 'brief' affair outside his marriage. The governor started carrying it in early April, shortly after telling his wife of 17 years that he had been unfaithful.
>
> Wisecoff, a Democrat, cited the pain his infidelity has caused his family when he announced last week that he would not run for re-election. He has declined to say whether he had the affair with Angela Mascia, a 35-year-old European projects manager for the West Virginia Development Office. But the admission to his wife and the writing

of the statement shortly followed the April 7 divorce filing by Mascia's then-husband, Phillip "Icky" Frye.

Senior administration officials confirmed the sequence of events surrounding the statement, which some of them helped to write. They refuse to comment on the record, but believe Wisecoff's actions reveal the governor's intent not to mislead the media about the improper relationship.

These officials also say Wisecoff, 55, was prepared to issue the statement to any reporter who asked for it. But the media did not know to ask the question until May 12, and only then because of an anonymous e-mail forwarded to Charleston's two daily newspapers.

The email's route from the Internet to front-page news is reminiscent of the role online gadfly Matt Drudge played in revealing President Clinton's affair with Monica Lewinsky to the world.

Three days earlier, conservative radio talk show host Stephen Reed received the e-mail from an America Online account using the name "Thewvsource." It linked the governor to Mascia, naming both her and Frye. It detailed the divorce petition and included its case number as well as where and when it was filed.

The e-mail described its author as a Wisecoff supporter "more than severely disappointed that he would have risked bringing further national scorn and ridicule on our state and that he's such a hypocrite in quoting the Bible in every speech."

I was fascinated by it," Reed said of the e-mail. "To this day, I don't have a clue as to who that is."

"An hour after he received it, Reed forwarded the e-mail to both the Valley Gazette and the Daily Mail. As it was late on a Friday afternoon, the Daily Mail's final edition had already hit the streets, and most of its staffers had gone home. Government offices had closed for the weekend.

"We weren't quite sure what to do about it," Gazette Editor James Haute said. "I've always been leery of reporters peering into the bedroom window of politicians."

Daily Mail Editor Nanya Friend declined to comment on whether her newspaper received the e-mail.

"We came in Monday morning and found we got a very detailed, anonymous tip," she said.

The Daily Mail broke the story that day, after a request for comment from Wisecoff's office released the statement.

"It didn't take very long for them to respond," she said. "It was almost like they were expecting it."

Friend said receiving the tip revealed that several staffers had independently heard rumors about an affair in the governor's office.

"I'm extremely surprised by the impact," Reed said of the anonymous e-mail. "To be quite honest with you, I wasn't aware that it was my forwarding it along to the newspapers that opened the whole ball of wax."

The governor's demise from extreme popularity three years ago to lame duck status reminded EagleClaw of the tremendous changes that must have impacted the lives of his ancestors in the state when the British invasion began.

The major question was how long could they endure, and how would they adapt. Like the governor, their primary goal in life, he said, was to put the family back together, not maintain goals of running, as the governor said.

And histories repeat themselves and people grow and survive and learn to re-culture themselves.

But the real question in the minds of the general population was much different: What about his plans to succeed Robert Byrd as US Senator someday? It was a largely undiscussed and unanswered question.

His family had moved out on him to Washington, but he claimed the dichotomy of wanting to put his family back together while being governor here. And life is filled with dichotomies.

And Humpty Dumpty sat on the wall, and Humpty Dumpty had a great Fall; yet,

All the King's horses and all the King's men,

Couldn't put Humpty Dumpty back together again.

And some projected he would resign before his 18 months was up, then the Speaker of the state Senate would take his place automatically. The speaker was an un-announced candidate for governor to date, but why should he be? He was a Democrat, as nearly all politics ultimately are in the state. But time was on their sides for people forgetting and forgiving. And should Bob Byrd die, Heaven forbid, the governor then appoints a replacement. Heaven forbid. What a deal, and in the interim folks would forget that he exercised power, one might say, over folks in the state ranging from a female state employee to given state-contracting small businesses. It was his best thinking at the time of the debacle. But "Icky" wouldn't forget.

But Democrats the next time would re-elect a familiar Democrat name to the US Senate again. History does, after all, repeat itself in the state, and the people practice acceptance as Democrats very well so long as they just recognize the name.

Most folks don't vote anyway, save for the machine politics of labor, coal and those naturally born Democrats. Those other types are called Republicans but seldom win elections.

EagleClaw remembered that after the battle of Pt. Pleasant, years after Mary Engles had traveled through the Kanawha Valley, stolen by the Shawnee from Virginia and taken to Cincinnati, then escaped back, the Shawnee had become not only ferocious but also wise enough to begin moving to areas closer to their capital west of the Ohio River.

They had to leave their homeland to put their families back together again, like Governor Wisecoff.

To stay and fight or to surrender and leave were the two options. Many decided to leave the valley surveyed by George Washington after the Battle of Pt. Pleasant. But many had mixed-blood relatives here. Leaving family has always been tough for all generations of peoples who have lived here in the mountains.

But that required moving has in several generations been forced on residents, whether Native American in the 18th century, coal miners in the 19th century; or residents today moving to North Carolina via the Hillbilly Highway or a dozen other states where the American economy takes them.

But as they leave others move in, and the ebb and flow

of peoples continues.

The Cherokee retreated south in the 18th century, although many returned to families here to escape the Trail of Tears. The Shawnee did much the same thing, crossing the magnetic Ohio river to rejoin relatives later here. Some time afterwards the Sioux tribal members journeyed to the area and continued through the 1940's at the actual encouragement of the federal government their leaving the reservations. The coal mines were booming then and the world needed whatever workers were available for the two world wars and for mining coal.

And thus one finds today 74 kinds of Native Americans living here or enrolled as members of the Appalachian American Indians of West Virginia tribe, unfortunately a tribe today as in disarray as the disparate cultures it was intended to help bring back together.

You see, at a recent historical juncture, many tribal leaders decided to grow politically within the tribe instead of spiritually. And thus Indians, as always, divided and conquered themselves, too.

After the Shawnee retreated out of Virginia closer to Chilecothe, Tecumseh and the Prophet, his brother, began teaching return to the old ways to unify Native tribes and in part to stop the ravages visited upon and nearly destroying their culture. "The old ways" meant a return to the spiritually-based culture and tribal practices of the past.

But many Shawnee remained in the mountains in these homelands where they had a little business left, including salt production and maple sugaring, especially in the Kanawha Valley and in the Summers, Clay and Nicholas County areas – and to remain near the burial grounds of their ancestors, holy places to Native peoples.

And history repeats itself in trends and cycles and circles of cultural and spiritual growth and decline and rebirth.

In Pt. Pleasant in 2004, the first Native American powwow in at least 210 years that we know of was held at Ft. Randalph and people again danced on the valley floor.

No shots were fired. All God's children were represented, singing and dancing and loving one another to thousand year-old songs. Entire cultures can and are in recovery in Vandalia, Appalachee, America. Aho!

Chapter Twenty One

Monsieur Pearbottom, Les Miserables

DR. PARKS WAS WALKING from the washer and dryer to the bedroom carrying one empty and one full laundry basket of clothes to be folded and put away when the front doorbell at his residence rang.

Holding the laundry baskets in one hand and opening the latch with the other, he saw none other than Nicholas Pearbottom holding paperwork.

"Mr. Parks I have here some subpoenas for you and the corporation for a civil trial in federal district court."

Dr. Parks looked him in the eye and remained stolid. "You never quit, do you," Parks said in an even tone of voice.

"Well these aren't mine this time; they are the Division of Highways."

"Ok, but why are you delivering them for a state agency. Of all the people who could have delivered these, say a deputy sheriff or a contract delivery service, why you?"

He failed to answer. "I don't have to have your signature this time; I just have to hand them to you, that's all.

You say civil charges – does that mean the same charges as the former criminal charges you guys couldn't even get a jury indictment on to look at your useless charges?"

"Yes," he replied, "essentially, but these are for civil but mostly the same. I can't discuss them with you. If I can just hand them to you I will have accomplished my purpose this time around." Dr. Parks reached out his hand for the papers and glared with his clear blue eyes into the face of the re-

lentless, but not resentless, criminal investigator agent.
He closed the door and left promptly for a 5:30 meeting at the Serenity Club. He lived just a few minutes away from it.

He sat by chance next to his lawyer for the Workers Compensation case against the state DED, where, six months after this continuing ordeal had begun, he had been hired, hurt on the job and hospitalized then fired as the direct result of "seven or eight" telephone calls to the governors office alleging that he was a "potential federal criminal,"– never mind that U. S. Constitution. Two weeks later the job position had been eliminated by title by the DED director, who was, of course, directly appointed by the governor.

He sat quietly during the meeting and simply listened in order to maintain some semblance of serenity he had become accustomed to regardless of circumstances in these 17 years practicing the program.

His lawyer spoke first, and, after speaking, glanced over at the legal paperwork which Dr. Parks reviewed quickly during the meeting. Afterwards, no words were spoken about the paperwork. The two trusted servants smiled simply and said hello, good to see you.

Such civil matters were never discussed before, during or after such meetings, only at the lawyer's office.

The month before Dr. Parks had helped a sponsee and his wife move to Erie, Pa. He was one of a dozen sponsees on the roost at the time and was a success for a one year sponsee. He had worked 12 steps and 12 traditions and the promises were beginning to come true in his life. He had lived at Dr. Parks' home for three months to finish a job while the wife moved on to start a good new job and set up the household. Times had become good for them.

Dr. Parks drove the moving truck, then took a rental car to Toronto to spend a couple days in R&R in that city he loved– and hopefully to again experience after this long period of his life *'Les Miserables"* at a Toronto theatre. Unfortunately, he was advised, the show had closed, but was still playing on Broadway if he happened to be in New York. He said thanks, and decided maybe he would get to see it in a future road show in some city "drivable" from Appalachia.

He had seen the stage production about seven years ago in London at the old King Albert theater, had loved it, and was spiritually renewed enough by its message content to require spending the next 3-4 hours walking through central London to re-balance his usually even-keeled emotions. He needed to see it again, he felt, in his present cyclical painstaking period preceding some level of spiritual growth from the pain of criminal charges and more to come.

Before going to Toronto, he had been ill advised by a bell clerk during preregistration. He had said the show still played at some theatre there. It had been bad information.

He had a real need to see the show again for this period of his life to let himself know that despite whatever happens in life there is another cycle of good coming so long as one keeps coming back.

He remembered the unstoppable pursuit of Jean Val jean by Inspector Javert and thought of Pearbottom. Both looked normal in the face, he thought, but that expressionless face masks a mind that is troubled, it occurred to him, and what drives those two– are they the same character? Who had appointed Pearbottom to maintain this false social order, he wondered.

He wondered if in the book Victor Hugo had identified the boss of Javert to complete a quantum theory of combining 00 and 01 and the resulting synergistic personality disorders resulting in the human mind, particularly a sick one untreated by a dis-ease.

He wondered if the term schizophrenia fit any or all the men, whether it be Javert, Reicht or Pearbottom. Some projections we can't make, he told himself, and that wasn't his opinion to hold anyway. He promptly drove home, called his daughter America and the two grandchildren and a girlfriend who had been seeking him out again for Friday night, and went on with life. It was a very pleasant evening.

The next day, Saturday, he slept in, went to Mustard Seed Group and met Son Gabriel for a few games of racquetball. It's a 'wristy' game that determines whether one wins or loses, he said to Gabriel after the game, standing outside the court sweating freely and smiling, grateful at his age to still be in good shape for the game of life.

Gabriel already knew that and confirmed it each time he beat dad, which was now most of the time for most games. But even a blind hog finds an acorn once in a while, as it had been said for generations in Appalachia, and dad had taken a set, finally. That weekend he had enjoyed all his "acceptable addictions," –but not necessarily in that order. The rock 'n roll that weekend included downloading a disk of favorites for playing in the van while going kayaking on the Greenbrier River. The disk's label became Kayak Backwards. It was a good palindrome out of the Native, American culture.

The phone rang about 8 am that Monday morning back in the office. It was a woman who identified herself by her first name and her company explaining they were hired by the state to collect back taxes.

"You owe us more than $6,000 in back taxes in Wheeling and Charleston for state sales taxes. Are you prepared to pay?"

"Mam, we provide professional services, and mostly to government entities, are not required to collect state sales taxes, and don't, so no, I am not and will not. What is your number and I will call you back," Dr. Parks said, adding this time he would like to receive something in writing.

She said the statement had been mailed to Wheeling and should be delivered soon. He did not reply, knowing the firm had not had a Wheeling mailing address for the past four years but knowing his present mailing address was on file at the state tax department for the corporation. Was Pearbottom at it again?

He suspected that Pearbottom or someone similar would appear at his door soon to ask him to either sign or come downtown to be arrested for not paying taxes. He called Barrister Al to make an appointment and left a message of his request.

Some things never end, he thought, but knew his bookkeeping service had filed quarterly reports for years that no sales taxes were collected for his professional services under the Engineering and Related Services federal and state professional categories for Standard Industrial Classifications.

"We shall see, shan't we?" he quoted his "always" sponse Ed H's long-term advice for not giving advice. After all, he would add, if I give advice I might have to take it. Instead, he just shared his experience, since all true knowledge always comes from the inner self by way of one's experience, or that of others. But he always also discussed potential options. Opinions were always better discerned by others, he believed.

The telephone rang again and it was Al Halberts saying immediately that Ms. Jackson had written a Summary Judgement against him and the corporation and that the judge had signed it.

"What, that's amazing. He can't do that and preclude the upcoming trial, can he? We weren't involved in any summary judgement discussion and I understand we have to be."

Al slowly replied that he had met at Jackson's request last week to discuss settlement and that he had simply said there could be no settlement on Dr. Park's request. So apparently the two had taken that discussion as a preliminary to the order of the court today– but that the language had no order to the clerk to prepare and to proceed on the document.

"I think the judge is lashing out at me for not performing any depositions and to your circular answers to Jackson during your deposition that you couldn't identify in her photos of tan walls where your samples had been collected. She believes you didn't collect the samples at all, any of the hundreds, and that you just made up the reports from your desk and got the samples from your basement or down the street somewhere."

"Al, this vivid imagination, how do we counter that? A Summary Judgement based on vivid imagination. Have they completely run out of material now?

"Yes, apparently, but we can appeal or go to the Fourth District Court of Appeals in Richmond. Which do you request?

"Appeal the Summary Judgement, demand our day in court, quote the U.S. Constitution as Bob Byrd is always saying, demand due process, and remind anyone who listens that the Goodrich family and Jackson and the Judge that we are prepared to go to television's 20-20, Richmond or otherwise exercise the fact that we have the right physiological anatomy to proceed to fairness. Then let's have that day in court," Dr. Parks replied.

Al said he understood and would be in touch. Three days later he called again to say the trial was delayed until March, but if we lost we would go to Richmond anyway, but that a new court date for the trial was in process. One of their key witnesses was ill, he said. He wasn't sure who it was, he said.

The circle and cycle of completion was now beginning to complete itself, and whatever the lawyer for the defense did or did not do, Dr. Parks knew that it was time to begin submitting his own documentation with the court clerk.

The judge had lashed out forcefully at Barrister Halberts during their last meeting, but had now also reversed himself on two counts of his own making, that the trial would not go forth as docketed, but that Dr. Parks could now submit his own material to defend himself to the court. He called on his good friend Charles Giorgio and the entire sets of defense documents except for the three technical reports were submitted as evidence. The three technical reports and attendant files were being saved for the jury's vision at trial, Barrister Al had suggested. They were the proof of the work having been performed, he said.

Some things do change radically if one keeps coming back with truth. A complete circle of the history of the case and the defense and offense for damages was now in order and was filed by the following motion to the Judge and Federal District Court:

> April 8, 2004
> Hon. Joe Bob Goodrich, Judge
> Southern West Virginia District Court
> Charleston, West Virginia 25301
> Re: Civil Case 12:12-1944
> Government v. Enviromental Consulting Services, Inc.
> And C. R. Parks
>
> Dear Judge Goodrich:
> I want to show my utmost respect, honor and gratitude to both you and the Court for your order for listening to my intervening 12 questions and 12 research items yet unanswered in the above-captioned civil case; and, more especially, for your reversing your earlier order that our defense material does not necessarily have to be filed through my lawyer with the court clerk.
> For over four years now, I have been Federally bullied after serving as an asbestos expert witness against EPA-Wheeling personnel whereby I went to Northern District Court for a client to say that EPA personnel there had not properly tested their own asbestos samples in the case styled Government v Batistelli. In the public schools today bullying is taught to our children by the following definition: "Bullying happens when someone unfairly uses power to hurt someone else over and over." That has been my experience with Justice here, and it is seen as one of our cultural traits which must be recognized and overcome.
> Batistelli was acquitted following my expert testimony of just telling the technical asbestos regulatory truth. The headlines attested his innocence. He, too, was set-up by EPA-Wheeling, according to his lawyer. Later, EPA-Wheeling personnel began delving secretly into our small firm's WVDOH contract work, which our small business had completed with only compliments for many years. Joe Dunn, an acquaintance of 17 years, stopped our firm's state contract with a one-paragraph letter based on a lie by not telling us the truth about the EPA scenario in the background.

Six months after our firm's primary contract was interrupted, I obtained a job at WVDEP. I had worked with outstanding ratings for 17 years earlier in life for the state in public and environmental health responsible positions, and desired to finish my state retirement for about 7 more years. But I was hurt on the job, hospitalized, but fired three days after the injury while on Worker Compensation medical benefits. I was told by my boss Bill Adamson, Esq., that "...seven or eight calls were made to the Governor's Office, including from EPA and others, stating that a potential federal criminal is working at WVDEP– that you'd better fire him before Bob Wisecoff is embarrassed by his working there." Several e-mails in my possession attest to these facts. They and various other documents are unintroduced materials at this time. Some of these documents are considered a part of the referenced Kanawha Circuit Court case which you tossed at Ms. Jackson's suggestion while I had no required lawyer, as you may recall, to defend me or the corporation.

After the firing, criminal charges against me, my two younger children, my business partner and the corporation were filed alleging "compositing" of asbestos samples, based solely on Nick Pearbottom's nonmiranda forced interview in my office; and, alleging "submitting false documents," supposedly that I did not have an accredited Ph.D. degree (I do); that Dr. GreyOwl Apperton was a principal in the corporation (he is an associate); that he had illegally worked in asbestos for us (he is a QA/QC organic chemist for our hazardous materials site assessment protocols); and, a litany of other laundry-list charges resulting from someone's vivid imagination.

After the US-DOJ ran out of material, they now allege, according to my expert witness following his deposition that I never even went to those sites to survey buildings for asbestos, even with two-inch thick submitted technical documents; with keys obtained there from WVDOH personnel; with drawings of buildings with dimensions; with photographs; with hundreds of analyzed samples; with interpretative data with integrated reporting of positive square footage of asbestos to be removed; and, with about three reams of unpaid ($25,000 tasking assignment) work performed by us based on my initial quality inspection work. The dichotomy is I am charged with "compositing" asbestos samples which I didn't collect in the first place?

What a stretch to imagine I never went there to inspect while tan wall photos after tan wall photos of structures were presented in my deposition. Several structures remain standing on the Huntington-Melissa Road project, but that portion of the believed "set-up" is not part of the charges, strangely; thus, our FOIA requests for my expert witness to establish veracity by visiting the remaining structures remain an unanswered question at the prosecution's suggestion. Is FOIA still a law?

My approximate $10,000 work in Logan was later resurveyed by a Pittsburgh firm, I was told by WVDOH personnel, at a cost of $57,000, amazingly, but resulted in my favor after that follow-on firm missed 5,000 sq. ft. of positive-asbestos (point-counted) plaster compound. Nevertheless, my work was used in a "worst-case scenario" Project Design by them after an Ohio firm was hired for their first contract here to remove the positive asbestos-containing material. Our samples are independently analyzed in Virginia at $6 a sample. Other firms charge the state $20. Nick Pearbottom told me he could charge us with fraud via interstate faxing, one of many threats to me and others, thus interfering with justice through intimidation of witnesses. He may be guilty of false swearing. It was later suggested I must have taken a bribe, since it was an $80,000 removal job for the positive plaster. That wasn't the first time I had found positive plaster in Logan. How was the other removed? Removal subcontractor Bill Judy said he absolutely did not complain to the state officials, but instead that Paul Gallahue, a former employee supervised by me, came to Judy first. Then Leonard Wumble, an asbestos "bean counter" for WVDED, denied a permit for my work for WVDOH. No permit for my work is required by the Code. The demolition contractor, from South Charleston, said he did not complain to the state technicians – they called him first and he was confused but didn't want any questions on his state road contract for removing asbestos. Prior to this incident these (all over the state) structures knowingly were bulldozed sometimes the day after I inspected, or worse were burned on site, common knowledge with WVDOH employees. Just ask them.

Perhaps those asbestos real violations to workers and public health should be explored by EPA and DOJ officials, rather than the professional consultants in business to do our part to have asbestos removed safely. It is a killer mineral, we all know. I have seen these structures being burned myself, yet the asbestos removal money was paid to the demolition contractors. Ask those employees who were on our subpoena list, or the state employee technicians in the WVDOH so-called Technical Section, who did not regulate our work. Our work was overseen very satisfactorily, they told us, by employees in the Consultant Services Section for many years prior to this fiasco. They never criticized our work to us. We consultants are the ones trying to contain the epidemic of asbestos in this country, to have it removed safely, yet the state "pays" demolition contractors to burn asbestos-containing building materials. It's another West Virginia story, of course, albeit one heard in other states also, no doubt.

Those initial US-DOJ criminal charges did not receive an indictment – no ham sandwich. We were assured by Ben Wanton, Esq., via Carol Jackson, Esq. and others that the Federal Investigation had ended. It hadn't. The prejudiced resentment would continue, as would the asbestos epidemic in this country. I personally know about death to asbestos, your honor. My parents were witnesses to the diseases last year. I am an asbestos worker, also, you may note. How many of these government proselytizers have ever conducted a building survey for asbestos? Are they even trained in the complicated field, or just have "opinions." Pearbottom asked me how to spell microscopist, one of the licensed fields of asbestos work. Marvin Reicht once asked me in Wheeling on the street what NESHAPS stood for. I don't know lots of things you and others know, but I know asbestos.

"I wrote the law for licensing professions 17 years ago in West Virginia. The minimum for the art and science of collecting samples properly is a high school diploma. It is the simplest yet the most complicated of the hazardous materials fields, in my professional opinion as a senior environmental scientist with a generation of experience and two (yes, accredited) degrees in the subject.

Carol Jackson, US-DOJ for EPA-Wheeling's Nick Pearbottom, later filed the same charges (civilly) against me and my firm after we refused again to "dog fall" to her. In state court, I had filed pro se a civil case against the state, et al for the very substantial damages occurring as the direct result of this personal vendetta built on a lie of two bureaucrats, one state one federal. Without a lawyer for my case, the state case was removed to your jurisdiction, then tossed by you. And the US-DOJ bullying continued.

"Between the criminal trial and the civil trial, Marvin Reicht, CID-Wheeling, whose office was 20 ft. from mine in the Methodist Building in Wheeling, where we both used to work for US-EPA Region 3 for many years, had a debilitating heart attack, I am advised. And, thus his alleged vendetta has continued since the year 2000 by his employee Nick Pearbottom. I have a copy of the EPA memo from Pearbottom to Reicht. I filed a police report of Pearbottom's appearance in the basement of my home upon an unplanned return trip from teaching at the Jesuit University in Wheeling. My neighbors reported he has stalked my house under the guise of delivering personally supoenas for his cases against me. He appears to me to have some kind of dishonest sexual aversion in his mind, based on our first unpleasant meeting near Wheeling, frankly.

"Your honor, we ask that you review my earlier-referenced state civil rights case in light of the following:
– the destruction of my West Virginia (US-SBA) Small Disadvantaged Business, which formerly wrote billable hours paychecks to seven employees;
–the arbitrary and capricious ending of the WVDOH federal Setaside Statewide asbestos building survey renewed contract, based on the synergistic destructive effects of the vendetta relative to Joe Dunn and Marvin Reicht, both long-term acquaintenances prior to the subjective ending of our work;
– my having been fired from employment (a Clean Water Act-required position as Ombudsman for Small Business Environmental Affairs) as a 17-yr. returning employee. fired while hospitalized and while on Workers Compensation; I was an at-will employee, but that status ended the day I was injured on the job; I am also a WV Civil Service-rated epidemeologist, but was paid $10,000 less per year than an epidoemologist hired the same week by the Wisecoff administration;
– and, my four-year-and-counting personal and business "imprisonment" as the direct result of this prejudiced resentment and legal bullying by pompous bureaucrats wrought against me and my Native American-owned small business for environmental technical consulting, employee hazardous materials training and related AE environmental work, including, of course, expert witnessing.

"Our situation is one that suggests perhaps a "real" Federal Investigation is now in order for removal of asbestos in buildings federally funded, such as those torn down overnight near my home on WVDOH property. And it certainly wouldn't be the first time an EPA official lied in court in West Virginia (the dog ate his college diploma story). The trail of civil rights and Constitutional violations is clear in our case from Charleston to Wheeling to the Philadelphia area.

Crazy Horse once said "Long Hair (Custer) came...they said we massacred him...Our first impulse was to escape... but we were so hemmed in we had to fight."
Respectfully,
Bob EagleClaw Parks, Ph.D., President

It was a lengthy letter, but represented the case to date. The letter was mailed after he gave it long thought and decided he couldn't do much wrong now by sending it.

The following week Ms. Jackson suggested in a requested order that Dr. Parks and his firm be fined between $143,000 and $198,000 for the $38,000 work performed on the contract over the last three year period. The judge wouldn't yet sign the order until a ruling in the federal judicial system was appealed and received from the Richmond 4th Circuit Court of Appeals.

The popular tee shirt was now being worn around the state with the slogan *"It's all relative in West Virginia."*

One week later a state judge issued a bench memo validating Dr. Parks' firing case at WVDED while on Workers Compesation benefits in defiance of state law. It seems Dr. Parks had not appealed the decision within 10 days while hospitalized and recovering. The judge chimed in with the administration which had helped elect him. It was an election year. The new administrative rule had been published without a date one month after the firing. But its all relative in West Virginia. It would have to be appealed on a basis of not being Constitutional, his lawyer James Cole had said of the Workers Comp case, now in state district court. But Cole was now suffering from leukemia, suggesting that Dr.

Parks find another lawyer for the appeal and suggesting Al Halberts as his new Workers Comp attorney. Was the collusion in the local "good ole boy network" continuing, as sponsor Ed. H had once suggested? He didn't know. He had been born at night in the dark, but not last night, he told a friend.

One week later, Dr. Parks was paid a visit by a local FBI Agent and a Federal Agent at his home. They were concerned that Dr. Parks had written letters in his own defense and filed them with the federal court clerk, now 14, in fact, they said. The figure included documents filed as portions of briefs. The purpose for their visit to his home, they said, was "not one of intimidation." It was protection of the Federal Court system in this state, they said. And a bluejay is red. Their "requested discussion" in Dr. Parks' living room was documented and faxed to others.

One week later Dr. Parks filed in state, district and the federal appeals court in Richmond, that foreign mother state, an appeal containing all the circles of information which now had blosssomed into six court cases, all of them on a down-hill slide to date. He also requested that all cases be combined, that the full record be reviewed as one integrated and wholistic event in his life. A timeline was provided for veracity.

"We are going to enjoy Richmond," Al had said, "...and finally all the things you have been telling me I now understand. Frankly, all the details of the several cases were fuzzy to me for at least two years, but I now comprehend them and I think we can present a good case. I am now attaching your submissions with my cover documents and we will let the record stand for itself," he said. He took calls on four other cases during the short discussion. He had many, many clients, he said. Included were 56 behind bars.

That very act of truth-bearing stunned Dr. Parks. He was pleased that Al had seen some light – even if it wasn't of the white light variety, not necessary to lawyers and judges much anyway. He was just happy they could finally put the facts together in one circle of information. Things could now get a little better a little sooner, he hoped. It would be four months before a trial in Richmond. The time was now at four years and seven months since the contract interruption. It was November, 2004. Bob Wisecoff had been replaced by a new governor, and the national political situation had turned from one of agressiveness to protectiveness against terrorist threats following the calamity of the Iraq war. All government officials at the federal level under the new administration had been ordered by the President to end quickly and settle any bureaucratic disputes in the federal court system all cases not relating to national security and to spend their time with vigilance against potential terrorist activities. Times had changed.

The court in Richmond took a studied review of the defense and orders were remanded to the Southern West Virginia District Court with words on the page suggesting remanding the case to state court and further suggesting that the state court come up with a combined settlement. The First Amendment still covers expert witnesses, "especially expert witnesses," they suggested. Some things do change, and change changes some.

The new governor, as new governors do, let it be known that he wanted all state civil cases being argued to "reach conclusion as soon as reasonably possible" in order to begin rebirthing a state economy which could no longer support itself, too burdened by its own bureaucracies' public argumentativeness. It was time to redevelop a state about to topple in its own perceived history, he had said. Real change was inevitable, he added, in the Mountain State.

All and parts of now seven law cases for Dr. Parks and his firm had now been assigned to one state circuit court judge and were being studied for remission to compromise settlements.

Dr. Parks had a third grandson, son Gabriel's. He had also completed a final draft of a novel biographical in nature and had blended circles of spirituality with life business issues of a Native American entrepreneur and had tied it all together with a recovery theme of both the main characters and the cultures those characters could not be separated. The novel was his experience, but had not yet ended. It was described as integrated and wholistic by reviewers, but the final chapter had not been written. Dr. Parks said his "crystal ball" in life was unplugged.

Chapter Twenty Two

On the Line

Dr. Parks had just completed reading a technical paper on vermiculite insulation by a scientist studying the subject yet again. The scientist had confirmed from studies that there are four asbestos related diseases extremely prevalent in Libby, Montana, and that the natural mineral, which contains less than one per cent asbestos, usually chrysotile, was a threat to public health and the environment. Asbestos was still being mined and now 23 million metric tons were still being shipped into the United States each year. Asbestos remains a powerful industry. Its epidemic killing of Americans remains just that. C.I. Pearbottom would have work a long time from it, no doubt.

Twenty five years ago that fact was known, but US-EPA had been politically pressured to not include the material as a hazardous material since the vermiculite insulation was less than the one per cent, the minimum standard set for asbestos for the country.

He remembered during the interview with Pearbottom he had said compositing samples in at least one arena was the correct thing to do and that was with insulation materials which are fibrous and the sample should be well mixed in order to obtain representative sampling for the "composite" insulation. New "facts" by US-EPA gave veracity to the comment.

Vermiculite insulation in the walls, not in ceilings, where it is usually found, was located in one of the Logan structures under question. But Pearbottom wasn't smart enough due to his lack of technical training, let alone experience, to ask the right questions. Dr. Parks was honest about it, but knew well that "anything you say can and will be held against you." He just didn't mention that the material composited was vermiculite. And now it all was an official EPA ruling by bureaucratic re- interpretation. Things can change with rules and people when the time is right, or not right, he mused to himself.

The newspaper that same day had referenced the vermiculite study to support an announcement that, lo and behold, after 25 years, the natural mineral vermiculite was, in fact, a hazardous material, but not before hundreds of people there in Libby, Montana and elsewhere died first –that slow, agonizing death of choking lungs filled with asbestos fibers laden with their own body's protective and fatal liquid.

Hundreds in the small town had died of asbestosis, lung cancer and mesothelioma and probably many more of present and future intestinal or other cancers throughout the body, wherever the blood stream sends small broken fibers of asbestos.

The toxicology of asbestos is such that the broken fiber pierces the nuclei of a cell, any cell, disrupting the genetic memory. The cell then grows in an aberrant chain in defferent directions, rather than just reproducing itself. And that aberrant growth in differing directions is what we call cancer.

The mineral even works it way through the placenta of pregnant women into the blood stream of unborn babies, it had been confirmed 20 years ago with the advent of Transmission Electron Microscopy, but Pearbottom had no concept of TEM analysis, he said. But because he "was EPA, he could make judgement."

In the interview Pearbottom had asked how to spell microscopist, one of the licensing professions for asbestos work, but couldn't get the pronunciation right, let alone the spelling learned in any basic asbestos training course.

It takes EPA a while sometimes to stop really obvious

human death tolls, he thought. Then in every Republican administration, it seems, some things go backward for public health and forward for industry and items such as Reicht and Pearbottom having to hold restaurant seats for the big boss and staid old engineering firms losing 25 year government contracts begin to occur.

And old studies get re-studied, such as the vermiculite report. Then pronouncements are made and pamphlets published. Then enforcement brownie points get sent in a whole new direction and defensive bureaucrats looking for raises need numbers and look for small, defenseless businesses and individuals to get the brownie points and the beat goes on.

"Dr. Parks– Al Halberts is on the line for you and he says it's urgent," Thom Botts had called out from the adjoining office.

"Al who? Parks had jokingly answered the telephone since he had not heard from the lawyer in a month of Sundays. "Hi, Bob. I have good news and bad news. Which first?"

He always took the good with the bad, he said, so good first and bad second.

"Judge Goodrich said the governor's office is willing to pay you what they owe you and don't want any more bad publicity after the last governor got caught with the female state employee and his wife is divorcing him and the election is over, so they'll pay. But they won't agree to reimburse for the three years' work you missed at the requested $74,000 per year to the corporation. But, they are willing to settle with you individually for having been fired while in the hospital on Workers Comp while you were working at DED. On the third charge of blackballing from state employment in the merit system, you as a rehire with the top score in the state as a merit system employee, they want that kept quiet but will pay three years back wages. And they will replace your state retirement and put you back in a position at DED if you agree not to stay there too long.

That one gets a little tricky, so be careful about saying yes too quickly. On the other charge against the state, tortuous interference with a business contract, that's turned out to be the biggie. Seems Joe Dunn has taken up alcohol and has come forward admitting in all the wrong places his resentment against you and your partner for starting that bi, gay, lesbian and transgendered group of 12-steppers in recovery. He thought you were 13th stepping some of the guys and/or girls, he wasn't sure which, he said in a taped deposition taken while he was under the influence. It was played for the EPA guys and they folded up their parity checks of dishonesty, which was clearly evident after the deposition, and now it seems Marvin Reicht just isn't right anymore, and Nicholas Pearbottom has removed himself back to Boone County, where he is under extortion and swearing to false testimony threats by the county prosecutor there. They're willing to just drop the charges. So all's looking good here, but there's a catch. The feds always want a cliffhanger until the end and Judge Goodrich needs to save face and wants you to end the corporation with a fine of $39,037, just as Pearbottom proposed that day in discussion with you and Ben your criminal lawyer in that meeting in the federal courthouse.

"I thought he was a judge, not a Justice prosecutor, Dr. Parks interjected. "Why would he suggest that when absolutely nothing has been done wrong by us, save the EPA bureaucrats' opinion that I simply told the truth as an expert witness in their asbestos trial in Wheeling."

"Bob, you're repeating yourself out of honesty, I realize. But you have to realize that justice in West Virginia is a parity check between those politicians in power at the time and those who run the court systems at the federal and state levels. You know Goodrich's family is ensconced in the gubernatorial administration in the state as well as in the state Democratic Party. Fanny Silers keeps printing that and it is common knowledge and once this settlement is made public the judge has to see that damages are minimized. That's really why this thing was in Federal court when it was clearly a state issue. They have just kept you on the line until such time as they hoped things might get better politically and then that sex scandal thing happened with the divorce of the state female employee and they really don't want this one to hit the press outside of West Virginia if they can help it. They say after the governor became known as the left-handed keyboard operator with the 500 e-mail incident, then the sheep in the x-rated manger scene, and other stories about West Virginia to hit the national press embarrassing to all us in past years, they don't want your story of the government trying to destroy an expert witness to be added to the list."

"So what's your response, Bob, although you don't have to give it all to me right now." Al asked.

"What happens with the suit against the professional liability insurance company for failing to represent us after we gave them thousands and thousands of dollars all those years and then when we needed them, nothing?"

"Bob, that's another day. If you don't have an instrument for a suit, just like the Western Environmental case, after you and your partner had done a Chapter 7 USC bankruptcy, you didn't have an instrument for collecting the $2.4 million damages except personally under a civil rights threat violation personally for you and your Indian business partner. I don't know what your settlement was there, but I do know you settled and can't talk about it, but that's another day and someone else's justice, not ours. I suggest your company plead guilty as the corporation but that you as the individual collect the damages, Al interjected.

"What if I reverse the process– keep the corporation and it could collect damages?"

"That's just not an option to the government, Bob. Listen, after I ran some calculations and I take my one third, all the thousands you have spent on other lawyers, the company passes through all it owes to you for putting your own meager resources into its defense for five years, and you pay your legal debts, you should clear number one your state retirement; about $100,000 for the four years; a cleared name, and return briefly to a job at WVDED. That's about the best I can do, I think.

"Al, that's a salary of about $25,000 a year. Have those two bastards really won without our knowledge?"

"Bob, look at it this way: what if you don't take the proposed settlement. The resources of the government are unlimited, you have been living in poverty and this will clear the air and you can start a new business for your consulting practice tomorrow. I'll help you with the papers and serve as your attorney for the new corporation if you want me to at my standard fee arrangement. What do you think?"

"Al," Bob replied, "...here is my answer: God grant me the serenity... and you know the rest."

That simple prayer, he had learned many times over the past 17 years, had a certain finality to it and allows one to move on with life as it is given by Creator.

"Al, here's my answer the best I can give it to you today, which is all we have, and it probably has something to do with the fact, as I have jokingly told you all these many months– that in life I have gotten my acceptable addictions down to sex, racquetball and rock'n roll."

"But not necessarily in that order?" Dr. Bob?"

"Yes, and I have already taken care of the first two for this day, so here's my answer out of the pages of your and my history, in the words of that Englishman Joe Cocker, I think it's high time we went–as into the courtroom for the trial."

"Enough said, Dr. Bob, I'll be in touch and send you a projected schedule for the trial even though we know the projected outcome on another day. Have a good one."

His lawyer's office was at the confluence of the Elk Tiskewah River and the Kanawha River. Several civilizations had towns there in the past including the unknown Natives called the Moundbuilders, who left hundreds of burial and ceremonial mounds which were leveled for industry by the white man. Then there were the Melungens, mixed Portuguese and Indians whose descendants still lived in the state and showed their ethnic characteristics of facial structure and skin and hair color; and later the Daniel Boone character lived there seven years; and, before that, the other historical characters which began with Gabriel Arthur and ended with George Washington and earlier some French came and went; then came the Virginian Europeans, including Charles and Andrew Lewis and 1,200 troops marching through on the north side of the valley, killing Chief Pocatalico along the way to Pt. Pleasant; then came many battles and the Clendenin and Morris Europeans moved in from Virginia and substantially lightened up the population, many of whom still live in the area today and know exactly who they are and how they got here.

But before the Civil War, then statehood, a major population drain of the Shawnee out of the area occurred. Tecumseh, or in English, Panther in the Sky, an astral event seen in the night sky at the time of his birth, the most prevalent thing in nature, was born near Clarksburg, he told local landed gentry. His family, as was the trend, escaped across the Ohio River and out of West Virginia and thus out of the country. Later, Shawnee Chief Blue Jacket followed out of a cabin near Richwood, some suspect, at his own will, rather than under capture, as his mixed-breed "white" family reported to neighbors.

In adulthood, Tecumseh tried to organize all the tribes about 1810. He became a spiritual leader and left legacies of those spiritual teachings used today in daily meditations for cultural, addiction and spiritual recovery throughout the United States. He's one of our American cultural heroes, but many of us are still to learn that fact.

The Shawnee had always fought back, while the Cherokee adapted to the English god, language, system of government and even had a newspaper in their own written language, thanks to the genius George Sequoyah Gist. It all worked until the white man discovered a little gold on their North Carolina land, and you know how some people are about gold. Indians don't wear it to this day, instead shunning its artificial value and broken hearts memories for silver as the preferred precious metal.

And getting them out and all Indians throughout the East, from Maine to Florida, after the gold was found, lead to the Trail of Tears to solve "the Indian Problem." Yet we name children's schools and counties after Andrew Jackson, one of our darkest presidents.

Alfred North Whitehead, Alfred E. Neuman and EagleClaw might suggest we "reinvestigate" who our cultural heroes really are before we give our children's schools their cultural namesakes. Andrew Jackson need not apply. Just because one is a president, or governor, or judge of others doesn't mean he deserves the label of a cultural model– especially for our children.

It was EagleClaw's experience that cultures of people, sports teams, schools, and even institutions not only come and go, but also can re-name and re-invent, and re-birth, themselves. And we might start with Mountain State, formerly West Virginia, formerly Virginia, formerly Orange County, formerly Augusta, formerly Vandalia, formerly Appalachee, formerly Turtle Island, he thought.

In at least five disparate history books noting the Native American cultural "problem" in the state's history, five instances of "the last Indian shot out of the woods" are recorded. Probably the victors could have written that the last fighting Shawnee at that instant was gone; the rest had intermarried and were still here as grandmothers; and, some had moved across the Ohio river to Shawnee territory, and some came back, and many never left. Many more Cherokee and Shawnee and other tribal ancestries of women and men and children exist in the state today in the state they are in.

The Kanawha River was the recognized traditional border between the Shawnee and the Cherokee, according to pre-history, for at least 150 years before Gabriel Arthur set foot in the Kanawha Valley. The Cherokee lived in the mountainous areas east and north to Pittsburgh and south to Georgia and west to Tennessee. The Shawnee lived in towns in the Kanawha Valley with trade routes into Logan and Mingo Counties and had a major trade road, US Rt. 35, north to Xenia, Ohio, going past their tribal capitol known as Chilecothe.

Treaty upon treaty was later broken and that story too is a part of our darker American history usually left out of the school textbooks.

King George III's Proclamation of 1763, to the relief of the Cherokee, pronounced there would be no more white settlement west of the Appalachian Mountains. The American Revolution ended all former European treaties with the Native Americans. Unfortunately, there was no way to enforce the former law. West of the Appalachians, 100 years later, in 1863, West Virginia became a state.

It has been said that this country was not founded on the Ten Commandments. It was founded on killing and taking land from Indians. Extreme denial, it is amazing. But that, boys and girls, is our true American history. It's just another lesson in acceptance as a spiritually-based principle, in the teaching of Indian country spirituality throughout our country, just another lesson of the spiritual principle of acceptance. Can we change it? No, but we can admit and accept it and go on to better things, like learning new spiritual principles and helping others. In return, we will reap the rewards– we guarantee it, EagleClaw would say to you.

In the Kanawha Valley much evidence remains of past differing Native groups, ranging from maps of mounds, to the people who still live here who trace their bloodlines to tribal lineages of all the other regional historical and prehistoric identified Indian tribal groups. And major trade routes crisscrossed the state from Canada to Florida and east to west. Those trade routes, which have been mapped, are now state and federal highway routes. They evolved that way.

Even much of the sociological anomalies have not

changed. According to writings of 18th Century Native Studies sociologists, gay, lesbian, bi-sexual and transgendered Indians were a known percentage of the population by birth and were fully accepted in the tribes just as they were born. Both then and now those people were called two-spirited, a term common in Native cultures in the United States today. We can learn from history if we listen, it has been said, because history repeats itself.

Many tribes moved westward as the Europeans encroached and spread diseases, including the Delaware, or Lenilanape, as they call themselves, who moved west to the Wheeling and Morgantown areas. And some would integrate with local folks along the way, but their leadership was forced on west later, eventually to Oklahoma. Their culture survives here and elsewhere not only through their own efforts today but also in part as a role model by Boy Scouts of America, whose eagle scouts emulate their regalia at powwows around the country. And here one might add the Ed.'s Note: Please see paragraph on sociology, above. It's all about respect and the spiritual principle of acceptance.

And new tribes, such as the Mingo, would organize and settle in various areas of the state, including Pocahontas County, the Northern Panhandle and the traces of the extended Shawnee Highway from Charleston south into Mingo and Logan counties, to again mix with their cousins, the Shawnee, Cherokee, Seneca, white settlers and other minglings of all God's children.

The Mingos, spelled often by the white language rationalization and justification rules as Mingoes, like Negroes, were mixes of Natives and Europeans and often escaped slaves or free blacks. Some blacks in this country were never slaves, even back then. Mingos were rejected by both main cultures. The root derivation of the term Mingo comes from "to mingle." Those people were never an indigenously recognized tribe. They evolved that way, after circular rejection. They were multicultural, one might say, before their time. They were popularly called half-breeds–

people different than "normal." The fact, miscegenation it was called, never set well in early America, let alone in Appalachia. Today those "Mingo" descendants are called mostly West Virginians. Sometimes they are called worse, depending on one's cultural point of view and experience and knowledge or lack thereof.

The Kanawha River, that respected traditional border between the Shawnee and the Cherokee, best translated as river of falling banks, was walkable in EagleClaw's dad's days at such places as the Red House Shoals, precluding no one from crossing it by canoe or walking on the rocks. It was a trade route crossing for Indians heading northeast to the ridges of Putnam County to Jackson County, present day State Rt. 34, and points beyond. Later, as the Europeans marched into the valley, the Shawnee there just moved out of the valley to one more ridge back to retain their own land holdings. Many of them still live there today – Appalachian American Indians.

EagleClaw remembered his own father telling him of crossing the river on Saturday nights to see a girlfriend at the Red House Shoals. Some things never change. And he told him that all the game fish in the Kanawha River he used to catch as a child, the gharr, the smallmouth bass, and some trout, had now returned to the river after two generations of chemical and coal pollution. They still aren't edible, but they're back and surviving and reproducing, just like EagleClaw's extended family. It all reminded him of his favorite Siouan expression, "Aho. Mitakuye Oyassin," translated "We are all interrelated" on this earth.

Siouan influence in the state has been long documented, beginning with the tribe of Chief Pocatalico. The linguistic name does not fit the Cherokee language group, is easily pronounced, but is somewhat foreign to both the Cherokee and Shawnee languages whose people surrounded them in the state. They were the Sioux Virginia Catawba. These folks' descendants today are all over three counties and call themselves Blackfoot, but don't know how they arrived here, just who they are. As Sioux, a co-mingling may have occured as yet unrecognized in the prehistory of the state. But many things are known and documented.

Chief Pocatalico's history was documented by O.O.White, former superintendent of schools, a coach and civics classes instructor at Poca High School. He wrote the history of Chief Pocatalico from known verbal history and taught it often to his high school civics classes. The written history may be located in the Poca High School yearbook called *the Pocatalico*.

The Virginia Catawba always planted catawba trees in the areas where they lived. Catawba fruit has been recognized by many cultures for their aphrodesiacal qualities and are purchased today in health food stores. On the lawn of Poca High School are catawba trees which "double aut" White always refused to allow to be cut in remembrance of Chief Pocatalico, whose grave remained until a few years ago on an undeveloped lot in a nearby subdivision. The two cedar trees planted at the head and the foot of his grave by Virginia Militiamen on their way to Pt. Pleasant stood there while EagleClaw was a child. Both the grave and cedar trees where Pocatalico was buried have in the last 20 years washed downstream from recreational boat use and lock and dam construction, which raised the river level substantially to include the former higher elevation of the burial site. The lot now has a house on it instead of an historical marker.

The Blackfoot prolific in the area know who they are, even though they don't know how or when they arrived there. They live in a broad geographical area from Putnam County along the Pocatalico River basin to its headwaters in Roane County and into Clay County – Chief Pocatalico's land. Many burial mounds remain on farms along the Pocatalico River and some have been robbed and the rest maintained in secrecy for that very reason.

EagleClaw had been given a large oil painting of the Pocatalico River with the cliff Chief Pocatalico was forced over by the Virginia Militia troops after he was shot and was trying to get back to his village on the other side of the river. He temporarily survived the gunshot wound, dived over the cliff but died on the other side of the Pocatalico river. He was buried where he died. His wife Amma and two teenage children, a girl of 15 and son of 13, and the tribe, moved into what is now Roane, Calhoun and Clay counties. One of the drunked-up European mililtia from Virginia and Lewisburg it is said by oral tradition had yelled "the only good Indian is a dead Indian" and shot. The classic line had followed instructions by the Lewis brothers to halt, that that was Chief Pocatalico, a friend, riding toward them. Later admonishments of the troops for drinking too much are recorded in historical documets written from their destination, Pt. Pleasant. Charles and Andrew Lewis and their 1200 troops then continued through eastern Putnam County to secure the land for the English.

A later book on Pocatalico published by a politician running for governor held that Pocatalico was but a myth, that the name Pocatalico had been invented, and that he never lived. He liked to visit in a later history of the town of Poca the many bars which developed as the Europeans moved in to cut the virgin timber of the area and mine coal. His theory helped assuage the cultural guilt and shame of stealing the land and shooting the Native Americans while enslaving the African Americans. He was into American history, he said, but that is his story. Truth always surfaces. It's just his story.

EagleClaw and his sister Raven-In-the-Snow once visited for smudging Pocatalico's gravesite. It was washed away. They then visited several burial mounds in the area, picking pawpaws along the way. Their Indian pawpaw loved pawpaws. The first mound they found had been recently dug into. In a hole about three feet in diameter they found a black plastic garbage bag containing three dead kittens someone had chosen to suffocate and dispose in the Sioux burial mound.

Grave robbing is a federal felony crime under the Native American Grave Protection and Recovery Act, NAGPRA. Native Americans often say to those seeking burial objects, "How would you feel if someone dug into your grandmother's grave under the guise of looking for artifacts?" The act covers all grave robbing as a felonious crime. County sheriffs are the assigned criminal investigators. A Deputy Sheriff was once quoted in a newspaper that he, too, liked to 'collect arrowheads.' Burial artifacts sell for thousands of dollars on the WWW.

The Ohio River and the Appalachee Mountains have attracted and held Native Americans before and after the last ice glacier melted and receded toward Erie, PA, about 13,000 years ago.

The trend is noticeable today as more Natives who have visited or driven cargo trucks over Interstate highways crisscrossing the mountains have returned to retire and live there because they feel an attraction. The green mountains have always had that magnetic pull for Natives and other natives, including today.

The only problem is it is hard to make a living there.

In the 1960's the state's hills and mountains served as a mecca for back-to-the-land hippie farmers from throughout the country, many of whom still live there. Today, the same trend has become noticeable to those with Native interests. Powwows now dot the state. The trend began about 17 years ago and may be expected to continue, if such population mini-trends may be projected based on experience. Many come seeking higher ground in the mountains and higher standards of living in nature. Appalachee has always offered that reward.

Thus, the state has both a history and a future rich in Native American culture. But mixed Native and other American bloodline peoples there have always been aware of that fact. But many others have not. A visitor cannot locate a single piece of statuary at the state capitol building or grounds of the Indian chiefs born or pivotal to the state's history: Tecumseh; Cornstalk; Blue Jacket; Red Jacket; Pocatalico; Logan, or Cornplanter or any other Native American so culturally identified – yet.

As the tribes moved west as the Europeans encroached, the Seneca spread out under British protection, with a town of over a thousand people at Ravenswood; the Sioux, Blackfoot, Virginia Catawba apparently accepting and friendly to Europeans coming to the valley to trade, became known in the Kanawha Valley and Pocatalico River basins; and several other tribal evidences prospered by manufacturing salt for preserving meat available in abundance from hunting here in the lush mountains, including the Miami in the upper Kanawha Valley. And and Shawnee have always been in Pennsylvania, Ohio, Virginia and West Virginia. That history is verified by archeologists today who follow the development of corn from South America north to its culmination with the growing of beans about 900 years ago in the Ohio Valley. That circle is compleat even today. Cherokee, whose war games for bravery documented capturing "coup" of adjoining tribes, were all over the southeastern United States from the mountains of Pennsylvania, south through West Virginia to the Kanawha River, west to Kentucky and south to the northern borders of Florida, where other tribal lands picked up. Over 8,000 identified tribes have at one time or another lived in America, government researchers tell us.

And thus, history and its lessons are learned best in trends as cultures comingling. We all learn and relearn lessons, sometimes quickly, sometimes slowly, EagleClaw had learned in his own history.

Chapter Twenty Three

A Corrupted File

BUSINESS PARTNER Thom Botts had left the firm during a time of slow business as a billable hours employee. He still accepted billable hours work for the firm and remained as a corporate officer. Some had wondered out loud how he had escaped named prosecution in the latter civil suit.

After the lack of work and interruption of the state asbestos contract, all job benefits by the firm were eliminated and employees assigned to billable hours pay only as overhead skyrocketed. The billable hours concept is used unilaterally by professional firms including professions such as lawyers, doctors, engineers and related professions– including fledgling and other environmental firms in the AE professional services industry.

And as a consequence, as overhead rates increase for administrative activities in periods of low work, overhead costs not only continue but grow exponentially whether work is performed or not – rent, telephone, professional liability insurance, as examples.

And the administrative-multiplier rises substantially, not decreases. It usually, in fact, in Dr. Parks' experience, goes through the roof. In government contracting, admin-multipliers are crucial. At the federal level, a business is reimbursed by an audited admin-multiplier, while at some state levels state administrators set a maximum admin-multiplier sometimes absurdly low – set by bureaucrats who view the dollar amounts as "getting rich" while federal contract administrators, more technically trained, understand the dollars as the price of doing business – within reason. And the feds award contracts based on the admin-multiplier factor at the beginning of the contract, then pay the bill. State bureaucrats, most of whom never receive contract administrator training, say "that's all you get" and the firms make a decision on bidding according to their rules. Many just won't work there; unless, of course, they are politicians or know one or are federal prosecutors who hold sway over "Federal Investigations" of their choosing.

Thus, the name of the game for businesses in the government contract arena is to get enough billable hours from all sources, and to keep overhead as low as possible in order to be competitive. It all works if one lets it. The problem comes when a won contract, with much investment costs before the first dollar is turned over, is interrupted.

Employees have to either be laid off or relegated to part-time work, then resign, and overhead kept to a minimum, and the profit idea factored into the admin-multiplier is just blowing in the wind. It's called the opposite side of working for the government. In West Virginia it's widely described that "if one is a small business and works for the state, the state will work to put one out of business." Its not negative, just many small business owners' experience. It gets repeated because it is popularly known. Small businesses are easy targets.

Botts remained the administrative manager for the small business for Dr. Parks' firm after getting a job working for the state. His final job act was to contract with a Certified Public Accountant firm to determine the company's audited admin-multiplier. It remained at 2.27, or an effective 3.27 with labor costs. It was very reasonable by federal standards, but was higher in view of the state's maximum of 1.6 or a "loaded," with labor, rate of 2.6. And the only decision to be made was once again paying the rent and the employees– but not growing a company.

Botts had as a man in his thirties inherited from his family tree and Appalachian culture of high-fat eating habits traits for heart and coronary disease, requiring surgeries in

Wheeling, Charleston, Washington, and valve replacements later as new technologies crossed the mountains.

He and Dr. Parks had remained friends through the years as well as business partners, with Dr. Parks retaining 51% shares and Botts at 10% owner and an administrative employee who also produced technical reports from drafts produced by technical staff, including asbestos survey report documents essentially as a clerical function.

The cultural backdrops of both men were similar. Each had been raised one county outside Charleston. Both were 3/8 blood mixes of Cherokee and Shawnee with 5/8 European bloodlines, as it so happens for many Appalachian Indians today. And each had other similarities, ranging from similar but disparate sexual preferences to comparable rates of recovery as parts of their cultures for the past 17 years. Both maintained an integrated but wholistic philosophy of life. Both earned respect.

The two worked well in a complementary manner in the environment in the office, with Dr. Parks directing the business contract and technical environmental arenas of work and Botts overseeing and producing technical reports and billing for those products. Botts knew computers and people and Parks knew hazardous materials and "protecting public health and the environment."

Both knew business service on one principle – producing and collecting payment for a product.

But when a prejudiced resentment interrupts a contract illegally for producing either widgets or for consultants, business stops and the lawsuits begin. Where all the players on any of the teams end up– sometimes in court, sometimes unemployed– the usual result, except for government bureaucrats, who are protected by the 11th Amendment to the US Constitution.

And in between or in the Courts, what happens when players on different teams side with the opposing team or its coach?

Dr. Parks had already given all the information any jury

would need, that the bureaucrats, driven by jealousy – that most awful of human emotions, about his small business, its former seven employees, his family, his corporation, his livelihood.

Honest friends on "the other team" had provided honest information sufficiently, if presented to a jury of his peers, should the court system allow, and could bring a stinging indictment not to his technically correct reports billed along pre-approved dollars, but instead to those bureaucrats supposedly protected in the government by the 11th Amendment. He knew that. The problem was how to get the information to a jury. That might take a while, he surmised, based on his experience.

His experience to date was that the criminal grand jury had not even indicted– no basis to continue. That made the state, which brought the charges, look guilty, which they were. Looking at the supposed but weightless charges, no ham sandwich, never mind that Pearbottom had attempted to intimidate witnesses, Mr. Botts and Dr. Parks the younger and other malfeasances. Prosecutors down through history had joked in-house that they could even indict a ham sandwich, thus the expression "not even a ham sandwich."

And never mind that not one but three lawyers contracted for justice delivery, had abandoned their client when they couldn't see a quick payday for themselves.

The lawyers, Yianni's boss at his firm and Ben Wanton for his firm, and later by default Al Halberts, all had urged Dr. Parks to dog fall before the trial and all just go home after their hounds had dived over a cliff together in the darkness.

No so, Dr. Parks had declared. The mass destruction of his small business, the state contract loss, the state job loss, the professional services losses to his small business, such as it remained, the years of 'imprisonment' to date of his life, the failure of his professional liability insurance company to perform because the charges, never in court let alone real, were denied by his Pittsburgh carriers – all were too real damages to let die by diving over an imaginary cliff while hunting imaginary foxes.

Elton John sang after recovery on his New American Tour starting in Philadelphia, "*I'm still standing,*" followed by wonderful successes with "*Philadelphia Freedom.*" Dr. Parks lived in Philadelphia when that historical recovery event occurred, and the memory was not lost on his own plethora of events leading up to this day.

Jackson at Justice had included, of course, Dr. Parks' children, and former employees, in the federal charges of "producing and charging the US Government for false documents." It somehow just didn't sound real impressive after all these years to Dr. Parks. They were words on a page.

And as one might suspect, then again appeared Pearbottom at Dr. Parks' door of his home late on that fateful Friday evening, demurely smiling as best as a dishonest government employee can when working an hour or two overtime for justification of a few more dollars on payday. They were not pleasant memories to Dr. Parks, but he maintained for the most part a level of serenity acceptable under the vendetta-driven circumstances. And again, acceptance was the key.

After two years, Thom Botts had expressed his deepest personal fears recently once again to Dr. Parks prior to a meeting: his worst childhood fear was one of being put in a jail cell.

"Where did that come from after a thorough 4th Step?" Dr. Parks asked.

I had a close call during the criminal jury proceedings whereby I was "talked to" and then they visited my offices at the state and the lingering possibility still exists with my being named with the new civil charges," he said.

"Tom, this is a civil charge. It is for money, not jail time, and I have ready to go a new lawyer for collecting damages anyway for the corporation. What's the issue?"

"Fear," he replied. "Sometimes our worst fears come true" he added as the two were motioned into the beginning of a meeting.

Dr. Parks and Botts earlier had discussed outside the same discussion meeting the need to update the computers in Dr. Parks' office, a task that Thom had always overseen.

Thom proposed that a fellow he knew who was a computer technician, not by trade but by claimed practice, come by and for about $50 install more memory on the computer with a modem and to install an icon and new drive system program on the older word processor. It was still used to place bids and for Dr. Parks' personal correspondence, including those to the lawyers. All the legal files had been compressed there.

"That sounds like a good idea, Thom, but remember all my legal correspondence is on that word processor and I don't want to lose the files in that directory and I don't want them transferred to the modem computer because the False Claims Act first sentence allows the government to wiretap."

"I know that," he replied, "but it's just such a good deal. The work has needed done for awhile and I don't have time to do it and it needs done. And for $50 he can add more memory and he has software that will make it easier for you to retrieve files."

"Ok, but remember that I want the system legal in all respects and I will want some hands-on instruction on how to use it and I'll pay him accordingly. Why are we not using our regular computer tech George, though?"

"We're late for the meeting, I'll see you about it later. I have to go to the bathroom first" Thom said, walking off into the church structure.

"Sounds like a wiener," Dr. Parks intoned with acceptance and agreement. "How about next Tuesday and your man can come by."

Mack the computer musician was there on Tuesday, laughing and hacking in an apparent legal-drug-induced stupor of sorts, it appeared to Dr. Parks, dutifully reordering hard drives, transferring files, including the legal files, installing two new memory chips for $20 each and calculating his expected labor charges, entering dozens of arcane commands foreign to only partially computer-literate Dr. Parks, and, upon leaving, had completely made unusable not one but two machines used by Dr. Parks.

"I'm sorry," Mack said on leaving. "I'll come back and retrieve everything and there'll be no charge whatsoever," he said as he quickly exited for returning to his regular job at the newspaper inserting advertising copy.

Some things require the prayer, "God grant me the Serenity..." and this was one.

"Thom, call me immediately, I am confused, a little upset, and I think, screwed. Both my tools for work have been rendered useless by your hacker friend Mack. It's a little unbelievable, but he has destroyed both machines in my office. What's the solution?" he left on a telephone message voice mail.

The legal files had been lost in a directory with corporate files on the non-modem machine. They had been filed numerically and numbers 1 through 37 were lost.

For "just in case" purposes, Dr. Parks had earlier downloaded them to disks. But by some act, they too had been "lost" in the subdirectory by the friend of Thom's, whom Dr. Parks was now referring to as "the hacker."

The disks were now gone from retrieval on one computer, and, he later learned, transferred to the modem computer but protected by a password. New computer technician time, Dr. Parks decided.

Using a commercial service, he was told by a trained technician that files are never truly destroyed, but that a period of time was necessary to retrieve them by specially trained personnel.

"And the disk is fine but the file has been corrupted," he had added.

Knowing other technically trained and trusted persons for retrieving the data, two techy friends were brought in, and, after short times, the information retrieved from the hard drive, refiled, and protected.

"Thom, I need to confront you on what happened with the computers. And by the way all data has been retrieved by two friends. What happened is my question to you, and I am asking for an explanation based on the obvious – i.e., the first principle that saves our lives, honesty," Dr. Parks asked poignantly.

"I wasn't there the four hours Mack was there, so I don't know."

"How about Saturday night when I came by the office and you and Mack were in my office with the housing and hard drive out of the word processor and you retrieved 1600 files but not the important legal document file?" Dr. Parks asked.

"I don't know. I just got back the corporate directory and the first 38 files didn't get transferred by Mack. I don't know why."

"But you knew that's where the important legal files were placed in a mixture of two locations. Why?"

Silence.

Do you still have a fear of being put into a jail cell because of the civil charges, Thom?"

He said, "As I've told you before, I am not allowed to discuss any of this with you and therefore, I just don't want to know– to know anything more before the trial."

"I find that very strange hearing that from you as a business partner and friend of 17 years." Dr. Parks replied.

"Well I don't want to go to jail and I don't want to know, and that's why I walked out of the meeting last week when you were sharing your week of good things and bad things, even in non-specific topical terms. But computers receive commands and sometimes things just don't go the way we planned. And as I told you before, I am not even allowed to discuss these things anymore with you. I have to go to the bathroom. You decide."

Dr. Parks after the meeting returned home, called his sponsor Ed H, related the continuing saga, and sponse replied, "...you decide. We don't know. But people are going to do what people are going to do. We shall see, shan't we?" Both signed off with the traditional RWLY they had utilized for years to signify "Remember Who Loves You...there are many of us and I am just one of them."

Dr. Parks slept well that night. The weekend before while the computer tryst was occurring, son Gabriel had a wonderful wedding replete with tuxes, pretty women, good food for all, drinks of differing varieties; daughter Jenny flew in from Alaska, bringing lots of King Salmon for everyone; dad picked-up at the airport; America's kids were specially outfitted for wedding roles; Dr. Parks 'cleaned up real good' in his own tux he hadn't worn since his last trip to the Greenbrier Hotel won while taking the kids on a fishing trip; and, an old girlfriend came to town; dozens of friends and family showed up, including Thom Botts, other old friends and grandparents; the father of the bride was on time; and, good music, good feasting and copious amounts of love and joy were had by all.

It was a good week and a bad week. Good with love and joy for a long-awaited weeding; not so good with crashed computers holding files important to the future of major law cases and planned court settlements.

But for all it was a wonderful, joyous weekend for Dr. Gabriel and his lovely, intelligent and 'just God's children' bride and groom, Dr. and Mrs. Gabriel Parks.

That family experienced great joy, then the wedding couple was off for a cruise honeymoon in the full-moon Caribbean; America and family went to the beach for a week; and Jenny returned to Alaska. Life is good, and all is well that ends well.

Reporting in to sponse that night, a life-long habit, it seems, Dr. Parks once again heard more endearing words: "And always remember and never forget: There are sick people, inside and outside these rooms. In fact, we are all sick to a degree or we wouldn't be in recovery. And besides, it's not what happens to one in life, it's how one reacts to it,

whatever 'it' may be. That's what's important."
Sponse said one more thing and they would 1 call it another day.
"It's a quote by a fellow named Munger which was written on the back of an envelope gifted to me by a friend. It says:
"All truth is an achievement. If (when) you would have Truth at its full value, go win it. He added:
"Truth does make me free. The richness in my life is a generous reward for courage.
"I pray for the grace to let go of my innocence by being honest, taking action, and admitting my mistakes.
'EagleClaw, you hold the truth, and all true knowledge comes from the inner self. Courage is not the absence of fear. You hold the truth. Now go win it. And RWLY."

Chapter Twenty Four

Working With Others In the Courthouse: Blowback

THE CIVIL TRIAL against Dr. Parks and his firm, with false charges brought by the state Division of Highways, had stopped one step short of the US Supreme Court. The state agency's lawyer was Tal Adamson, Esq., a bureaucratic placebo, in whose name the allegations were now, on paper, being driven. His and Pearbottom's depositions had been taken, of course, by Carol Jackson, as primary evidence. Dr. Parks was not privy to the depositions. But behind the scenes remained the EPA-Wheeling criminal enforcement officer, Pearbottom, representing his now reported disabled boss Marvin Reicht.

Marvin S. Reicht had taken a dislike to Dr. Parks while he surveyed hazardous wastes sites in Wheeling, then lost a major asbestos court case in Federal District Court. He had parlayed the criminal charges to civil charges after Joe Dunn had made a bad bureaucratic decision to spend $57,000 re-surveying Dr. Parks' work of $10,000, and the results tilted to more embarrassment, then the division's engineer spilled the beans to Dr. Parks.

Then Joe Dunn himself was hoisted up and out. Then Ben Wanton shared the EPA memo from Pearbottom to his boss in Wheeling. It ended the criminal charges, but the EPA-Wheeling henchmen then convinced the Justice Department to parlay the very same charges to a federal civil charge. It was pure abuse of power by "the government," i.e., the so-called U.S. Justice Department, against a small

Native American firm, essentially unable to defend itself. The Goodrich family was in charge politically for the states administration.. It all again loomed in EagleClaw's life. And history was repeating itself, with only the dates and facts changing, it seemed.

But it was a pique in Mr. Reicht's career. That verb is defined as a feeling or fit of resentment stemming from wounded vanity or pride. Pride is the very first of the Seven Deadly Sins, EagleClaw had been taught in his spiritual program. And he now understood why the Prophet had instructed the Shawnee to no longer trade pelts for English mirrors because they promoted vanity.

But all on Creator's Earth, *did he say all?* that goes around comes around. All life is circular, not linear in straight lines of history by facts and dates, as the Europeans once led us to believe. EagleClaw no longer defined "cultured" as Western European culture. He had a new pair of glasses.

Yet he had to remain an instrument of his Creator, now that he knew who his Creator was. He could not dog fall, in the words of the Virginians. His sponsor had told him so, and sponsors have the final word. They knew. And EagleClaw knew.

In subsequent years and now into the fifth year of the continuing saga, Ms. Jackson took depositions using dozens of photographs of tan walls in nondescript buildings attempting to use them to get EagleClaw to "admit" he had not collected samples on those walls. She was a frustrated woman as EagleClaw answered in circular, as in compleat, answers that tan walls are tan walls but that he had collected by the national standards under 40 CFR Part 763 the required samples not just for walls but six additional categories of suspect asbestos-containing building materials in the dozens of buildings. Ms. Jackson repeatedly referred only to a portion of the technical reports. EagleClaw said those portions of reports cannot be interpreted as a stand-alone page representative of the total calculations for positive and to-be-removed asbestos containing building materials. The reports are integrated and wholistic and the whole must be viewed by a trained asbestos technical person, not interpreted by laymen. They are technical documents used by the next trained profesional up the asbestos line, the certified and licensed Asbestos Designer. But she just didn't want to hear the truth. It was not a part of her legalistic cultural concept. Her mind was closed for some reason he didn't know.

EagleClaw constantly reflected on that day in Wheeling in federal court speaking truth to EPA legal representatives in the courtroom who just didn't want to hear what their own rules required. The law that day did apply for environmental affairs in the courtroom in WWVA, he recollected to himself. EPA-Wheeling was wrong, but that was at trial with a jury.

Marvin Reicht had entered the courtroom gallery and quietly sat in the back row in District Court in Wheeling seven years ago. In that courtroom, Reicht whispered notations from federal environmental law documents visible to Dr. Parks, and shuffled technical pamphlets produced by the National Institute of Occupational Safety and Health, NIOSH, at is locations near Wheeling and Morgantown.

Last month, while delivering a subpoena to Reicht, EagleClaw had learned from Dottie that he had the major heart attack after the failed criminal trial loss in Charleston.

According to other friends, Reicht was in Philadelphia at the staff meeting writing a required critique of the court loss for the criminal charges of compositing asbestos samples by some Indian, then billing for them as False Claims Act violations. He had dinner the night before at a Philly French restaurant with friends Mike Springer and Rudy Shoup, who called him regularly.

The "whistleblower" act, originally intended to protect government whistleblowers, was now touted by government bureaucrats in the law enforcement field as "a new arrow in the quiver" for environmental law enforcement by bureaucrats. The law allows first, however, for wiretapping. It is a useful tool for deceitful bureaucrats looking to build a prejudiced resentment labelled law enforcement. Their arrow was now out of the quiver and had been shot at EagleClaw.

Reicht in court in Wheeling that day had shuffled quickly from state licensing law to copies of the Code of State Regulations, CSR, to the National Emissions Standards for Hazardous Air Pollutants, NESHAPS. Reicht had once stopped Dr. Parks on the street in Wheeling to ask what the acronym NESHAPS represented. He was now charging him with violating that law and utilizing reference codes for the EPA Asbestos in Schools regulations as a linkage in federal district court. European cultured people use mixed emotions often to shoot their arrows at others from their cultural quivers, EagleClaw surmised and smiled. Some things never change with some folks, he could see and smiled.

Dr. Parks had been charged with violation of Subpart M of NESHAPS – that he had "composited" materials already composited by the manufacturer and were thusly labelled on the asbestos sampling form called the Chain of Custody.

"After all it said so on the inspection sheet where all samples are either 'bulk' or 'composite' samples," Pearbottom had said in the forced interview in his office years earlier.

They had been identified as composite building materials by the sampler certified and licensed for such work at the time the samples were collected. They were composite materials mixed by someone for that purpose, specifically mixed troweled-on plaster consisting of limestone mixed with an adhesive mixed with asbestos for tensile strength, he had replied on the witness stand. Yes, they were composite structural building materials. The jury seemed to understand the simple explanation in a non-technical way. Dr. Parks as an expert witness had learned to communicate to the jury, usually comprised of non-technically trained human folks who could understand any technical issue if it were explained in a down-to-earth manner. It was one of Dr.

Parks' fortuitous qualities as a good expert witness in the hazardous materials fields. Honesty always and respect for all minds were revered traits practiced by him to the best of his Creator-given abilities. It's called respect. His favorite culture is based on that one word.

Dr. Parks thought it interesting that the CSR, with a minuscule reference to the federal NESHAPS rules for asbestos, had even been included in the federal charges. Dr. Parks had drafted then shepherded through the state legislature those very licensing requirements 17 years earlier in his career before he left employment by the state for promoting compliance for protecting public health and the environment at the federal level. Many bureaucrats are practiced at garnering information about individuals they work with, then using that same information against them, Mike Springer had once told Dr. Parks. And history repeats itself, he knew.

What a circular argument in the name of vanity, vindictiveness and false pride in the name of law enforcement in the environment here in an Indian valley still polluted with dioxins and all other manner of hazardous materials, he thought.

He considered it one of life's real dichotomies that a federal bureaucrat combined with a state bureaucrat who then stated to Dr. Parks and his lawyer in a conference that he didn't know anything about asbestos, but that the regulatory agencies would not issue a permit based on a state law he had drafted 17 years before. When he had renewed his current annual license, the program manager and he had a conversation on the case. He was guilty, not of compositing, as charged, he was told, but instead because he had not completed a "reproducible inspection" by the schools management plan requirements for the buildings to be demolished. Rationalization and justification, ever present in the human condition, come in many forms in life, he had observed.

He was charged civilly, or not so, he was also told, for

violations of the False Claims Act. Perhaps someone should look in his own European mirror for a reflection of truth, he thought but didn't verbalize. He wondered again who the Relator, or the Whistleblower, was. No one said.

Al Halberts had called to say he had a surprise in the mail, that Judge Goodrich had cancelled the scheduled trial and had ruled with a bench memo instead on a motion by Carol Jackson that Dr. Parks was guilty and liable for expenses to the Court of $195,000.

All (did he say all, and in writing, as the first-page footnote poignantly stated) the ruling was based on submission of charges by the government, alleging that Dr. Parks never went to the sites, that he had just made up the two-inch thick technical documents for the assignments from his desk– never mind that photos of structures had been submitted; that he had picked up keys from Division of Highways personnel near the sites; that drawings of dozens of rooms for dozens of structures, photos attached, had been submitted; that hundreds of samples had been collected and sent to an independent laboratory and results received back and had been matched with drawings, to scale. Never mind any part of the defense – it had not been submitted in advance by Al Halberts. The federal prosecutors had it all for the criminal investigation proceedings – but not from Al Halberts again.

The news had been received on April 1, but was not an April Fools Joke. It happened.

Dr. Parks then submitted to the court the defense, documents, asking 24 unanswered questions. He included drawings comparable to contract requirements. But those facts of the case Al Halberts had retained for the trial. No trial in Charleston would now be held. The judge had reversed himself three times to date and the rumor had spread that he had begun "forgetting" some things in life. Ms. Jackson provided the secretarial judicial paperwork titled Motion, he was advised, and it was signed.

The promised trials became more broken promises in

the land where a popular tee-shirt was worn regularly now, the one inscribed *In West Virginia It's All Relative*. The good old boys hated the tee-shirt. The tee shirt slogan initially garnered the wrath of the governor as a suggestion of incest in the mountain culture, but the governor had already allowed folks to see him as a dart target. The criticism of the tee shirt allowed instead sales to skyrocket– and a few more guffaws to the governor caught sending 500 e-mails to a state female employee allowed a few more laughs and a couple more newspaper editorials.

The judge had sent a personal letter to Dr. Parks saying he understood his frustration with the federal government. "The case against you and your small business is closed as to liability," the letter said. Three legal minds interpreted the letter to say "It's over," and relief was apparent to Dr. Parks and friends. But it was short-lived. April Fools Day came and went. The decision was immediately appealed to the Fourth Circuit Court in Richmond.

One week later Dr. Parks was napping in the afternoon when a knock was heard at the front door of the residence. He answered to find an FBI Agent and a Federal Marshall at the door. He summarized the event in a letter to Al Halberts, then sent copies to be filed in the official record.

Trial preparation had been completed for the Richmond US 4th Circuit Court of Appeals decision to remand all matters relative to what was now called Government v. Parks et al, and a second court case called Parks, et al v. State of West Virginia. Both were combined and the two forces remanded their efforts to a settlement with an effort at restitution by the two state agencies WVDOH and WVDED. The powerful delivering unto the powerless had prevailed in the Mountain State, disregarding the "suggestions" of the 4th Circuit Court in Richmond, and the trial would instead be held in Southern West Virginia District Court.

"All rise," the bailiff had said, and those in the courtroom, and the galleries, empty except for Reicht and Pearbottom, and two other men in black suits and brown hats. Each wore a pen with a circle and a triange on the lapel. All rose to honor and portend respect for the proceedings.

"*The United States v. C. R. Parks, and, his Environmental Consulting Co.*, who are charged with fraud against the government of the United States and with, uh, I believe, compositing composited building materials which may have contained, or which, yes, definitively did contain, according to Dr. Parks laboratory report by an independent laboratory, positive fibers for ASBESTOS," he audibly emphasized.

"How do you plead, Mr. Parks?" the federal prosecutor asked.

And so the trial awaited now many years had begun.

Al Halberts asked to address the Court. Shortly into the proceedings he said, "Your honor, I object to the jumping ahead format of the proceedings in this courtroom today. I further object to the summarizing of the inopportune description of law violations as provided by your Justice Department attorney."

"And I further object to the perpetrators of this proceeding and by the apparent EPA personnel description of the alleged sampled material." Dr. Parks' lawyer stated.

Judge Goodrich replied he would take the description of the material as presented to him into consideration since it could, in his initial opinion, sway a jury verdict due to irrational reference to the word asbestiform instead of the collective asbestos.

The attentive jury had been substantially objected to for Dr. Parks' firm by the Justice lawyers for about half the number of selected jurors. Many had worked or had relatives who had worked in the chemical valley the Indians had called the Kanawha, the "land of a culture of Moundbuilders for their honored dead." Jurors there often related asbestos to deaths in their family experiences in the valley filled with the hazardous mineral placed throughout chemical manufacturing plants there for the past 50 years. It was literally still blowing in the wind much of the time.

Many of the juror's families had died slow agonizing

deaths of asbestos lung diseases, as had EagleClaw's father two years ago. So had his mother's death arrived during the debacle of a trial fostered for the EPA-Wheeling bureaucrat by the US-DOJ. Dr. Parks had held his father's and mother's hands as they belabored their last breaths, suffocated by asbestos infested aveoli from working years in valley chemical plants with thousands of yards of asbestos-coated pipelines filled with organic pesticides, including Dioxin, Agent Orange and multiple other chlorinated hydrocarbons now identified as carcinogens.

At 15 years old, his father worked in the Plymouth coal mine, breathing the black air. But he had inherited good genes, O-positive blood, it was learned in his last years, was a survivor, and was a good man. His name was of the English culture, Charles Barby Parks, but his soul was now one of asking for and getting forgiveness, that top on-the-beam emotion.

While interviewing and learning from the potential jurors for duty that many had relatives who had died as a result of asbestos diseases, Ms. Jackson was elated. Her only *voir dire* jury selection issue was that none had ever contracted with the state, much less having their jobs eliminated when Democratic governors changed. Her motives were singular and purposeful. She could win.

Many of the jurors, Dr. Parks surmised, had an inherent respect and inherent fear of the very word asbestos, based on experience of disease and death from the four asbestos diseases from working in either the chemical or mining industries in the valley for the past 20 to 50 years.

The remaining population there has an abnormally high rate of exposure, resulting in a parallel high rate of asbestosis, lung cancer, mesothelioma and organ cancers in concentrations much higher that the norm in much of the rest of the country, the jury was instructed by Ms. Jackson. "One more fibre could cause cancer," she had rightfully stated to build her case before the trial.

A positive asbestos sample could thus, she surmised,

conjure up guilt by association and make a statement based on the pain of slow death and disease suffered by past family members with the jurors. They wouldn't want that.

Over the next two days, expert witness testimony of the type Dr. Parks himself had often given in various court systems and medical hearings and legislative hearings was repeated by government employees looking for a raise and enjoying several days and nights out of their offices.

EPA lab chemists from Illinois were flown in to try to sway an opinion unnecessary to presenting factual data, such as was definitive point-counting of small percentage asbestos containing samples necessary to "prove" they were asbestos minerals and not just cotton fibers. They were, Dr. Parks testified, as he had that day in Wheeling.

"Of course that is required," Dr. Parks the Senior Environmental Scientist and author of asbestos legislation now 17 years old, and asbestos expert witness, had testified. He carefully quoted the law to the chagrin of the US Justice lawyers present. He now understood what he had heard many defense lawyers say in the past, that the US Justice Department is a misnomer for the agency. The agency should simply be called what they represent – government prosecutors out to win their case, right or wrong.

In his spiritual program, that key word Justice is the principle behind that final house-cleaning step in 12-step programs. But it was an unanswered question today.

He had looked the jurors straight in the eye as he answered technical questions from memory and refused to acknowledge opposing government lawyers as the receivers of information intended to confuse the jurors, instead opting to answer by looking straight at the jury individuals.

Frustration had begun to set in with the mind-set of the Justice lawyers assigned to the prosecution and especially to Jackson.

Carol, a farm girl from Jackson County, at just 20 years old, had applied and been accepted based on personal references to the state's only law school. The school is known for perpetuating itself in the state. And she intended to supercede the Judge someday. She was a rather masculine-appearing barrister cum secretary persona Justice prosecutor in her case for proving fraud of the United States against Dr. Parks and his corporation. No doubt she believed *in her mind* she possessed an inherent right to judge, to blame the victim, and to prosecute her case based on her beliefs, including her cultural mores. After all, are there others here on this government land? She didn't think so.

She was presently asking questions requiring standard technical answers, but would later move toward perceived finality with the fraud charge for creating false document questions, the billing for sampling, Dr. Parks suspected.

On cross examination, she asked Dr. Parks questions regarding himself and two hourly personnel and their methods of sampling.

Following the four-year decline and destruction of the small minority-owned business, he said, little work had been performed by him.

His seven year old firm, he answered, had competed against a major Pittsburgh firm for the earlier contract, and won based on the state's decision from a scoring system based on technical skills, talents and abilities for finding and quantifying building materials to be removed before demolition where asbestos was present in the manufacturing process. They were a well qualified firm on the contract, he had answered her.

"Does the word asbestos scare you, Mr. Parks," Jackson asked, glancing at the jury members with eyebrows raised and a firm scowl in her jaws and a legs-spread standing stance.

"Scare me – no. Do I respect the fact that someone else put it there and that it must be first found and then removed and disposed properly? Yes."

Jackson was quick to twirl after questioning, giving an air of in-charge defiance she hoped would relay to jurors that this woman was in charge and in position.

"Mr. Parks, are you married or single?"

"I was married for 17 years and I have been single for 17 years."

She paused momentarily to pick up a paper document her male assistant held in abeyance for her questioning of the accused. Dr. Parks maintained eye contact with her continuously during the questioning as well as with her assistant. He wondered what the two were thinking as he maintained a slight smile and wondered if his attitude exhibited honesty, his first principle now ingrained in his psyche for not only maintaining serenity but in fact his life-giving sobriety and spirituality – words he would always think but seldom verbalize, especially here in a courtroom setting.

He admonished himself to pay close attention to the questions. Prayer and meditation, he told himself, have their proper place, but he wasn't sure here in the courtroom testifying truth to government Justice employees who work on the brownie point system for raises and promotions, he thought, might not be the correct place to be inattentive, while seeking Creator's will for himself.

And to ask that God of his understanding for Step 9 Justice at this late date might be a little too presumptive of who was in charge, after all. An entire culture and ethnicity of ancestors had not received justice in this valley. Did he think his situation warranted more?

"*Come si, come sa,*" he thought to himself. "God's Will will occur with or without EagleClaw," he surmised.

"Mr. Parks, why did you list a Dr. GreyOwl Appleton as an officer of your firm when he was not?" Jackson asked.

"Dr. Appleton is listed on the state's version of Standard Federal Form 254-5 for our firm in the broad category for such purposes as *associate*, which he was and is" Dr. Parks replied, looking first at Jackson then making eye contact with as many jurors as were looking forward at the time.

"What kind of asbestos work did he perform for you?"

"None. He performed hazardous material QA/QC– quality analysis/quality control– technical review for accuracy, if you will, for organic chemicals laboratory analyses for five hazardous site survey jobs on that form alleged to include fraud in the criminal investigation." he said.

Bang, went the gavel of the judge, who had lightly tapped it before to bring the court to order.

"Strike that from the record. No reference is to be made by any of you to any other court matter which may or may not have been brought to clear Mr. Parks and his firm of any wrongdoing." the judge admonished to all present.

The jurors looked askance at each other and one handed a short note to another and nodded as if to say "afterwards" to his neighbor.

"Your honor," Jackson spoke with held breath, I move for a break in proceedings so that Mr. Parks may be instructed in proper protocol in the rules of civil procedure in this courtroom today."

"Objection, your honor," said Al Halberts for the first time in the proceedings, rising to speak.

"My client simply stated fact as questioned and I see no need for a break in continuity for such presumptive allegations by Ms. Jackson's suggesting to the Judge that my client be given instruction in proper procedure by her. That's just not normal proceeding, it is not necessary and could be presumptive-appearing to the jury. I might suggest that perhaps she should be the one instructed that one does not instruct my client Dr. Parks in this or any other courtroom. That decision is one for your discretion, your honor, and a request is filed that the jury not be presumptively swayed by Ms. Jackson's management control mechanism as I would label it today, your honor."

"Sustained. Please continue answering the questions, Dr. Parks." the Judge replied.

"Mr. Parks, is that correct, which would you prefer to be called as a title, Mr. Parks," Jackson asked, without offering the logical alternative.

Dr. Parks replied that he does, in fact, hold a Ph.D., from a state board of education-accredited institution, the California Department of Education, although that accreditation status, like schools themselves, come and go, but that the institution was accredited upon his graduation.

He did so on purpose anticipating Pearbottom's allegations earlier that he did not possess a Ph.D. degree except from some African university he had located in a database in order to allege that he had no Ph.D. degree.

You may call me either, he had replied, but "just don't call me late for dinner." A few smiles from opposing sides and a couple jurors gave anecdotal humor relief to the tenseness observable by some in the courtroom– not at Dr. Parks' trite answer, but instead from embarrassment, it appeared, that one who earns such a degree earns minimally the respect to be called the standard title without having to be asked.

Inadvertently, score one for our team, he thought.

The questioning, mostly along technical and financial lines for the corporation, continued another 45 minutes and Dr. Parks continued his even-keeled responses, sometimes smiling and answering but usually formally simply saying the answers as he remembered to questions fired relentlessly by Ms. Jackson.

In the balcony the two EPA-Wheeling employees and two former statehouse employees in dark suits now observed the proceedings from the courtroom gallery seats.

On break, Dr. Parks' lawyer asked him if he was holding up emotionally as well as he appeared to be physically. Yes, he answered, adding that he and his son Gabriel had played some good racquetball the evening before after his son left the hospital and before a meeting, he added.

"I have good serenity today after practicing all of my 'acceptable addictions' last evening," he commented with a smile.

"Hmm," Al replied, "...but not necessarily in that order I believe it is time to return to the courtroom. Continue doing what you are doing and we will be ok, I believe," Al said.

"I don't know how to do anything else, Al."

Next called to the witness stand was local EPA Criminal

Investigator Pearbottom. The CI's face appeared to be that of a straight male in a white shirt and dark tie with a black suit and shoes. His hair was crewcut and his non-distinct face offered the appearance of a given man on the street appearing as a standard government employee just doing his job, in his opinion.

His face appeared to be that of a normal individual, oiled and with a slight mustache and new goatee with sandy brown hair of the average American white male of about 37 years old.

But his body, wide at the hips with his suit-coat buttoned, caused drawing of the fabric at the hips and crotch. It served contrast to the upper body and facial appearance. The fabric in his trousers appeared to be at best insufficient for his 6-foot frame. His wrists curled to the inside as he gingerly stepped up to the witness stand.

He answered the defense attorney's questions in short if not staccato sentences with no additional information provided beyond a basic answer to Al Halberts' poignant questions on his technical expertise training in the broad field of asbestos analysis, removal and control as a hazardous waste in the environment.

"Were you a former deputy sheriff in Boone County?" Mr. Pearbottom.

"No not Boone. I worked as an investigator in the next county, Lincoln, and was deputized for specific duties at times," he replied.

"Why, then, Mr. Pearbottom, did you say you were a deputy sheriff to the county prosecutor, not an investigator hired on a federal training program for the unemployed in the coalfields for displaced workers?"

"I was deputized at times and completed my assignments under supervision for the time the paid training was offered by unemployment compensation through the sheriff's department. The county sheriff signed our checks."

"Who was you employer, there, Mr. Pearbottom."

"The County Commission issued my paychecks but I

worked out of the sheriff's offices at the former county courthouse jail location."

"I see. And the sheriff is the county treasurer. Before that you worked for a coal corporation and after the County Commission training program you applied for a federal civil service position and EPA-Wheeling called you to do work in close proximity to Charleston and Southern West Virginia counties. Is that correct, Mr. Pearbottom"

"That's right and I was hired to do investigator work in sometimes unsafe and or unknown environments."

"I see," Halberts said. "Mr. Pearbottom, have you ever been in the basement of Dr. Parks residence in South Charleston, and if so, the approximate date and time of day or night"

"My attorney said I don't have to answer that question, at least not directly, sir, but I have been in his office structure for investigatory purposes and for interviewing him at his will and pleasure to ascertain law enforcement for asbestos purposes" Pearbottom replied without changing expression.

"Mr. Pearbottom, I have here a document which I will label two-A for the record indicating that on approximately Feb 24, 2002, Dr. Parks returned home from teaching at Wheeling Jesuit University on a Saturday evening about 10 pm and believed someone to be in his basement as he returned unplanned after canceling a trip to see his girlfriend in Cincinnati. Are you or were you aware that a police report was filed that he saw a person leaving his basement then scurrying down a backyard sidewalk and that the report was electronically filed but never acted on by the South Charleston Police Department?"

"No, sir, "Pearbottom replied. "No, what, Mr. Pearbottom. "No, that you were or were not that person in his basement in his absence or no that the information was never reported to your agency even though Dr. Parks suggested the silhouette seen scurrying down the sidewalk appeared to have been your distinctive body shape from the back appearance?"

"Uh, I don't know, Mr. Halberts. I, uh, yes, had to investigate allegations that he may have been storing information or additional asbestos samples in his basement just in case this matter went to trial which it has, obviously." Pearbottom replied.

"Did you, in fact, as you said yes to my question if I heard you correctly, secretly enter his basement to search the premises and accidentally get caught after he locked his doors and later found them unlocked after your exiting in, shall we say, a state of excitation, Mr. Pearbottom"

"I obviously have sworn to tell the truth as best I can as a federal criminal investigator so long as I do not implicate my agency or supervisor in any illegal activities, but I had the right to enter and search the premises, I was told, and was just following orders of my boss in Wheeling."

"And were your orders to search his office, or his private residence, or both, for search and seizure of potentially contraband or evidential material which might be brought to court as evidence here today?" Halberts quizzed quickly.

"Yes, I mean, I was told I could search for contraband under the fraud act and records if I found any not submitted by the corporation for review and such." Pearbottom answered.

"And what did you find to bring us here today, Mr. Pearbottom"

"I didn't find anything evidentiary, as I told my boss in Wheeling."

"What were you looking for, Mr. Pearbottom"

"Whatever I could find because we knew he was making money on the state for his company. Have you looked at how much he billed the state for a simple asbestos building inspection. You obviously haven't..."

"Objection, your honor," Ms. Jackson interrupted. The state's witness is being led and the government objects."

"Sustained," Judge Goodrich answered."Continue, Mr. Halberts.

"Thank you, your honor."

"And Mr. Pearbottom, you searched under cover of the night for evidence. Did you do so with a warrant or of your own volition?"

"I had no warrant but our wiretapping of his computer and fax lead us to believe he had some asbestos in his basement which he could send to a lab and file a false claim on," Pearbottom said.

"False claim for what, sir?" Halberts asked.

"Well my boss believes he is guilty of the False Claims Act because he knew he has a medical and paramedical professional license as a Registered Sanitarian by the State of West Virginia."

What, pray tell me Mr. Pearbottom, does that have to do with the False Claims Act? Yes, Dr. Parks has been a Registered Sanitarian for 30 years, a former chair of his state licensing board, well respected in the field, but that field in no way regulates asbestos, to my knowledge and belief, anywhere in the United States. Yes, there is a licensing act which Mr. Parks once drafted and introduced and became law and it is administered by the Department of Health, but it is by no stretch of the imagination regulated as Registered Sanitarian activity. It is even in the environmental health section of the state department of health, but has no correlation to the 100 or so Registered Sanitarians working and licensed in the State of West Virginia.

"Was that your or your bosses or perhaps a lawyer's stretch of opinion with the U.S. Justice Department for bringing this action in this honored courtroom here today against Dr. Parks and his small business, Mr. Pearbottom"

"That was my understanding, sir. I didn't make the decision I just followed orders out of Wheeling, and did my investigative work assuming I was operating under the law of the land.

"I learned in Lincoln County in training to do what I was told by my boss and that's what I did. I know Mr. Parks was charging too much money and making a haul for just looking at those old buildings that had to be torn down anyway for new highways using federal funds.

"But the asbestos had to come out first and no one wants to hurt workers or the environment if the asbestos isn't identified and is disturbed and becomes friable and gets into a persons breathing zone then causes cancer or is carried home on their clothing for other family members to breath and..."

"Objection, your honor," Ms. Jackson intoned. "Leading the witness again."

Smiles appeared throughout the courtroom as if to say no, not leading, he's leading himself, and this case, to the hanging platform all by himself with or without a motive proposed in the cross examination.

In the gallery seat Reicht shuffled his seating position uncomfortably from one rounded cheek to the other, again looking askance at best at his investigating employee who had just run his mouth much too far for his comfort, but at the pleasure of the defense lawyer.

Al Halberts had rather enjoyed with or without prompting on his part the court evidence to justify a prejudiced resentment on behalf of two government bureaucrats– evidence of the variety called "lost down a dark alley and still running" approach.

Pearbottom had presented that evidence and the now nervous and overly talkative federal criminal investigator had run amok once again.

Dr. Parks whispered at the break that perhaps Pearbottom should run for president of the West Virginia Deputy Sheriff's Association. "Just all in good subcultural fun," he said to his attorney "with all disrespect applicable to the trade."

Judge Goodrich noted that it was nearing lunch recess time and that after two days of witnessing and cross examination that he believed both sides should probably either rest or allow the information to the jury for a decision. The jury members stretched quietly, trying not to show disrespect for the system but no doubt feeling that conclusion to this presentation was due soon, if not by some quicker design.

Lunch went well for Dr. Parks, who was joined by business partner Thom Botts and son Gabriel on break from hospital visiting rounds and on his way to an interview for a physician supervisor program in the southeastern part of the state.

Gabriel had learned to kayak while in medical school in that part of the state and he would likely go into practice and build his dream home there in the near future.

"How's it going, dad?"

"Ok, I think," his dad replied.

"It is about the same as what you and Thom had to go through during the criminal trial where the jury failed to even give a ham sandwich to the federal prosecutor, let alone indict someone. The EPA bastards, oops, name-calling is not in my repertoire, the EPA-Wheeling employees as well as the Division of Highways person seemed nonplused that they aren't doing so well, or that's my opinion. Al may differ, but we allow for that here, especially before the jury verdict this afternoon, hopefully, don't we Al?"

"I agree, Bob, but I have learned we just have to wait and see. I never try to outguess a jury till the verdict is announced."

Returning to the courtroom, the judge rose and all were seated and the jury, meeting during lunch at their group decision, had already returned to the courtroom, apparently with the foreman and with a decision in hand.

"Mr. Foreman, what sayeth the jury of Dr. Parks' peers relative to counts one, two and three of the federal fraud allegations, first for Mr. Parks himself as an individual and secondly and separately as charged, his corporation, which provided contractual services to the State of West Virginia which uses federal tax dollars at the 90 percentile rate to carry out its work?

Your honor, on the first and second and third counts of

fraud in billing; and on compositing asbestos materials for sampling; and, the third count for billing for those allegedly composited samples: NOT Guilty, as charged.

Silence permeated the courtroom as all parties peered without any real expression at the Foreman. Dr. Parks very slightly nodded his head in acceptance and without directed response.

"And on the first, second, third and fourth count against Environmental Technical Corporation, the jury finds that the proceedings are without proof that any crime was committed in sampling, no false representation of technical personnel was proven, and, that no allegedly false billing occurred, and that no causative evidence was presented for ending the contract as a prime contract by the state or federal representatives. Thank you."

"All rise," Judge Goodrich said. All rose, then all adjourned. "I will announce additional comments to each of the parties in writing in the near future," Judge Goodrich said. "Court dismissed."

Outside, Al Halberts was the first to say that the good news only got better by the "juried comments" of the foreman and the judge, and that the contract was essentially broken illegally by the state.

By some strange design, Al had convinced the judge after the governor's "500 e-mail" fiasco to allow the five points of Dr. Parks' damage suit to be re-introduced as evidence into the civil trial, and Judge Goodrich had by surprise and legal kindness agreed, admonishing the objections of Carol Jackson of Jackson County to "hold her horses" when she vehemently objected and questioned Dr. Parks' veracity.

"That seldom happens," he quickly added and smiled.

"We shall see, shan't we," Halberts said to Dr. Parks.

Next day an interview hastily put together by Fanny Silers was printed in the morning newspaper alleging that a state contract had been illegally broken by a department head of Wisecoff's staff at the highways division. A followup investigation had been promised to the reporter via a telephone call after the court case was reported by the wire service to the newspaper and confirmed in draft court records.

"Governor Wisecoff's staff claimed no knowledge of this issue since they do not get involved in contract operations of the various agencies" a staff member named Gabriel Burden had replied. "We just don't get involved in state contract issues," he was quoted.

"Then who does in state government, wonder," Al asked of Dr. Parks.

"I think you know the real answer here, Al. Hear no evil, see no evil, know no evil" with government contracts in West Virginia. Let the feds do the enforcement after the fact, if anything, in fact, is ever found wrong by the state investigators," Dr. Parks replied.

"And how about state worker opinions that something is not right, or that someone seems to be making a little money compared to their state salaries and the technical issues are irrelevant for opinions, I suppose, is that part of the story here too, Bob?"

"You guessed it" Dr. Parks replied. Those two technicians, Euless Gallahue and– what's that other red-faced, gray-suited, white-suited technician at DED named, oh yes– Wumble– they have important opinions. I suggest we go after them personally next, just to send a message," Dr. Parks suggested. "We'll call it the pompous bureaucrat case," he laughed.

"Not quite yet – let's see what the Judge says in his allocation of justice in our case, and maybe then you can write a letter to them and their bosses just asking some pertinent questions and let them stew a while, then maybe we'll do a court filing against them individually and see if there is an additional personal settlement proposal– one never knows. We shall see, shan't we?" Al replied.

"Al, thanks again, and we'll see you soon. Let me know what you hear and I'll do the same."

"Thanks, EagleClaw."

"Thank you, Al. And Aho! Mitakuye Oyasin! We are all interrelated."

ISBN 141203316-0